THIS TIME IT'S FOREVER

Timing is Everything Series, Book 4

CHRISTINE MILES

Books by Christine Miles

ADULT CONTEMPORARY ROMANCE

Timing is Everything Series

Last Time We Loved (Book One)

First Time We Laughed (Book Two)

The Time We Met (Book Three)

This Time It's Forever (Book Four)

YOUNG ADULT

Pacifica Academy Drama Series

Me, Shakespeare and the Anti-Love Club (Book One)

The '68 Camaro Between Kenickie and Me (Book Two)

Teddy Brewster's Hold On Me (Book Three)

Silver Bells for Me and (Saint) Nicolas (Book Four)

You and Me Dancing to Gershwin (Book Five)

Summer in Winter Wonderland (A Cozy Mystery)

Chapter One

THE SOUND OF FABRIC TEARING, followed by a gasp, followed by a whiny moan forced Felicity to drag her eyes from her phone.

The maid-of-honor's face turned several shades darker than her coral, strapless gown. "I'm so sorry," she said to the bride. "Your dress wasn't this tight at that last fitting."

Felicity held onto the fact the bride had skipped the *final* dress fitting for an impromptu, single-girls hurrah in Las Vegas a few weeks earlier which hadn't even been her bachelorette party. That had just taken place the previous weekend.

The flushed bride squeezed her eyes shut. "Ohmygod, ohmygod. This can't be happening." The young woman's eyes flew open and settled on Felicity. "What are you going to do about this? You're the one who recommended that place for custom dresses." The bride gestured at herself. "Considering what my parents spent on this dress, I would have expected it to be made of a much higher quality."

Felicity met the bride's sharp gaze while swallowing the less-than professional reply of "*And maybe you should have ordered the proper size instead of one smaller, promising you would lose ten pounds even though I said not to count on that.*" The shimmery, satin wedding gown had been favoring skintight from the beginning.

The maid-of-honor's shoulders relaxed, clearly from relief at not being the one under fire for the dress mishap.

Felicity forced her mouth into a smile, slipped her phone back inside her crossbody phone case, and focused on her assistant who immediately handed over the mini sewing kit.

If not for Lynn Delgado, Felicity wouldn't have made it this far and long as Denver's number-one coordinator for premier weddings.

Felicity held up the kit. "I always come prepared for every possible challenge. All you have to do is turn around, I'll get that tear fixed, and we'll get this wedding underway."

The bride's posture relaxed as she curtly nodded, then again faced the full-length mirror.

Minutes later, Felicity completed the last stitch, tied the ends of the thread into a knot, and firmly patted the spot twice. Perhaps even a tad too firmly based on the bride—still facing the mirror—narrowing her eyes into slits.

Felicity grinned. "All finished and practically new again." She stepped backward. "I'm needed in the banquet hall, but Lynn will be close by if you need anything."

After pressing the sewing kit into Lynn's hand, Felicity strode from the room and closed the door behind her. She leaned back while shaking her head that had started to ache.

Yet another lovely bridezilla making Felicity question her long-term career choice. Her younger brother voicing his incredulity at working with the specific clientele who hired her to plan their idyllic Denver, Colorado weddings filled her weary head.

Felicitous Wedding Creations had certainly cinched her financial present and future, and for that she'd always be grateful.

She released a slow sigh and straightened.

But the bridezillas and demanding parents and extravagant weddings had started to take a toll on her physical and mental well-being. Her business hadn't started out that way, though.

A long time ago in another life she'd been the hopeless romantic planner of intimate weddings all about genuine love.

She stared at the floor.

A completely different, much darker, and unexpected life twist was affecting her emotional and mental well-being, as well.

Her phone buzzed inside her phone case and she withdrew the device.

Last load of flowers being placed on tables now.

Felicity managed a slight smile at Jillian Castillo's message.

She enjoyed working with a handful of vendors that included Daisy's Bouquets, her first choice when it came to florists for all of the weddings she planned. Since partnering with the small, women-owned shop over a year before, Felicity hadn't been disappointed with them, their bouquets, or ability to adapt to last-minute changes due to challenging brides and their mothers.

Felicity responded with, *Thank you! I'm on my way.*

She deeply inhaled air into her lungs and squared her shoulders.

Simply a few hours left until the reception began and she could leave the rest of the evening in Lynn's fully capable hands. Then she could shed the *fairy tale* wedding coordinator and be Felicity—daughter, sister, aunt, and single dog mom who now preferred cozy fleece sweatpants and sweatshirts to power business suits.

The second she stepped into the banquet hall, however, her mind cleared of everything but her job and the beauty before and surrounding her which made her genuinely smile.

The room lined with windows offered uninhibited views of Boulder and the Denver city skyline. The bride and groom had lucked out with a crystal-clear Saturday evening for late March. Coloradans never knew what kind of weather to expect in the springtime months, particularly March. Though decidedly brisk outside, Felicity would take a day like this over anything else synonymous with early spring weather in Colorado.

The bride…and mother-of-the-bride…had opted for bouquets with bright-white and coral roses; the latter giving the space illuminated with natural light pops of color amidst the equally white linens, polished silverware, and gleaming flatware and glasses.

Once the sun set, the venue's staff would light each votive candle sitting on the guests' tables, as well as the head table. Between the city lights beyond the windows, the overhead lighting that would be set to low, and lit candles, the banquet hall would flicker with warmth and dreaminess and utter perfection.

Felicity's smile slipped.

"*Santo cielo*," Jillian murmured from Felicity's left side. "It's going to be absolutely beautiful in here tonight."

She brought back her smile and faced Jillian. "The flowers are brilliant."

Jillian arched her right eyebrow. "All we do is give you and the bride what's asked of us."

Felicity's smile deepened. "You do much more than that." Without a bit of doubt. "From what I've heard, my brother and Peyton have had a fabulous time in Durango with Campbell and her family this past week." She laughed. "It sounds like Scott would love to live there someday."

That really meant after his daughter, Peyton, became eighteen and left for college. But with her being only in kindergarten, a life-changing move wouldn't happen for a while.

"*Si.*" Jillian grinned. "We're looking forward to hearing all about the trip when Campbell's back on Monday. We've definitely missed her around the shop."

Lynn appeared at Felicity's right side. "We're ready for the bouquets and boutonnières."

Jillian nodded. "Hayley is grabbing those from the van right now and will head that way."

Lynn focused on Felicity. "The dress repair is holding up nicely so far." She smiled. "Well done, Boss."

Though what Felicity had told the young bride about always being prepared for any challenge had been sincere, she couldn't remember a time when she'd utilized the mini sewing kit due to a wedding gown tearing at the zipper from being too snug.

She'd been a wedding coordinator for nearly ten years and found it somewhat amazing she could still run into the adage "There's a first time for everything."

Jillian turned from them, then stopped. "Oh, I have something for you." She reached into her crossbody phone case and withdrew a small envelope folded in half. "This is for you."

Felicity grasped the envelope. "From Daisy's Bouquets?" She unfolded it and slid her pinky nail into the slight opening at the edge.

"No." Jillian stepped back. "Someone left it for you on one of the flower carts."

Felicity halted.

"Hayley found it a few minutes ago and gave it to me."

Felicity slowly turned the envelope over—

Her breath became lodged in her throat because she recognized that font; her name in thick, black, capitalized letters.

FELICITY MAYHEW

"Is everything okay?"

Felicity's heart hammering her chest caused Jillian's voice to sound miles away.

She cleared her throat and tore her gaze from the familiar, eerie typeface. Her eyes locked with Jillian's, wide with confusion and some concern. "Did Hayley mention seeing who dropped this off?" Felicity glanced at Lynn, her eyes also round but from shock.

Her assistant happened to know the font, as well.

Jillian shook her head. "She just said she found it on the cart. Felicity, what is it?"

She lifted her chin. "Nothing." Though she wouldn't be at all surprised if Jillian could hear her heart beating inside her chest. "Thank you, Jillian. I'll see you next week?"

Jillian stayed silent for a few seconds before, "I'm off next Saturday, so I'll see you in two weeks."

Felicity smiled. "I hope you have a lovely week."

Jillian lingered for another few seconds, then turned and left the room.

Lynn stepped in front of Felicity. "It's been so long since the last one arrived, I assumed he or she had gotten bored or decided two nasty messages were enough."

"Well," Felicity murmured, "apparently that's *not* the case."

She also had no idea what she'd done to deserve this harassment.

"Do you want me to open this one?" Lynn quietly asked.

"No." She paused, then reached into the envelope and withdrew a single white piece of paper with the familiar thick, black capitalized letters.

Just like in the two previous envelopes she'd received, a message had been centered on the paper. Another hateful, nasty, threatening message.

DESTRUCTION CAN BE THE CAUSE

OF SOMEONE'S RUIN.

I'M READY TO BE THE CAUSE OF YOURS.

Felicity stared at the words.

What could she have done to upset someone to this extent?

She planned extravagant weddings and lived alone with her dog. She also didn't date and only had a few close friends. She could very well be considered the definition of an independent, Twenty-First Century, workaholic woman.

Lynn pulled the paper and envelope from Felicity's trembling fingertips. A second later she folded it back up and shoved the paper inside the envelope. "You need to tell Scott about this *and* show him the other letters."

Felicity vigorously shook her head. "No. I can handle this." Her brother had also been through more than enough last month.

At that moment, a face appeared in Felicity's mind. A rather handsome face belonging to a man who was good friends with Scott *and* a Denver police officer.

A man who'd nearly let his enormous animal eat her dog when she'd met him for the first time at Scott's place over a month earlier. Recalling the man's striking, dark features which had held a hint of arrogant amusement at her irritation with him and his animal that night, Felicity narrowed her eyes. But he just might be who she truly needed right now.

"Felicity," Lynn softly said, "this person is showing they're not going away. The messages are getting more ominous, too." She sighed. "I understand why you don't want to get Scott involved, but you have to—"

"I know what I have to do." She snatched the envelope and slipped it inside the front pocket of her phone case. "More accurately, I know who I have to talk to."

Not her first choice by any means, but going to him with this would be loads better than causing her brother or other family members to worry. They, especially her mom, didn't need that in their lives. Not after what Felicity had been through with her ex-husband.

"I'd love it if you'd go with me," Felicity continued. "First thing Monday morning?"

Lynn nodded. "Of course I'll go with you."

She'd probably have to call the main line to find out if he'd even be in the police admin building Monday morning. Maybe make an appointment, if necessary? No matter what, it was officially past time for Felicity to get a professional involved. She'd also make him swear not to tell Scott. If he didn't agree to her non-negotiable terms, she'd go to another officer to help her with this problem that happened to be the much darker life twist she'd been trying to forget.

⊏⊐

A FILE LANDED on Ian's desk with a *plop*.

He glanced up to find his partner standing on the other side of the cubicle.

Detective Larry Walsh's weathered face formed a deep frown. "Forensics already came back on little Adrian."

"Little" meaning not quite six-years-old, the reason for the rush on DNA results. *Little* also known as the same age as Ian's goddaughter, Peyton.

Ian sat back and waited. Based on his partner's expression, he already knew who had caused the boy's untimely death by asphyxiation.

Larry rubbed his thick, gray goatee. "Mom and Dad's DNA were all over the little guy and his clothing."

Ian mentally went through every swear word in his vocabulary.

Larry sighed while shaking his bald head. "Hospital records show history of abuse, too."

No surprise there, either. But *holy shit*.

Ian had reached detective grade in December while still on the Grand Junction, Colorado police force and had never imagined ending up as a rookie detective in Denver.

For many damn reasons.

Being called to a crime scene involving a deceased little boy who'd been discovered in a dumpster wasn't a common occurrence in a city like Grand Junction. The fact the boy had died and been discarded as if a piece of trash at the hands of his own parents made Ian want to punch a hole in the nearby wall.

Yeah. He'd seen some messed up, downright disturbing shit while in combat. But *nothing* could prepare any true human being for seeing a little kid the way they'd found Adrian.

His jaw tightened at the image before he asked, "So why the hell aren't we already picking the asswipes up?"

Larry glanced at his watch. "Happening as we speak."

Ian frowned.

"Captain wanted them picked up at the same time. He sent patrol who were in the area of where the parents work, respectively."

Ian shook his head. "They suffocate their kid some time in the last week, toss his body into a dumpster, and go to work on a

Monday morning like everything's normal." There couldn't be a hell dark or rotten enough for people like Adrian's parents. "I don't know if I'll ever get used to that level of evil." Especially in a situation like little Adrian's.

"You won't," Larry quietly stated. "But your skin will continue to get thicker."

Though coming from a veteran Denver PD detective in the major crimes division, Ian still couldn't find Larry's words comforting. Not even a little bit.

"It's taco and beer night in the Walsh household," Larry continued. "You interested?"

Ian cracked a smile. "Only if Stella is invited, too."

Larry released a quick laugh that sounded close to an actual dog bark. "That would be a question for Tess. I'm not getting involved in a battle between my wife and partner."

Ian opened his mouth to once again defend his dog's actions the last time she'd been allowed in the Walsh home when a uniformed officer appeared at the entrance of his cubicle.

"Two women are here to talk to you, Stafford." The guy—more like kid—grinned. "A *smokin'* hot redhead and brunette. I tried really hard to offer my help, but they only want you."

Ian caught his partner fighting a smile comparable to the kid's.

"The redhead said you're good friends with her brother."

Ian froze as his memory shoved him several weeks into the past.

A "smokin' hot redhead" with a brother who was like a brother to Ian. Only one woman fit those descriptions and his frown deepened at the clear memory of when they'd met.

"And did you think to get her name?" Larry asked. "Or are you young *and* stupid?"

The kid's round face turned the color of a cherry tomato.

Ian stood. "Larry, ease up. I know who it is." The real question was what the hell had brought her to the Denver Police Admin building on a Monday morning looking for him.

The kid shuffled away.

Larry unleashed a shit-eating grin. "I love screwing with the rookies."

"And the rookie detectives," Ian tossed at him while leaving his cubicle.

Larry's grin grew.

"Hopefully this won't take long because I want to be present when the uniforms bring in those two worthless pieces of shit."

His partner's grin transitioned back into a deep frown.

Between the heart-wrenching, sickening case of little Adrian and the unexpected visit from his buddy Scott's *charming* older sister, this week seemed to already be headed in the direction of forgettable. And it wasn't even ten in the morning.

Chapter Two

"IS THAT HIM?" Lynn quietly asked.

Felicity turned her head left and her eyes locked with Ian Stafford's, dark with the absolute definition of smoldering as he strode toward them.

Dark and smoldering like the rest of him.

She straightened and cleared her throat. "Yes."

His clearly toned physique, broad shoulders, and bedroom eyes didn't make up for his hint of arrogance mingled with defiance. Something Felicity had *not* found attractive the day they'd met at Scott's place. Nearly allowing his monstrosity of a dog to almost eat her little Princess Belle hadn't helped their initial meeting, either.

"You failed to mention," Lynn murmured, "his *GQ* good looks."

GQ good looks only enhanced by his black suit, white dress shirt, and purple tie.

She stood and Lynn followed her actions.

He stopped in front of them and smiled, his bright-white teeth standing out against his skin as dark as his eyes and black, neatly trimmed facial hair. A five o'clock shadow at nine-thirty in the morning. Felicity also couldn't help but notice the smile didn't reach his eyes.

He also had to be remembering when they'd met.

"Hi," he said to Felicity before focusing on Lynn. He held out his right hand. "Detective Ian Stafford."

Of course Detective Ian Stafford had one of those voices that could melt ice cream during a Colorado blizzard.

Lynn's face flushed while she grasped his hand. "Lynn. Delgado." She laughed and continued to hold his hand. "It's incredibly nice to meet you."

Felicity pressed her lips together at Lynn's almost breathless statement.

Like her, Lynn happened to be the definition of a workaholic and not because of Felicity. Being single with few friends and her family living out-of-state—unlike Felicity—work happened to be Lynn's number-one focus.

Ian gently tugged his hand free from Lynn's whose eyes remained locked on him.

Felicity shook her head.

She'd never seen her assistant and closest friend react this way to *any* man since settling in Denver two years earlier.

Ian refocused on Felicity. "This is a surprise. And can't be a social call." That flicker of arrogance and defiance passed through his eyes, followed by a smirk.

Felicity lifted her chin.

No matter his *GQ* good looks, Detective Ian Stafford stood a little too tall on his pedestal.

"It's not social in the slightest," Felicity replied. "Is there somewhere we can talk?"

His smirk faded. "Follow me."

Moments later they were enclosed in what appeared to be an empty office and seated at a round table. Though the office had windows with a direct view of numerous beige cubicles, the blinds offered some privacy from several police staff, including officers in uniform, who'd been watching them closely…for some reason.

"This isn't about Scott and Campbell, is it?"

Felicity fell silent at Ian's question laced with concern.

He'd been active in helping Campbell, and by extension Scott, over a month ago at catching her ex-husband who'd been harassing and stalking her. The *wanker* was still sitting in a jail cell somewhere in the Denver Police Admin complex while the justice system worked its magic to make sure he never went near Campbell again.

And by extension Scott and his little girl, Felicity's niece.

"I assure you they're fine," she answered. "They came back from Durango yesterday."

In that respect, Felicity owed Ian quite a bit. He also appeared to be quite good at his job, another reason she'd instantly thought of him on Saturday.

His face relaxed and he grinned. "I'll give him a call later." He slid his gaze to Lynn, still focused on him, and back to Felicity. "So how can I be of service, Ms. Mayhew?" The flash of arrogance returned.

Felicity narrowed her eyes.

His arrogance must have gotten him into trouble numerous times throughout his life and certainly wasn't earning him any points at this precise moment in time.

"I have a slight…problem." She reached into her purse, withdrew the three letters, and placed them on the table in front of him. "I received the third one on Saturday while working a wedding and realized I'll need some assistance with this matter."

"And you thought of me?" His grin deepened. "I can't tell you how flattered I am."

Felicity leaned forward. "*Mr.* Stafford—"

"*Detective* Stafford."

"This isn't a joke," she continued. "I would appreciate it if you'd take this seriously."

Ian glanced at the top envelope with her name in big, block, bold font on the front and back at her. "You're right." His smirk again disappeared. "My apologies."

She gave him a curt nod.

Ian opened the first envelope which also happened to be the first letter she'd received. As he read the short note, his forehead formed a frown that deepened while he read the remaining notes. He then slid the last letter back into its envelope and concentrated on her.

"Any ideas on who you've pissed off lately?"

Something about the question and the way he'd asked it caused Felicity to snap, "I plan fairy tale weddings for a living, *Detective* Stafford. It's not typically the kind of work that results in pissing people off, as you so eloquently put it."

Silence settled between them while she and Ian's hard gazes remained locked.

From the corner of her eyes, Felicity caught Lynn tightly folding her hands in her lap.

"I didn't say it had anything to do with your line of work, Ms. Mayhew."

She pursed her lips.

Fine. She'd silently concede that point.

"I'll rephrase the question," he added without breaking their eye contact. "Is there anyone in your life you can think of who doesn't like you very much?"

Felicity could think of two people and one of them happened to be sitting right in front of her. The other person, however, couldn't be behind the notes.

"My ex-husband doesn't like me very much." But the narcissistic ass would never waste his valuable time on writing and leaving nasty notes.

He'd also never had any problem with being rotten to one's face, including hers.

"And where would he be right now?"

"Still in London." Right where he belonged and another reason he couldn't be behind the letters.

Ian raised his eyebrows. "Well, unless he has someone here helping him, he's out."

Felicity sighed. "Detective, believe me when I say it's not him.

And not just because he lives in London," she added under her breath. "I honestly don't know who could be doing this."

Ian sat back. "So no angry ex-boyfriends, lovers, one-night—"

"*No*," she ground out. "I've been focused on my business since I moved back to the U.S. when my divorce was final over three years ago." Not entirely the truth, but not exactly a lie.

Still, that particular…international fling…had nothing whatsoever to do with her current problem.

"She's right, Detective," Lynn offered. "It's been Felicity, the business, and me."

Ian slowly nodded while keeping his gaze trained on Felicity.

Though the intensity of his dark eyes piercing her made her want to look away, she'd never give him the satisfaction.

"How did you receive the other two notes?" He pointed at the short pile. "You said you received the latest one on Saturday while you were working a wedding."

Felicity glanced at Lynn who gave her a tight, but encouraging smile.

"The first one was sent to my office here in downtown Denver."

"It arrived with the mail," Lynn added.

"And the second one?"

Felicity hesitated before replying, "That one was left on my doorstep. I found it in the morning—it was a Sunday—when I left to walk my dog." One of the few things in her life she thoroughly enjoyed that had been tainted a handful of weeks ago.

Ian straightened. "This person who's harassing you with threatening notes knows where you live?"

Felicity managed a quick nod in response to his statement dripping with incredulity.

"And you're just now reporting it?"

She lifted her chin. "Since I have no idea who on earth could be doing this, I figured the individual would simply get bored and go away."

"That's not how stalkers operate, Ms. Mayhew."

She opened her mouth to once again defend herself when he asked, "How long has this been going on?"

Felicity looked at Lynn who answered, "A little over a month."

Ian released a quick breath that sounded on the fringe of frustration.

"Like I just said," Felicity enunciated, "I thought the person would get bored."

"And you probably haven't said a word to your brother," Ian said as if she hadn't spoken.

She clenched her teeth, then replied, "No. Believe it or not, I'm quite capable of taking care of myself, Detective. And there's no reason for him to know now that I've come to *you* for help with this matter."

Ian's eyes widened. "You want to keep this from Scott."

"Yes. If it's a request you"—she pointed at him—"can't agree to, I'll find someone else to help me." She lowered her hand. "Scott's been through more than enough and now he's genuinely happy for the first time in a long while. You know it as well as I do."

Ian remained silent, but his posture did relax a fraction.

"I won't let this interfere with his happiness," she finished, catching Ian's gaze.

Silence descended in the office, outside of the steady din of voices and ringing phones beyond the closed door.

Felicity once again eyed Lynn, watching Ian.

After a few more moments of silence, Ian picked up the envelopes. "You've made a compelling argument, Ms. Mayhew. But I'll only agree to your terms under one condition."

"I'm listening." She held her breath.

He leaned forward. "If this starts to go in a really ugly direction —and I'm not saying it will—you have to tell Scott."

She slowly expelled the air from her lungs.

It certainly wasn't an unreasonable stipulation. If this did indeed start to go in a "really ugly direction" she'd have no choice but to tell him.

"Agreed."

Ian stood, and she and Lynn followed.

"I'll send these to the lab to check for fingerprints and DNA, but I have to be honest." He walked around the table. "Getting any kind of hit or finding anything in general is a long shot."

Felicity nodded since she'd suspected the same.

"In the meantime," Ian continued, "I need you to really think about who could be doing this. That's going to be your best shot at finding and stopping this person since he or she obviously knows you pretty damn well."

Yes. *Obviously*.

Felicity briefly closed her eyes and said, "I already told you—"

"She'll do it," Lynn answered. "We'll start brainstorming today."

Felicity glanced sharply at her assistant, focused on Ian.

Normally, she didn't mind Lynn taking control of matters. It allowed Felicity to concentrate on other, usually more important things. But that was work. This was her personal life and no one knew it better than she, Felicity Mayhew.

"I'll check in with you in a couple of days." Ian reached into his inside, suit jacket pocket and withdrew a small notebook where he removed a business card. He handed it to Felicity. "Call me at any hour if anything changes. What's the best way to get a hold of you?"

Before Felicity could answer, Lynn reached into her purse and retrieved two business cards. "Her contact information as well as mine." She paused, then added, "*Both* include our cell numbers."

"Thanks." He stepped toward the door and opened it. "I'll walk you out."

In spite of the tension between them, Felicity couldn't help but savor the relief shrouding her at getting Detective Ian Stafford involved with her slight…problem.

No, they didn't necessarily like each other. Nonetheless, she knew he'd do everything within his power as a detective to find and put this person away before it became really ugly. With that thought, she deeply inhaled air heavy with freshly-brewed coffee and a little too much men's cologne while following Ian.

Surely this wouldn't go in an ugly direction now that she had help.

For the sake of her sanity, she had to believe that.

———

IAN SAT at his desk and set the letters down, then again retrieved the first one Felicity had received. He knew this particular note had been the first one since she'd numbered them.

ANGER IS A STRONG FEELING OF HOSTILITY.

I'M READY TO SHOW YOU WHAT THIS MEANS FOR YOU.

Ian frowned while placing the concise, but clear message back inside its envelope. He then retrieved the second one.

PHYSICAL AND MENTAL SUFFERING.

YOUR PAIN WILL BE THIS GREAT.

His frown deepened as he absently slid the paper into the envelope.

It couldn't be a coincidence this particular note had been left on Felicity's doorstep. This person wanted her to know how *physically* close he or she could get to her.

He next re-read the most recent note.

DESTRUCTION CAN BE THE CAUSE

OF SOMEONE'S RUIN.

I'M READY TO BE THE CAUSE OF YOURS.

"So what the hell was that all about?"

Ian raised his head to find his partner standing on the other side of his cubicle, almost exactly like he'd been when Ian had left to meet with Felicity and her assistant.

"It appears my buddy's sister has an unwanted friend." Ian handed Larry the letters. "It's been going on for over a month and the jackass also knows where she lives." He pointed at the envelopes. "Note number two was left on her doorstep."

Larry grunted while reading the letters.

When he finished, he handed them back to Ian. "Jackass, huh? To me it stinks of a jealous woman. She get herself tangled up in some kind of love triangle?"

Ian sat back. "According to her and her assistant, her work is her life right now and has been since she divorced three years ago."

It was perplexing, too, when Ian really stopped to think about it.

In spite of her razor-sharp tongue and eyes, he couldn't ignore the fact Felicity Mayhew happened to be a *smokin'* hot redhead with curves in all the right places. Being only a few years older than her brother put the lady in her late thirties.

That seemed way too young to be living for work.

"So there's an ex-husband," Larry stated.

"Yeah. Sounds like it was an acrimonious divorce, too." Ian glanced at his partner. "But the guy lives in London." Which certainly explained her slight, British accent that had come through a few times during their meeting.

Larry stepped back. "I'm still leaning toward jealous woman. She got any ideas on who it might be? It's clear they know her."

Ian shook his head. "But I told her to give it some real thought and I'd check back in a couple of days." He stood. "In the meantime, I'm going to take these charming notes to the lab."

"I wouldn't get my hopes up they'll find anything."

"They're not." Ian stepped out of his cubicle. "They bring those scumbag parents in yet?"

"En route."

Ian nodded. "I'll make this quick."

The moment Ian stepped into the brisk, late March air, he took a long, deep breath. He then walked into the sunshine and slid his gaze over the stark city skyline.

Denver, Colorado.

Getting the job as detective and moving here had been an unexpected life change. But staying in Grand Junction had ceased to be an option in late December.

He headed for the Crime Laboratory housed in a different building, but in the same complex as police admin.

He'd told Larry that Felicity had been through what sounded like an acrimonious divorce. Something Ian could absolutely understand, though he'd been through a break-up.

But it sure as hell had felt like a divorce.

Anger. Betrayal. Bitterness. Fighting. Even some tears. And all while separating their belongings. Separating their lives which had been entwined since high school. Then he'd really gone off the deep end the day he'd marched into the Grand Junction police station, sealing his fate with their police force.

Ian inhaled another deep breath.

In truth, he was damn lucky his captain—the definition of a good man—had been so understanding. He'd been Ian's much-needed ally and the reason he'd gotten the job as detective with the Denver PD.

If not for Captain Arthur Potts, Ian's law enforcement career would have ended that day he'd stormed into the station to confront the person he'd trusted and treated like a brother for years. The only other friend in Ian's life who held those distinctions was Felicity's brother, Scott.

Ian paused outside the crime lab doors and focused on the letters.

He didn't like keeping something like this from his good buddy. He knew how close Scott was to his family, especially Felicity. The lady had, however, made a damn good argument regarding Scott's happiness. The guy did happen to be over the moon for his girlfriend, Campbell, and vice versa. Scott's daughter, Peyton, loved Campbell as much as Scott. The two absolutely deserved each other and their happiness. But the person behind these letters was *not* going to go away like Felicity hoped. It never worked that way and something about what the notes contained seemed too calm and deliberate.

The person seemed to be biding their time until they struck for good and more notes would surely follow until then. Felicity's harasser fell into the category of unpredictable and that's what made him or her scary. He and Felicity had made an agreement, though, and he would honor it.

Ian released a quick breath and opened the door.

Fingerprints. DNA. Long shots for sure. But he had to start somewhere and maybe he'd get lucky.

Chapter Three

FELICITY CURLED into the corner of her couch and picked up Princess Belle, her tan, miniature poodle. While hugging her dog's warm, soft body close, she stared at the notebook she'd set on her coffee table beside her wine glass. The blank, bright-white page stood out against the table's dark wood, then Ian's request drifted once more through her weary mind.

I need you to really think about who could be doing this.

Easier said than done. Everything she'd told Ian that morning had been the truth.

She, Felicity Mayhew the creator of fairy tale weddings in the Denver metro area, had no life outside of her work. Her closest friends were Lynn and, ironically, Scott's ex-girlfriend, Shannon, who was also Peyton's mother. After Felicity had divorced her ex-husband and left London, she'd possessed zero interest in men. Her face warmed, however, when she remembered her physical needs and desires catching up with her during her first vacation in too many years.

Officially reaching burn out at the beginning of February, she'd handed Lynn the business reins after Valentine's Day and taken herself to Cancún, Mexico for a week of sunshine, turquoise waters, white sand beaches, rest, relaxation...and a bit of revelry in the evenings.

A grin teased the corner of her mouth while she set Princess Belle beside her on the couch. She then leaned forward and picked up her wine glass.

The revelry had included making *friends* with a handsome, single gentleman from northern California staying at the same resort and also on his own.

Felicity sipped her red wine as the memories of letting go that entire week returned.

The trip had, without a doubt, been exactly what she'd needed and wanted. Her grin vanished, though, when another, decidedly less pleasant memory replaced those of her trip.

She'd returned to work on the twenty-third and the first note had arrived on the twenty-fifth with the mail, like Lynn had told Ian.

He or she obviously knows you pretty damn well.

Ian's words were a gross understatement. But who the hell could it be?

Who could so clearly despise her to the point they wanted to harm her physically, mentally, and emotionally?

Felicity shuddered when she pictured the second note laying on her welcome mat, right outside the front door of her home mere blocks from the Cherry Creek Shopping District. Then she'd opened the note, still the most threatening one of the three.

As a single woman living alone, she'd always been vigilant about keeping windows and doors locked, specifically at night. Princess Belle barked at everything and everyone as if she were a ferocious watch dog which definitely kept Felicity on her toes. But at the end of the day her little Princess Belle was just that—a little princess.

Since the notes had started, Felicity had become obsessed with double and even triple checking her front door locks, windows with easy access into her home, and the door that led to the garage. Thinking about it made her stand and walk the few steps right, into the small foyer, to again check the front bolt and handle which were, of course, locked.

She shook her head and returned to the couch where Princess Belle again curled beside her, followed by a sigh. At least one of them felt genuinely safe, secure, and content.

That happened to be what Felicity despised most about this person and the notes.

They'd taken away her sense of safety and security even while at home, the one place she should feel safe and secure.

Once again she racked her brain for someone—*anyone*—in her past and present who she could have inadvertently angered.

Yes, she'd dealt with her fair share of difficult brides and mothers and the occasional difficult groom. But she'd long ago accepted that most of these demanding attitudes stemmed from nerves and a need for perfection on the most important day of their lives. Or their children's lives. Some clients, however, were simply *wankers*. She'd certainly dealt with her fair share of them while partnered with Stacia Marsden, youngest daughter of one of the most wealthy and successful businessmen in the Denver metro area. At the same time, he'd attained that distinction by being ruthless; an attribute he'd passed on to Stacia.

About a year ago this same time, Felicity had reached her limit with the woman and severed their partnership, no longer wanting to be associated with the Marsden name. Though Stacia had pitched an impressive hissy fit and declared Felicity's business would suffer, she'd walked away—

Felicity froze.

Stacia Marsden. The Marsden family.

Her eyes widened as she recalled her last meeting with Stacia in the woman's office.

If looks and words could kill, Felicity would have suffered a painful death that day.

She frowned.

Why wait a year to act on the anger and resentment, though? It didn't make sense. Unless Stacia's anger and resentment had been building over the last twelve months since Felicity's business was thriving? She even received occasional calls from individuals wanting to hire her for planning events. She and Lynn always politely declined since they were weddings only.

Felicity straightened.

Stacia's business *was* event planning. She'd even tried to expand into wedding coordination, but had been unsuccessful. One of those reasons happened to be Felicitous Wedding Creations.

She absently sipped her wine.

Could Stacia Marsden really be capable of leaving and sending nasty notes? Though without question the cliché, rich, entitled brat, Felicity had never gotten the "violent" vibe from her. But what about her all-powerful, ruthless father? Stacia was not only familiar with Felicity's business and had been in her office, but the woman also knew where she lived.

Before Stacia had turned to and embraced the dark side, they'd been friendly partners. It's how the woman had ended up in a relationship with Scott, though it had been brief.

Felicity continued to roll the possibility through her mind several more seconds before reaching for her phone. She needed to run the idea by someone first; the only other person who'd been right beside her from the beginning of the Stacia Marsden partnership until its bitter end.

"Hi," Lynn quickly answered. "Is everything okay?"

"No new notes if that's what you're really asking. And I just had an epiphany."

"You have my attention."

"Stacia. Marsden."

Silence fell on Lynn's end before, "Not an implausible idea, considering her background and *lovely* personality. But that was a year ago."

Felicity stared into her wine glass. "I thought about that, but you know as well as I do we're still thriving despite what she said. Plus, she's been unable to expand into weddings."

"True." Another pause, then, "If it were anyone else, I'd say it's a stretch."

"But Stacia is a Marsden," Felicity interjected. "She proved that a year ago."

"Yes. But she's a *Marsden*," Lynn emphasized. "Taking this to Ian could go in a different type of ugly direction."

Felicity sighed. "Lynn, what choice do I have?" And wouldn't that be such a Marsden family thing to do. A dare, so to speak, as well as a damned if you do go to the police and damned if you don't. "I've been racking my brain all night and she's the only person who makes sense. Her temper is terribly explosive." Probably just like her father's, too.

"Okay. Call Ian first thing in the morning."

Felicity relaxed into the couch cushions. "I will. Thank you for listening."

"You never have to thank me for that. But…I have a question for you."

"I'm listening."

"Would you mind if I called Ian, but for social reasons?"

Felicity halted.

"His smile, the eyes, that voice, the suit"—she laughed—"I sure hope he's single."

"He is," Felicity stated, envisioning everything Lynn had listed about Detective Ian Stafford. "Handsome, for sure, but a little arrogant for my taste." With that hint of defiance, too.

"You just don't like him which is why I'm sure you won't mind me calling him?"

Felicity finished her wine. "Of course not. He's all yours."

Though she couldn't honestly say she did like Ian, picturing him fulfilling a woman's physical desires and needs wasn't a terrible image. At the same time, she knew very little about her brother's good army friend who'd moved here a tad suddenly from Grand Junction.

"Then I guess I'll be calling Ian tomorrow, as well."

Maybe Felicity had judged Ian a little too harshly the evening they'd met at Scott's townhome. But it had been the day she'd hit burn out, and Scott hadn't been returning her calls or texts. Then she'd found out why. He and Ian had been dealing with Campbell's unstable ex-husband who'd been in the area.

She managed a smile. "Going out with Ian will be good for you."

"He has to say yes first. Call me if anything happens, okay?"

Felicity's smile became more genuine at Lynn's tone turning concerned. "I will."

She set her phone and wine glass on the coffee table and again picked up her dog.

While squeezing Princess Belle to her chest, Felicity closed her eyes and mentally placed herself back on the white sand beach of Cancún and listening to the ocean waves.

Being there happened to be the last time she'd felt at peace with herself and surroundings and she couldn't help but wish herself back to that idyllic moment in time.

IAN REACHED into the pocket of his running pants and withdrew his buzzing cell phone. At the unfamiliar local number he answered, "Detective Ian Stafford."

"Hello. It's Felicity…Mayhew."

He glanced at Scott, standing no less than a foot away from him while stretching his legs, and faced Sloan's Lake, a body of water, park, and neighborhood in Denver. The city's skyline loomed in the distance.

"Good morning. Do you have something for me?"

"Yes. Stacia Marsden. An absolutely *dreadful* woman I used to be in business with who has an equally dreadful family."

Ian fought a grin at Felicity's slight British accent while saying the word dreadful. "Would that be the reason you're no longer in business with her?"

"Precisely."

"So things didn't end well between you two." He looked over his right shoulder and caught Scott watching him closely.

"Not even a little bit."

Ian held up his left hand and mimed one minute to which Scott replied with a nod. He then faced the lake once more. "When did this happen?"

"It's been a year. But you need to know, being new to the Denver area," Felicity added, "that the Marsden family is quite rich, powerful, ruthless, and they don't forget what they perceive as disloyalty."

Damn. Were they involved with the mafia? Still, it qualified as a challenge and exactly what he needed to continue proving himself at work.

He grinned. "Well then this should be a lot of fun."

Silence fell on her end, followed by, "Are you being serious right now?"

Her faint British accent again came through and shit if it wasn't mildly attractive.

"My partner and I will look into her and the family." *The family.* There was a movie title in there somewhere. "I'll be in touch. Again, you can call me any day or time if you receive another note." Or worse. However, Ian didn't feel the need to add that to this conversation.

"I will."

He was about to hang up when he heard, "Thank you, Detective."

The call ended, and Ian stared at his phone.

The beautiful lady with the sassy mouth and fiery hair had actually thanked him.

He shook his head and shoved his phone back into his pocket.

"Everything okay?"

Ian faced Scott. "Yeah. Just a work call." At least that couldn't be considered a lie. He thumbed over his shoulder. "You sure you're up for this after a week off, Professor?"

Scott jogged past Ian, toward the path that lined the lake. "We spent a good portion of the week skiing, Detective. So try to keep up."

They fell into a synchronized rhythm beside each other.

Due to the semi-early hour, the dry air felt nothing short of brisk. As they jogged, their breath came out in bursts of white puffs. The still rising sun would eventually melt the frost on the grass, but the day's temp wasn't expected to get out of the forties. Though in a dry climate with the sun shining, it never felt that cold. At least, not to Colorado natives. Or those who had lived in the state for a substantial amount of time.

"It sounds like it was a good trip," Ian stated. And damn if his good buddy, who he'd known since they were little more than kids in the army, didn't deserve it.

Scott grinned. "It was great. Seeing Campbell with her mom and brother and being so happy. She never stopped smiling and laughing. They loved Peyton, too, and vice versa." His grin slipped. "But they occasionally called her *Britt* which I'm still wrapping my brain around. And the reason why it's no longer her name."

Ian nodded.

Britt being short for her real name, Brittany, that she'd legally changed to Campbell as a way to hide from her shit bag ex-husband.

"So when does the lady get to meet the rest of the Mayhew clan?"

They veered left, still jogging in sync.

"We're going down there Easter weekend." Scott laughed. "If my mom had it her way, we'd be going down next weekend when I have Peyton again. But Campbell has to work, and Easter is only a few weeks away. We—I—also need a break from the road and driving."

Ian sensed Scott's gaze before, "Enough about me, Detective. How's it going? Really?"

He knew what his buddy was actually asking, but could only

manage, "Great. The job's starting to click. Good people, too." He eyed Scott. "No complaints."

"I'm glad to hear it, but that's not what I was asking."

"I know."

Silence settled between them.

Ian understood Scott, like Ian's family still in Grand Junction, had to ask because of concern. He had lost almost everything back in December and had barely begun to put the pieces back together; the biggest pieces being his relocation to Denver and job with the DPD.

"You need to get yourself back out there," Scott continued. "Denver's a great place to do it, too. I don't have Peyton this week, so pick a night and I'll be your wingman."

Ian smirked. "I'm sure Campbell would love that."

"Actually, I'm sure she'd love to go with us and help since she's told me a few times she doesn't understand how you can be single."

Scott, however, knew why Ian happened to be single and why he'd left Grand Junction.

Betrayal leading to heartbreak had a way of shutting a guy down for an indeterminate amount of time. The betrayal Ian had experienced from two people he'd blindly trusted had nearly shattered him.

"Ian, Candace and that asshole don't deserve you giving them any more attention and thought than you've already given them since December."

He glanced sharply at the lake. "I know that and I don't want to talk about this." Because he still couldn't shake the feeling of utter stupidity on top of the betrayal.

How had he missed the woman he'd known and had been with since high school, and also planned to marry, screwing his married partner for months?

Shit, he had to be one of the most clueless, trusting men on the planet.

"I'll drop the subject," Scott threw back, "after you pick a date to go out this week."

Ian narrowed his eyes. "You're not going to let this go, are you?"

"Hell no. And it's not like I'm expecting you meet *the one* and get married the next day."

"Gee, that's a relief."

"It's about moving forward and having fun and getting to know Denver a bit better." Scott stopped which forced Ian to do the same. "We both know you need to do this."

Ian released a heavy sigh.

It wouldn't necessarily be bad to go out on a Friday or Saturday night in his new city and with a good friend. As much as he loved his dog, Stella, and her company, getting out of his rental house and being a wholly different type of social would be a damn nice change.

He also couldn't help but wonder if he even knew how to be single after years of being with Candace. He'd never really thought about whether he could be considered charming and desirable by women. He'd only had eyes for Candace.

Going out as a single guy in Denver could turn out to be an eye-opening experience and exactly what he needed as a way to start truly moving forward.

"Ian, come on. I don't have all day and neither do you so pick a date."

He frowned. "When did you turn into such a pushy bastard?"

Scott shrugged. "Probably from spending way too much time with Felicity."

Ian didn't know Felicity very well, but pushy seemed a bit too kind a word to describe her sharp personality and eyes and her entire sassy package, for that matter.

"Fine. You win, Professor. Friday night." He paused, then added, "If, of course, nothing comes up at work." Now that he was a detective, this really rang true.

Always on the clock, for better or worse.

They once again fell into their synchronized jogging.

Okay. He actually had something social—that didn't include hanging out with his partner and family—to look forward to this week.

Felicity had given him a name with regards to her harasser. Sounded like this Stacia Marsden could be a legit possibility, too. He'd talk it over with Larry when he got to work. If the last name happened to be as important as Felicity had stated, his partner would probably have some good insight.

Maybe this week would actually end up being better than forgettable.

Chapter Four

"I CAN'T TELL you how excited I am that *the* Felicity Mayhew is going to be my wedding planner." The newly engaged young woman, who didn't look old enough to drink much less get married, released a round of giggles. "It's going to be the most perfect day of my life!"

As she continued to laugh, Felicity smiled and focused on the mother-of-the-bride seated beside her glowing daughter. The two were seated in front of Felicity's executive glass-top desk, a gift to herself when Felicitous Wedding Creations had grown to the point of needing office space. "I'll have my assistant draw up the contract that will contain everything we discussed"—she turned her smile on the bride-to-be—"including all of your wants and needs for your wedding day."

Wants and needs that included arriving at The Brown Palace Hotel in downtown Denver in a horse-drawn carriage that resembled the one in *Cinderella*. The young woman wasn't picky about which movie version Felicity drew from for inspiration.

The bride-to-be giggled some more and quietly clapped her hands.

Felicity kept her smile in place.

She—they—seemed like pleasant enough people who'd probably

be happy with what Felicity eventually came up with in the coming weeks.

"Oh!" The young woman reached into her Prada backpack and withdrew her phone. "I have to text my fiancé the *awesome* news."

This young bride-to-be, however, had the enthusiasm and energy of a puppy who'd just lapped up an espresso shot.

"When can we expect to see the contract?" her mother asked while her daughter's thumbs rapidly hit her phone's keyboard.

"Within two days."

Felicity stood, followed by mother and daughter, though the girl's eyes stayed focused on her phone. Felicity then held out her hand which the older woman grasped. "I'm looking forward to bringing your daughter's wedding vision to life."

"Thank you for everything, Ms. Mayhew." She released Felicity's hand. "Stacia Marsden actually approached us about planning the wedding since our families are distant friends."

Felicity froze.

"Between your impeccable reputation and experience," the woman continued, "it was obvious we had to reach out to you." She leaned forward. "It's no secret Stacia can be quite…temperamental."

Temperamental. That was certainly one way to describe the woman.

"One should also never mix business with friendship, even distant ones."

Felicity's smile deepened.

Yes. She and this particular mother-of-the-bride would get along just fine.

As soon as they left her office, Felicity sat and her gaze drifted left to her light-oak credenza situated under the lone office window. Her view of another building certainly couldn't be considered spectacular, but she still smiled since moving into this space one block off of popular and busy 16th Street in downtown Denver had been an absolute high. As had the awards she'd received for wedding planning she'd placed on top of her credenza due to the sunlight the area received.

Felicitous Wedding Creations had definitely come a long way from where she'd started, planning intimate, cost effective weddings in and outside of the London area.

Intimate, cost effective, *romantic* weddings.

Her smile slipped and she dragged her gaze to the copious notes she'd taken during her meeting that she needed to organize for Lynn. She also had to get on the phone with her contact at The Brown Palace Hotel regarding the couple's preferred wedding date in June of *next* year. There were additional phone calls she needed to make and return. Last-minute details for an enormous wedding this weekend had to be finalized.

Enormous weddings. Horse-drawn, *Cinderella* carriages. Influential families.

In actuality, her business had come a long way from realistic and romantic. At some point, she'd ended up being a planner only wealthy and prominent people could afford.

She frowned at the notes she'd taken.

A handful of years later, Felicity couldn't shake the feeling it no longer felt satisfying. On top of those realizations, she'd somehow acquired an enemy, as well, which led her thoughts to Ian and his partner speaking to Stacia Marsden about the horrible notes.

The fact Stacia had recently lost yet another wedding to Felicity only fueled her belief the woman had to be behind all of this. Who else could it logically be?

She halted when another epiphany hit.

The first note had arrived here at her office not only after her return from Cancún, but on the day she'd secured the wedding of a state representative's daughter. She'd just received the third note, mere days before securing *this* wedding of a young, local socialite to the son of a family who owned half of a professional Denver sports team.

Two large, important weddings involving VIPs any planner in the Denver metro area would kill to have on their schedule.

Kill.

She cringed.

Certainly not the best word choice when she recalled the truly awful second note.

Stacia must have also reached out to the state representative's family and daughter, which led Felicity right back to who else could it be? The Marsden family would not react well to Denver PD detectives showing up to question one of their own. Of that Felicity was certain and she cringed once more. But like she'd told Lynn, what choice did she have?

After she'd given Ian the bare minimum with regards to the Marsden family, he'd responded that it "should be fun" talking to Stacia. His glibness had caught her off guard. At the same time, Felicity couldn't help but admire his overall confidence. Though it often went in the direction of maddening arrogance, Ian Stafford did emanate integrity and a certain amount of fearlessness. He seemed to be the kind of officer—detective —who would do whatever it took to solve a case. He'd demonstrated that when it came to finding and arresting Campbell's ex.

He actually appeared to be a good man. Reliable and loyal and quite personable.

His easy, bright-white grin drifted through her mind.

Lynn's interest in him was definitely understandable, and Felicity wondered if her assistant had called him yet. She was currently out of the office meeting with their newest partner, an up-and-coming caterer.

From what little Felicity had heard from Scott, Ian had been in a years-long relationship with a woman that had abruptly ended in December. Then he'd moved to Denver. There seemed to be a chance Ian may not be ready to date, but she hoped for Lynn's sake he'd say yes and they'd have a lovely time. It would be good for both of them no matter what happened.

She refocused on the notes.

They weren't going to organize and type themselves.

She moved the mouse to wake up her computer at the same time her cell began to vibrate and ring. When she saw the caller's name, however, she hesitated for several seconds before releasing a heavy sigh and answering, "Hi. Shouldn't you be in class?"

"I'm leaving my office now," Scott replied. "I'm calling to ask why the hell am I calling *you*? I've been back since Sunday night and I haven't heard from you. I never have to call or text you. Is everything okay?"

No, it surely wasn't. But Felicity had zero intention of telling her younger, yet extremely protective brother a damn thing until Ian had caught the rotten person. It's the main reason she hadn't called Scott since he'd returned from Durango.

"I'm fine," she lied. "I'm just incredibly swamped at work. We are easing into wedding season." Those statements weren't at all lies, which eased her guilt a fraction. "But I do want to hear all about your trip."

"Okay. Happy hour at our favorite place this Thursday night? I'm sure you know Peyton's with Shannon."

She did know that and happy hour this Thursday night sounded blissful. She simply didn't think she could sit across from Scott for two or so hours and pretend her life hadn't changed for the worse in the last month. One of Scott's closest friends knew it, though.

"Rain check?" She briefly closed her eyes. "This is a terribly busy week for me."

Silence fell on Scott's end, followed by, "I understand. Check in next week?"

"Of course." She forced her mouth into a smile. "I'll try my best not to work your girlfriend too hard this Saturday."

He laughed. "I'm going to hold you to that."

Felicity lowered her phone and ended the call.

It truly was for the best she kept Scott and the rest of her family in the dark about the notes. With Ian's help and Lynn's support, she could handle this unforeseen twist in her life.

Everything would be fine.

Thinking about Ian caused her to picture him talking to Stacia, possibly even presenting the notes to the woman?

Felicity always kept her cell close, but today she'd also max out the volume. She would *not* miss any calls, specifically from the detective.

CAPTAIN ALAN GELLAR'S THICK, black eyebrows damn near reached the ceiling before his robust upper body started to shake from hearty laughter. "The daughter of this city's richest, most pompous asshat sending her number one competition threatening notes." He continued to laugh.

A little over a month into the job, Ian still didn't know his captain that well. He seemed to be the definition of a good man, like his last captain. Checked in with his officers and detectives when appropriate, but also knew how to stay out of the way. That told Ian the man trusted his staff to do their job. But he had yet to figure out the man's reactions and quirks.

Sometimes he merely grunted after a quick check in and walked away. Sometimes he offered thoughts and advice. Sometimes he'd take a moment to get into a heated conversation about Denver's hockey and basketball teams. And sometimes he simply burst into laughter.

Ian dragged his gaze from his boss which collided with Larry's.

His partner lifted his shoulders and went back to picking at his jagged thumb nail.

Larry, who'd been working for him for years, seemed to be saying he hadn't figured the man out, either. He also didn't seem overly concerned about it.

"That family needs to be taken down to the depths of hell and left there." Gellar straightened. "Your friend has no other thoughts on who could be threatening her?"

Ian shook his head. "No. According to her and the assistant, she's a workaholic who plans fairy tale weddings for a living."

The man nodded. "Believe it or not, I've heard of her."

Ian raised his eyebrows before again looking at Larry who had stopped his nail picking.

He hadn't thought much about Felicity's career as a wedding planner. But the fact their captain had heard of her meant she must have built quite a name for herself in the Denver area.

It was something Ian couldn't help but admire, too.

"If you've got piles of money to burn on a wedding, she's where all the local brides go." He released another round of hearty laughter. "My niece wanted to hire her for her big wedding in Estes Park, but my brother almost went into cardiac arrest when they started talking money. Anyway"—he pointed at the notes Ian held that were copies of the originals—"tread lightly with the Marsden woman. My guess is she'll call her daddy who will swoop in with his fancy lawyers before you can introduce yourselves."

Ian silently stood.

It's not like he or Larry could argue that point.

"I'll call her office to see if she's actually there," Ian said as he and Larry headed back to their cubicles. "Being an event planner, she could be anywhere in this city."

"Yo, Stafford!"

Ian glanced sharply to his left to find a uniformed officer leaning against a nearby cubicle. Another uniform stood with him.

"There's a woman here to see you."

Larry stopped and faced him. "*Another* one?"

Though Ian had no idea who the woman could be, he grinned. "What can I say? It's not easy looking this good." He gestured at himself.

Larry's eyes rolled sideways. "And to think Tess has been bugging me to let her set you up with some girl she met during her yoga class." He snatched the notes that were in plastic baggies from Ian's fingers. "Guess this means I'll be tracking down Princess Marsden."

Ian laughed quietly while leaving the heart of the Major Crimes Unit. He stopped in his tracks, however, when his gaze locked with Lynn Delgado's who was waiting outside the doors to the unit; the same area she'd been yesterday only with Felicity.

Lynn gave him a warm, but borderline shy smile. "Hi."

"Good morning." He frowned and swiftly closed the large gap between them. "Where's Felicity? Is everything okay?"

"It's fine. I mean"—she paused for a few seconds, then sighed—"nothing new has happened since we were here this time yesterday."

Ian's shoulders relaxed.

"This is actually a social visit."

Their gazes caught once more.

She brought back her warm smile, but Ian caught hesitancy flash through her large eyes.

Oh, *shit*. Was she here to ask him—

"I was wondering if you'd like to meet up for a drink sometime this week?"

Yep. She'd shown up here to ask him out.

"You're new to Denver, so I thought you'd enjoy seeing what the city has to offer at night." Her smile deepened. "Have you spent any time in LoDo yet?"

A sense of déjà vu settled around Ian. And why the hell were people suddenly so concerned about his personal life?

"There are some bars down there with great happy hours."

Okay. With her deep brown eyes, long, thick dark hair, and subtle curves accentuated by her gray business suit, Lynn Delgado definitely qualified as easy on the eyes.

"Or we could meet up in Cherry Creek if LoDo doesn't interest you."

He'd also agreed to go out with Scott this Friday night as a way to ease back into the dating game. But could he really be ready to go on an actual date with an attractive woman who was apparently interested in him?

"Or we could catch the Hogwarts Express to Platform Nine-and-Three-Quarters."

Ian blinked twice. Upon realizing he hadn't said one word since she'd asked him out, he had the good grace to laugh.

"You are still with me." Her grin became a tad flirtatious. "Personally, I think the last option sounds more intriguing than drinks during happy hour, but that will have to suffice."

He returned her grin. "You must like Harry Potter."

She lifted her shoulders. "Only because of my niece and nephew."

Attractive. Witty. Smart. Independent. He'd be insane to turn down Lynn Delgado. And it was one evening. Unless, of course, they happened to vibe even more on a date.

Would that necessarily be a bad thing?

Her smile slipped several notches. "Did I catch you at a bad time? I had planned on calling, but I was at a meeting not too far from here and when it ended I thought—"

"You're fine. I promise." He slipped his hands into his pockets. "You just caught me off guard." *Shit*, was that the truth.

"In a good way, I hope?" She brought back her flirty smile.

He laughed. "Definitely. Meeting up for a happy hour this week would be great."

It's not like he had a damn thing to lose.

"Excellent. Will Thursday night work?"

"As of right now, yes. But so you understand, I'm always on the clock."

"Of course." She stepped backward. "I'll text you a place and time."

"Sounds good."

With a final, flirty smile, she turned from him.

Grinning, Ian walked back into the unit.

Scott would probably be shocked by Lynn coming here and

asking Ian out on a date. But he'd also be happy at this real step forward and away from what Ian had left in Grand Junction. His grin faded, however, at seeing Larry's forehead stuck in a deep frown.

"We have a big problem, Casanova."

Ian stopped and leaned against the opening of his partner's cubicle. "What happened?"

"Princess Marsden is currently in Tahiti with her mom and sister and won't be back at work until Monday."

Ian nodded. "Okay. That sucks. We'll just have to talk to her when she's back."

"If only it were that simple."

Ian remained silent.

"The person I spoke with added '*the Marsden family has become aware of Ms. Mayhew's allegations and that Ms. Marsden won't be speaking to us without a lawyer present.*'"

Ian's mouth fell open. "What the hell? How could they be so many steps ahead of us?"

Who was this family?

"I don't know," Larry muttered. "Regardless, we're stuck until the princess returns."

Ian gritted his teeth.

This didn't make sense. Felicity had probably told Lynn her suspicions before she'd told Ian. He'd brought it to his partner, and they'd gone to their captain.

What the hell was going on here?

"I'd call your friend to give her the update," Larry added. "I'd also warn her the Marsdens have already lawyered up."

Ian walked into his cubicle and dropped into the chair.

None of this felt right and now he had to call Felicity with bad news.

As he stared blankly at the computer monitor, darkness shrouded him when a horrible question penetrated his muddled thoughts.

What if the Marsdens had a good "friend" with big ears working for the DPD? It could be anyone, too. And what if he'd bitten off more than he could chew when it came to this family? He was a rookie detective in a major city determined to prove himself. But to what extent?

On that thought, Ian clasped the computer mouse. Within a second the monitor came to life. Better to learn as much as possible about the enemy before going into any type of battle.

Chapter Five

FELICITY GLANCED at her phone's screen for what had to be the millionth time and sighed.

Still no word from Ian about meeting with Stacia Marsden.

She shoved her phone inside her purse, then stood and picked up the oversized bag that worked as her mobile office.

After spending most of the day on the phone, she was beyond ready to go home, walk her dog, and sink into a hot bath. Lynn had offered to head to The Halcyon Hotel in Cherry Creek, the site of this Saturday's opulent wedding, to do a final check with the on-site coordinator.

Felicity had been all too happy and relieved to hand that over to her assistant…who'd been smiling like a teenager in love due to her date with Ian Stafford.

She heaved her bag onto her shoulder and left her office.

Though she knew the night out would be good for both of them, envy tugged at her soul.

Having almost no life outside of family and friends, swearing off the male species after her acrimonious divorce, and the grueling hours had put Felicity where she currently existed in Denver's world of lavish weddings.

She locked her office's main, glass door and headed for the elevator.

At seeing Lynn's schoolgirl smile all day over a date with a handsome man, Felicity couldn't help but miss that feeling. The excitement combined with nerves and possibilities and attraction.

She stared at the digital numbers above the elevator doors counting down.

Five...four...three...two...one.

The doors opened.

She continued to stand in the elevator.

The only thing waiting for her at home happened to be her little Princess Belle. She loved her dog dearly. She had no problem calling herself a proud dog mom. But Princess Belle wasn't human and after years of a bad marriage followed by singlehood, Felicity couldn't ignore the pang of loneliness.

She stepped from the elevator when the doors started to close.

The loneliness had started at seeing her brother finally and so perfectly matched. Now Lynn, who was more than her assistant, had a possible love connection on the horizon.

Her phone started to ring, and she stopped to withdraw it from her purse.

It had to be Ian—she frowned at the out-of-state, California number.

Her shoulders fell.

It was probably a wedding call and though she felt compelled to not answer, she cleared her throat and said, "This is Felicity."

A pause, followed by, "Hi. It's Perry Cantrell."

Felicity froze at the smooth, familiar voice she'd never expected to hear again.

"From Cancún?"

Her mouth inched open.

He'd actually kept her phone number? The only reason she'd given him her number was so they could easily find each other on the massive property before they'd *really* connected. It hadn't taken very long for that to happen, either.

"Are you there?"

"Yes!" she blurted out. "Hi." But unlike him, she'd deleted his number after they'd parted ways the day he'd left Cancún.

He laughed. "It sounds like I've surprised the hell out of you."

More like he'd shocked her speechless.

Why on earth would he have kept her number? They'd befriended each other on social media, but had never discussed ever reconnecting via phone or in person. It's why she'd deleted his number.

"Is this a good time?"

She gave her head a hard shake. "Yes. I'm…leaving work for the day." She released a quick laugh. "And yes. You have definitely surprised the hell out of me. How are you?"

Not a scintillating question. At the same time, her brain had become befuddled.

"Not too bad. You?"

"Good." She cringed. "Just up to my neck in work right now." And dealing with a person who wanted to harm her, but of course she wouldn't share such information.

"Work. That's actually the reason I'm calling. I'm going to be in Denver next week for a week-long conference. I didn't know they were sending me out there until today."

She smiled.

"Of course I instantly thought of you," he easily continued. "How could I not after Cancún?" He laughed once more. "I actually wanted to reach out much sooner, but it didn't feel right since we never talked about staying in touch. Beyond Facebook."

Her smile deepened. "It's nice to hear from you." Not at all a lie, considering the direction her life had gone since returning from her blissful, tropical trip.

"And that's nice to hear."

Felicity could hear the smile in his voice.

"So does that mean my lovely friend from Cancún will be able to fit seeing me into her busy schedule and show me around Denver while I'm there?"

She nodded while her mind tried to recall her schedule for next week. "I'm pretty certain I can make that happen."

He'd be at his conference while she worked, which would leave them the evenings.

He did live out-of-state. But they'd had a fantastic time together throughout the idyllic week and she had no reason to believe they wouldn't click all over again here in Denver.

"Excellent. I get in Sunday night, but the conference starts at seven-thirty Monday morning. Maybe we could meet up Monday evening for dinner?"

Anticipation shimmied through Felicity as she said, "It's a date."

"Great. I'll check in with you Monday." Another pause fell on his end, then, "Felicity, I'm really looking forward to seeing you again."

She laughed quietly. "Me, too."

The call ended and she stared at her phone.

Had that just happened? A handsome, successful software engineer she'd connected with in Cancún, Mexico of all places had kept her number and would be in Denver all next week?

She burst into laughter.

Lynn would never believe any of this. For once, Felicity Mayhew had something to look forward to in her workaholic life. With she and Perry living states apart, however, it would never be anything serious. She had no time and interest in a long-distance relationship.

Felicity dropped her phone back inside her purse.

That didn't mean they couldn't have fun here in Denver. She damn well deserved it, too.

With a huge grin, she pushed through the building's lobby doors —and into Ian Stafford.

The door struck his forehead with a *thunk*.

"Oh, I'm so sorry."

He stumbled back a few steps, onto the sidewalk.

Felicity followed him. "Let me see your head."

He held out his left hand while he rubbed the spot with his right. "I'm fine."

"Are you sure?" She grasped his wrist and tugged his hand down to fully inspect his forehead. "Maybe you should sit down."

Ian lowered his gaze which locked with hers.

Silence settled between them while his dark, sultry eyes pierced her as if he were trying to read her mind.

Her breathing slowed.

A short stream of people walked around them while having a loud conversation.

"I played football in high school," he murmured without breaking their eye contact. "I still play with my dad and brother every Thanksgiving and Christmas. I was also in the army for years and spent fifteen months in Afghanistan."

Yes. He had. Just like Scott. They'd been in the same unit.

His mouth eased into a grin.

A rather enticing grin, at that.

"Trust me when I say I'm fine." He stepped back, severing their gaze. "But I appreciate your concern, Ms. Mayhew."

She sighed. "Please call me Felicity."

They hadn't exactly hit it off the day they'd met. Still, Ian appeared to be a genuinely kind, loyal, hardworking man with integrity to spare.

"Alright. And I guess I'll let you call me Detective Ian."

She narrowed her eyes.

None of that changed the fact he also had arrogance to spare.

He slipped his hands into his pockets while his grin faded. "We need to talk and I didn't want to do this over the phone."

The exhilaration she'd been enjoying before plowing into Ian left Felicity as if a balloon's opening had been released.

Of course he'd shown up here with bad news. Had she really expected anything better?

"Are you leaving work for the day?"

She nodded. "The building doesn't have parking so I'm headed to my car."

"Then we'll walk and talk."

Ian fell into step beside her.

Grudgingly, she shoved Perry's exciting call and news to the back of her mind to refocus on her detestable reality.

AS THEY REACHED HER CAR, a bright-white, shiny Mercedes SUV, Ian finished giving Felicity the frustrating news.

Between the SUV, the designer-label bags, and black heels and business suit that fit her curves perfectly, the lady sure as hell seemed to be doing a-okay. Maybe a little too okay when it came to the person harassing her. In that respect, the Marsden woman seemed to be the most obvious choice. Larry had also offered the opinion the notes reeked of a jealous woman.

But could it really be that simple?

Felicity opened the driver's side rear door and placed her bags on the seat. She then slammed the door shut. "Of course that damn family has somehow already found out and gone to their lawyers." She leaned against her SUV. "I should probably expect a lawsuit, too."

Ian leaned forward. "I wouldn't take that on as a concern just yet. She has to return to Denver before anything else happens."

She nodded while staring at the ground.

"But because of what I discovered on my own about this family," he continued, "I have to ask are you absolutely positive there could be no one else behind the notes?"

The Marsdens weren't mafia, but they did own a good portion of the Denver metro area. And owning people, especially VIPs, always came with that kind of power.

Always.

Felicity slid her gaze to his. "If it was anyone else but the Marsden family, you wouldn't be asking me that question again."

He lifted his shoulders, unable to dispute her statement.

She straightened. "Unfortunately, Detective, Stacia is the only person who would be jealous and petulant enough to send me harassing notes. She also has the *means*?"

Means clearly equalling money and the right daddy to help her do the dirty work.

Still, Ian had to exhaust other possibilities Felicity may not have considered. Going into battle with this family could prove disastrous and soul-crushing for the lady who'd created a thriving business and notable name for herself.

He and Felicity were really nothing more than acquaintances. But she sure as shit didn't deserve to lose everything she'd built and created because of a spoiled rich girl essentially throwing a tantrum because she wasn't getting what she wanted. At least, that's how it seemed from his perspective coming from a more modest background.

"What about other wedding planners?" he persisted. "You and the Marsden woman can't be the only two in the area who are in this line of work."

"We're not." She sighed. "But we appeal to a very specific clientele."

"Important rich people." More like rich people who thought they were important.

"Yes." She shook her head. "I know it sounds elitist. And *I* didn't start out that way."

Ian fell silent at her quietly spoken last sentence.

It almost sounded as if she could be battling some regrets. Perhaps due to the notes?

She lifted her chin.

It was a defiant action she'd done a few times in front of him. Something that more than likely had frustrated the hell out of her parents when she'd been a teenager. Fiery hair, light-brown eyes full of passion, and chin turned upward. Like she looked right now.

He couldn't help but grin softly.

"I'm sorry, but what about this are you finding amusing?"

And there was that hint of British accent which seemed to only complement all of *her*.

Ian shook is head. "Not a thing." He needed to snap out of it. As a single man, he also needed to get the hell out of his house and away from Stella. "I understand what you're saying." His captain had even stated brides with access to money trees go to Felicity to plan their over-the-top weddings. "Okay. We'll get in touch with the Marsden woman once she's back in town. I'm still waiting on fingerprint and DNA results from the letters. But like I said, I'm not hopeful. I'll be in touch next week." He turned to head back the way they'd come.

"Detective?"

He stopped and glanced over his left shoulder.

Their gazes snapped together.

"Lynn told me you're going out for drinks Thursday night."

He shot her a quick smile.

"Lynn's much more than my assistant."

He nodded, though he could sense where this was going.

"She's also a dear friend who works as hard as I do." Felicity leaned forward. "She deserves a man who will give her his undivided attention beyond a first date."

He narrowed his eyes, understanding her implication perfectly.

Apparently, Scott must have told his sister some aspect of Ian's break-up weeks before he'd moved to Denver and most likely due to Felicity's pushiness.

She opened the car door. "I hope you two have a lovely evening."

Ian faced forward and continued to head in the direction they'd come from.

He hoped they had a "lovely evening," as well. Because he deserved it. But if he and Lynn Delgado ended up sharing no connection whatsoever, he sure as hell would not waste his time or hers by going on another date. He'd already wasted too many years to count on a woman he thought he'd known inside and out. He also couldn't help but suspect she'd cheated on him while he'd been gone, fighting for his country. But not one person in his life, including Candace, had ever admitted to such a thing.

Either she'd hidden her infidelities really damn well or she'd actually been faithful.

Ian gritted his teeth.

Knowing how well she and his former partner had hidden their relationship, he had a feeling she'd just been that sneaky. Regardless, Ian wouldn't string Lynn along if there ended up being nothing between them on his part.

They both deserved better, no matter having that awkward conversation.

His phone began to ring and he reached into his suit jacket pocket. At the name on the screen, though, his steps faltered.

Holy shit, this couldn't be good.

He hesitated a few more seconds before answering, "Hi."

Maren Gregson sniffed, then said, "Hi. Can you talk right now?"

The fact she'd been crying only amplified Ian's dread.

He walked a few steps to the left, off of the sidewalk. "Yeah. What happened?"

She continued to sniffle. "Candace is…pregnant."

His breath left his lungs.

"They're…going to Hawaii to get married now that the divorce is final."

He briefly closed his eyes as his worthless ex-partner's now ex-wife softly cried.

"I asked that cheating, lying *bastard* for years to take me to Hawaii and now—" Her sobbing replaced where that statement had obviously been heading.

Ian gripped his phone so hard he half expected it to burst into dust. "Maren, take a breath." He racked his brain for something else to say to the woman who'd also been knocked sideways by the selfishness of two people they'd loved and trusted. "Where are you right now?" Not that he could do a damn thing being five hours away from Grand Junction.

"I'm…at home. I couldn't go to work today."

"Is someone with you?"

It had been no secret Maren had slipped into a deep depression after Candace and his ex-partner had planned the four of them going out to dinner—days before Christmas—where the cowards had then dropped their nuclear bomb. But the social setting hadn't stopped Ian or Maren from giving everyone in the restaurant a gossip-worthy show.

Maren sniffed twice and released a humorless laugh. "Ian, I'm fine…in that respect. The medication my doctor put me on is helping."

He loosened his grip on the phone. "Good." He rubbed his eyes. "I'm sorry I left so quickly." More like sped from Grand Junction as soon as he could without a backward glance. "We're friends, too, and I wasn't thinking clearly." More like thinking of himself.

"Don't you dare apologize for taking care of yourself," she scolded in a surprisingly strong voice. "And you getting the hell out of Grand Junction has inspired me to do the same."

He lifted his head.

"That and finding out those two are on their way to *happily* ever after."

His jaw tightened. "Maren, those two will never be truly happy." Of that Ian felt certain. "What are your plans?"

"I'm moving to Phoenix to be closer to my sister and her family. Our parents spend half the year down there, too. They're down there right now, as a matter of fact."

Ian managed a slight smile. "I think that's great, Maren. Really."

He had hated leaving her in Grand Junction to cope with everything with no family support. She had friends, of course, but Ian, and by extension Candace, had become a part of the Gregson household. Friends who had become family which only added to the betrayal.

"I'm going to give my two-week notice tomorrow," she added around a sniff. "I've already started packing up what the *bastard* didn't take when I kicked him out in December."

Ian had almost kicked Candace out of their rental house, but instead packed up his stuff and Stella's a few days after they'd dropped their bomb and went to his parents' house. Then he'd stormed into the Grand Junction Police Department which changed his career course.

Leaving where he'd grown up had definitely been hard, but Ian now had zero regrets since Maren seemed to be on a positive path forward.

"I plan on being out of here the morning after my last day at work." She laughed bitterly. "I can't and won't be here when those two get back from their trip."

"I know," he murmured. "Call me anytime for anything. I don't care what it is. If I can't answer, leave a message or text and I will call you back."

"Thank you, Ian. For everything." A pause fell on her end, then, "Now that you're no longer together, I have to tell you I always thought you were way too good for Candace."

Ian stared at the tops of his black loafers.

This wasn't the first time someone in his life had admitted such a thing.

How could he have been so blind and foolish when it came to the *real* Candace?

"Something about her seemed…phony. And cunning." Maren huffed. "Now I know why I always felt that way."

"They deserve each other," he muttered. "If I don't hear from you sooner, call me when you get settled in Phoenix?"

"Sure. And you stay safe out there in Denver, Detective Stafford."

He cracked a smile. "I'll do my best."

After hanging up, Ian dropped his phone back inside his suit pocket.

Pregnant and getting married in Hawaii.

He shoved his hands into his pockets and started walking once more.

They sure as shit weren't wasting a second which told Ian the main reason Candace had stayed with him was that she'd viewed him as being better than nothing.

Better than being alone.

During their lengthy time together, they'd discussed marriage but the timing had never been right for *her* while he'd been in the army. He'd never really pushed the topic, either. Only once had she been determined to set a wedding date.

But he hadn't been on the same page as her during that difficult time in *his* life.

His footsteps turned heavy on the pavement.

The cheating signs had been there that had included all the nights out with her girlfriends, even when Ian hadn't been working. He'd simply not wanted to see them. But now he knew. Lesson learned. And it would never happen again. He'd lost way too much valuable time on the wrong people—wrong person—and needed to start living again.

Life was too damn short. Trite for sure, but it especially rang true in his line of work.

Felicity's parting comment drifted through his mind.

I hope you two have a lovely evening.

No matter what happened between him and Lynn, meeting her for drinks was a necessary step forward and anticipation settled around him for the first time in weeks.

Chapter Six

AS IT TURNS *out I couldn't wait until Monday to text you. How's your week going?*

Felicity smiled at Perry's message.

"Who in the world just texted you? You almost never smile like that."

Her head snapped up where she found her good friend, Shannon Glenne, watching her with round eyes.

"Aunt Felicity, when can I come over and play with Princess Belle?" This from her five-year-old niece, Peyton.

Felicity flashed them quick smiles before texting Perry, *Not too bad. Your week?*

She tapped send, put her phone face down on the restaurant table, and picked up her beer. "You've seen me smile like that multiple times." To her niece she said, "You can come over anytime you want to play with Princess Belle." She reached out and tickled Peyton's waist, then laughed when she burst into her little girl giggles.

Her niece had inherited a few physical attributes from her brunette, blue-eyed, beautiful mother, but she absolutely favored Scott—the Mayhew line in general—with her copious strawberry-blonde hair, bright chestnut eyes, and smile and laugh.

Felicity and her two siblings had been the same shade of red when they'd been Peyton's age which had darkened to a rich auburn in adulthood. She had no doubt the same would happen with Peyton as she grew older and into a head-turning beauty.

"You conveniently didn't answer my question," Shannon persisted before taking a sip of her beer. "Why so coy?"

Felicity swallowed a drink, then said, "Why so nosy?"

"What are you two talking about?" Peyton nearly whined.

"Nothing important, Sweetie." Felicity returned Shannon's glare, set her glass down, and sat back.

At least once a month, when Shannon had Peyton, they did a girls-only night at child-friendly restaurants located between where they each lived. Tonight they'd met up at a low-key burger and beer place, Felicity's favorite type of restaurant since she could shed the designer suits and heels and updos for jeans, a T-shirt, sweatshirt, sneakers, and simple ponytail.

She glanced at Peyton. "I'd much rather talk about your mom and Adam's wedding."

Peyton smiled. "I'm going to meet all of the Disney princesses on the big boat."

"I know you will and I'm terribly jealous," Felicity replied.

"Campbell said the same thing. Did you know Cinderella is her favorite princess? She looks like Cinderella, too. I don't know why Daddy won't let me call her that anymore."

Felicity laughed and eyed Shannon, shaking her head.

"I can't wait," Peyton continued. "Mommy, when do we leave again?"

Shannon pushed a strand of hair behind her daughter's right ear. "Not until June. Right after school is out for summer vacation."

Peyton's drooping shoulders matched the expression on her angelic face.

"Will you at least tell me *his* name?" Shannon asked, now focused on Felicity.

At that moment, Felicity's phone buzzed.

"Don't you dare pick up that phone without answering my question first."

Felicity sighed. "*His* name is Perry." She swiped her phone off of the table.

The week is going painfully slow because I know where I'll be this time next week. He'd also added the winking emoji.

"Perry. Why does that name sound familiar?"

Felicity somehow managed to keep a poker face while replying, *It will be nice seeing you again.* She once more placed her phone on the table, face down.

"Tell me why that name sounds—" Shannon gasped. "*Cancún Perry?*"

"Mommy, what's a Cancún Perry?"

Felicity leaned forward. "Shannon, I love you dearly. But now isn't the time to have this conversation." Her phone buzzed as if to emphasis her point.

Shannon's eyes became slits. "You're right. But you're under strict orders to call me when you get home and tell me everything."

Felicity nodded while grasping her phone.

Likewise. And if the conference wasn't starting so early Monday morning, I'd suggest meeting up for dinner Sunday night.

Grinning, she typed, *I guess we'll just have to be patient.*

"Speaking of little life twists," Shannon continued. "I heard Ian is going on a date tonight with your Lynn."

"She's not my Lynn, and yes."

The waitress appeared with their food.

Felicity leaned back as the young woman set down the plastic basket containing a juicy bacon-cheese burger and seasoned fries. The sight and smell made her mouth water. "Did Scott tell you?"

She only allowed herself food like this once a week. Her healthy curves could quickly become unhealthy with little effort and something she'd battled since becoming a *woman* oh-so many years ago.

"Yeah," Shannon answered while cutting Peyton's much smaller, plain cheeseburger in half. "After he talked to Peyton, we chatted for a bit and I asked how Ian was doing." She laughed. "I was so happy to hear he was going on a date with Lynn and that she asked him."

Felicity remained silent while munching a French fry.

"Uncle Ian's on a date with Aunt Lynn?" Peyton looked at her mom, then Felicity. "What's a date?"

Felicity smiled and pointed at Shannon using a fry.

"Honey, just eat your dinner."

Peyton sighed, picked up one half of her cheeseburger, and took a dainty bite.

"It especially made me happy," Shannon added after eating her own fry, "knowing what Candace did to him." She shook her head. "Scott always liked her way more than I did."

Felicity frowned. "All Scott told me was that Ian had been through a bad break-up and it was one of the reasons he'd decided to move here." And quite suddenly, too.

"Bad break-up is a gross understatement," Shannon muttered. "In any case, I'm so glad he's here and far away from that bi—woman." She cringed and glanced at her daughter, closely watching and listening to them.

Felicity smiled at Shannon stopping herself from calling Ian's ex something far worse.

For reasons she couldn't fathom, curiosity regarding the clearly ugly details of Ian's break-up with this woman named Candace swirled through Felicity's mind. Perhaps because one of her closest friends happened to be on a date with him at this precise moment in time?

She'd known enough about the break-up to…gently…warn him not to take it out on Lynn, who didn't deserve to get caught in the middle of any lingering hurt tand drama on his part. Though he hadn't said a word, Felicity had seen understanding flash through his hypnotic, dark bedroom eyes—she frowned at her food.

Hypnotic, dark bedroom eyes? Where the hell had that come from?

Incredibly tall, dark, and handsome fit Ian Stafford's looks. But she didn't even like him.

Or did she?

His support and determination to get to the bottom of her harassment case while they stood beside her car filled her head. Now knowing he'd been mistreated by his ex-girlfriend caused her frown to deepen. What she did know about him, and had seen and experienced firsthand, didn't amount to his ex having reason to treat him badly. Then again, she knew from her own experience people like that didn't need reasons to mistreat the ones who loved and cherished them the most.

They were simply awful and selfish and had no idea what it meant to be a human being.

"Text Lynn and see how it's going," Shannon suddenly commanded.

Felicity stared at her friend.

"Don't look at me like that." Shannon wiped her hands on her napkin. "What if she's having a lousy time? A text from you could give her the out she may need."

"Can I text Uncle Ian a joke my teacher told us today?" Peyton asked. "He told me he loves my jokes."

"Later, Honey. I promise." Shannon continued to stare at Felicity with raised eyebrows.

With her own heavy sigh, Felicity picked up her phone.

Perry had responded to her being patient comment with, *Easier said than done, but I'm up for the challenge. Have a good night.*

She sent him, *You too*. She then went into her texting thread with Lynn and tapped out, *I'm with Shannon and she wants to know how the big date is going.*

"Done." She dropped her phone into her purse. "Are you happy?"

Shannon laughed and nodded.

By the time they were saying goodbye in the parking lot, however, Lynn still hadn't replied.

"She must be having a great time," Felicity said to Shannon while giving Peyton a long, tight hug. "Not a huge surprise, either." Bad break-up aside, Ian Stafford emanated good guy with a hint of bad. And she couldn't help but think he had to be awfully good at the latter.

"You're right." Shannon pulled Felicity in for a hug. "I've always thought he was a catch." They released each other, and Shannon grasped Peyton's hand. "If not for *Cancún* Perry and Lynn, I'd encourage you to go after him."

Felicity waved her hand in the air as if shooing an annoying fly. "Hardly. We have absolutely nothing in common. He's also much too arrogant and on the rebound." Another undeniable fact about Ian Stafford made her add, "And he's a *police* detective."

After losing her father in the line of duty, who'd been a detective with the Colorado Springs Police Department, she'd sworn to never get involved with a man in law enforcement. Her family—her mother —had lost so much that horrific night twenty-two years earlier.

Shannon's grin faded. "I understand." She lifted her shoulders. "But when your British comes out, that usually means you're feeling a bit too passionate about the subject matter."

Felicity buried the still painful memories and crossed her arms. "Makes perfect sense since I do feel quite strongly about this subject. I would also never do something like that to Lynn." She blew her niece and Shannon a kiss, then waggled her fingers. "I'll see you soon."

"Don't forget to call me when you get home."

Felicity nodded. While heading toward her car, Peyton's high-pitched, "Mommy, what's a Cancún Perry?" reached her which made her shake with quiet laughter.

She walked behind her car, toward the driver's side—and halted.

Her laughter died in her throat while her smile became a straight line at the envelope tucked under the windshield wipers.

With her heart hammering her chest, Felicity slowly approached the front of her car.

It had to be another note. What else could it be?

She gave the other parked cars a cursory glance and of course happened to be the only one with something tucked under her car's wipers.

Her hand trembled as she reached for the note, but then she stopped to give her surroundings a more thorough look.

Nothing but parked cars and a couple walking into the restaurant. It was too dark to see beyond the lot lit up with the usual lights. An eerie silence settled around her.

With a deep breath, she swiped the note from her windshield, opened the driver's side door, slid inside, and shut and locked the doors. Now within her silent automobile, staring at the all-too familiar typeface on the envelope, Felicity heard her rapid heartbeat.

FELICITY MAYHEW

Her lower lip trembled upon realizing while she'd been inside the restaurant, spending quality time with her little niece and mother, a good friend, darkness had been lurking nearby.

Way too close to her and her family.

She carefully opened the envelope and removed the piece of paper. Tears immediately blurred her vision at the latest hateful message that had been left for her less than a week after the last one. They weren't only getting closer together, but more threatening based on the note she held with her still trembling hand.

Ian had given her explicit instructions to call him if she received another note. She hated the thought of interrupting his date with Lynn, but he'd been clear and she, Felicity Mayhew who had been determined to face as much of this on her own as possible, had reached scared.

She blinked her eyes clear, dropped the note and envelope in the passenger seat, and set her purse on top of both. All she wanted at this moment was to get home quickly, lock herself inside, and set the alarm. When those two things were done, she'd call Ian and try not to crack before, during, and after talking to him. She could not and would not let this break her in half.

IAN REACHED into his suit jacket pocket to retrieve his phone that had buzzed.

Scott had texted, *How's it going?*

If Lynn hadn't excused herself to go to the restroom, Ian would have ignored his cell altogether. But since she still hadn't returned, he replied, *Okay.*

Not the most descriptive, flattering adjective he could have chosen but accurate. And it wasn't Lynn's fault. He'd unintentionally set the tone of the date by being almost an hour late because Larry had stuck him—the newbie, rookie detective—with paperwork his partner had called a "teaching moment." Though the bastard had high-tailed it out of there after a cursory explanation of what Ian needed to do, not bothering to ask if he had any questions.

That doesn't sound good. Must mean we're still going out tomorrow night?

Ian had texted Lynn he'd be late, but then he'd gotten lost trying to find the damn bar tucked into the heart of Denver's lower downtown area near the baseball field. A place he'd spent almost no time since moving to the city a little over a month ago.

He typed, *Maybe. I'll keep you posted.*

Because of getting stuck at work, he hadn't been able to go home and change. He'd walked into the bar a disheveled, stressed-out mess while trying in vain to fix his wrinkled tie.

All of this on top of battling first-date-with-a-woman-in-years nerves.

He spotted Lynn returning to their spot at the actual bar and dropped his phone back inside his suit jacket pocket.

Lynn, on the other hand, looked damn good in a snug, black dress that landed inches above her knees. She'd also done something with her hair to make it wavy and bounce around her shoulders. She'd apparently spent time getting ready for their date while he'd shown up looking like he'd fallen asleep in his suit, rolled out of bed, and came right to the bar.

It hadn't been all his fault. But still. Not the best first date impression.

"Is everything okay?" she asked while sliding onto the bar stool. "I saw you put your phone away."

She crossed her shapely legs. Which Ian tried extremely hard not to *really* notice.

It'd be just his luck he'd come across as a lech in a wrinkled suit.

"Everything's fine." He picked up his glass and swallowed the remaining bourbon.

She leaned forward…and placed her hand on his knee.

Ian eyed her hand and lifted his gaze that caught hers, focused on him and curious.

"Can I ask you a very personal question, Detective?"

He swallowed before saying, "Only if you start calling me Ian." Charm courtesy of the bourbon finally kicking in. But better late than never on both counts.

She laughed and kept her hand on his knee. "*Ian*, how long has it been since you've been on a first date?"

Holy shit, he really was coming across as an inexperienced high school kid on his first date ever with a pretty girl in a tight, black dress.

He caught the bartender's attention and signaled for another round since Lynn had finished her wine before going to the restroom. He then loosened his tied.

She withdrew her hand and winced. "Was that too personal? It's just you seem a little—"

"Nervous? Uncomfortable? Utterly clueless?" He paused, then added, "Maybe all of the above?" He had the good grace to laugh. "It's been a *very* long time."

Her smile deepened. "How long were you and she together?"

Wow. She actually didn't know about the break-up. He wasn't certain how much Felicity even knew, but it was obvious she hadn't shared any of it with Lynn. At the same time, it would not have been her place to tell Lynn his business.

The bartender set their drinks down and removed the empty glasses.

Ian slowly turned his glass. "Since high school."

Lynn's eyes became round which then matched the shape her mouth had formed.

"And how old are you? If you don't mind me asking, of course."

"I'm Scott's age. Thirty-four." He cracked a smile. "Though I'm older than him by two months." And yet another reason he considered Scott his second *brother*.

"So are you recently divorced?" she asked while picking up her wine glass.

A harmless, logical question. Nonetheless, it still rubbed the healing wounds within.

"Believe it or not, we never made it to marriage."

She frowned. "After being together since high school?"

The incredulity in her question made Ian smirk. Because it was incredulous. But it hadn't always felt that way. "I joined the army right after high school and we were nowhere near ready to get married at eighteen."

Lynn nodded and sipped her wine.

"We talked about marriage later. While I was in the army. Then my unit—the same unit as Scott's—was deployed to Afghanistan. We were there for over a year." He swallowed some bourbon. "When I miraculously came back, I was nowhere near ready to get married." Something Candace had never understood, either.

The one time she'd been determined to set a date was during his darkest days dealing with his demons after he'd come home. The fact he'd returned unharmed had been a sign to *her* they really were meant to be together. At least, that's what she'd told him.

"And then…?" Lynn's question trailed into silence.

He sighed. "And then—" His phone started to ring. He set his glass down. "I'm sorry, but I have to make sure it isn't work."

She continued to sip her wine as Ian once again retrieved his phone.

He froze at the caller's name. "It's Felicity." He lifted his gaze—and caught Lynn's eyes fill with exasperation before rolling sideways. But the exasperation turned into concern so quickly Ian couldn't be certain he'd correctly interpreted her initial reaction. "Something must have happened because she knows we're together." He stood, carefully watching Lynn whose face remained set in concern. "I'm going to take this outside. I'll be right back."

"Of course. And you're absolutely right." She set her glass down. "Something must have happened or she wouldn't be calling you now."

The way she put a slight emphasis on the last word tugged at Ian's instincts now on high alert while he answered, "Hi. Did something happen?"

"Yes," came Felicity's clipped response as he walked out of the bar. "I was at dinner with Shannon and Peyton. When I returned to my car, there was another note. It was under the windshield wipers."

Her voice breaking apart caused Ian to stop in his tracks.

Strong-willed, independent, sassy Felicity Mayhew was scared.

"Where are you?"

She cleared her throat. "I'm locked inside my house with my dog."

A dog that wouldn't scare a fly, much less an unstable intruder with an agenda.

"I'm terribly sorry to interrupt your date with Lynn, but you did say to call—"

"Don't apologize. I'll be there soon. I just need to tell Lynn what's going on and pay the tab." Ian also wanted to see how Felicity's good friend and assistant would react to him abruptly ending their date due to her boss's stalker striking again. And so quickly after the last time.

"Detective, you don't need to come over. I assure you I'm fine. Truly."

Like hell. The latest note's contents and the fact it had shown up while she'd been having dinner with Shannon and little Peyton had, and for good reason, rattled her. But he said, "I need to see and collect the note. I'll get your address from Lynn." And would she offer to have him follow her to Felicity's house or simply hand over her boss's address?

"I can drop the note off in the morning at your work. My office isn't too far from there."

Damn, the lady sure as shit could be stubborn.

"Are you actually trying to talk a cop out of doing his job, Ms. Mayhew?"

Her deep sigh reached him through his phone.

"It's Felicity. And no. I just hate that this is interrupting your evening."

He turned to look inside the bar, but he couldn't see Lynn.

Maybe Felicity's call had actually been perfect timing.

"I appreciate it." At that moment, he recalled a pretty important detail about the Mayhews. "But you and your family know firsthand a cop's never off duty."

Silence fell on her end before, "That is true. Thank you, Detective."

"It's Ian. And Felicity?"

"Yes?"

He continued to stare inside the bar. "I will find and stop whoever's doing this to you." He ended the call, but continued to grip his phone.

What if Felicity's number-one enemy happened to be the person closest to her? A situation like that certainly wasn't unique. He'd definitely run it by Larry in the morning. Perhaps even do some digging into Lynn Delgado. It probably wouldn't hurt to keep her close, either. Though the hair, eyes, and shapely figure now held zero appeal.

Chapter Seven

FELICITY GRASPED the mug of tea Lynn handed her and sunk into her couch cushions. Once Lynn sat with her own mug, Felicity gave her a tight smile. "Thank you for being here."

Princess Belle jumped up and settled her tiny body between Felicity and Lynn.

Lynn shifted onto her left side and tucked her legs beneath her. "When Ian said how upset you sounded with this fourth note, it was a no brainer to have him follow me here." She clasped Felicity's free hand and gently squeezed.

Upon reading the newest note and shoving it into his suit jacket pocket, Ian had insisted on checking in and outside Felicity's home which he was still doing.

"I know, but I am terribly sorry for ruining your evening."

Lynn gave her fingers another squeeze, then released her hand. "No apologies. Ian made it clear you were to call him if you received another note and warned me he's always on duty."

Felicity sipped her tea.

Yes. Always on duty. A harsh reality of law enforcement life. As was the chance a person would never see their loved one again when they left for work.

"Felicity," Lynn quietly began, causing her thoughts to scatter, "this person is officially stalking you."

She nodded while staring into her mug, tonight's bold, black, all caps message appearing in her mind.

SAFETY IS BEING PROTECTED FROM DANGER.

YOU CAN NO LONGER FEEL SAFE FROM ME.

Hadn't she recently been thinking of safety? No longer feeling that way even while at home being what she despised most about this horrible person who clearly hated and wanted to harm her. The fact Ian had taken it upon himself to inspect her windows and doors and walk her property meant he, too, felt the threat had become serious.

"Maybe," Lynn continued, "we should consider working out of your home office until this person is caught?"

Felicity whipped her head in Lynn's direction. "And what if he-she is never caught? Then what?" Though Ian had sworn to find and stop her harasser, there was only so much he could do with little evidence and info to work with.

She remembered enough from her father's career as a police officer, then short time as a detective, they followed the evidence and leads. But if those went cold, so did the case. Ian had already admitted he didn't expect the lab to find fingerprints or DNA. The only person she could give him happened to be the daughter of an extremely powerful and wealthy man.

Tears burned Felicity's eyes as frustration and vulnerability shrouded her. But the feelings didn't stop her from saying, "I *refuse* to let whoever this is completely take over my life." She also loved her office and its location close to great shopping and restaurants. "You know how hard I—we—worked to get that office space." She blinked her eyes clear. "On top of making it ours." She shook her head. "No. I will not hide in this house."

Lynn opened her mouth to respond when the front door burst open.

Felicity jumped as Princess Belle started barking. When Ian came striding into the house, however, her dog stopped, leapt off of the couch, and sprinted right for him. All while wagging her almost non-existent tail.

She narrowed her eyes at the traitor though Ian never even glanced at her dog.

He sat on the arm of the lounger situated to the right of the couch. "I think it's time we told Scott what's going on."

Felicity leaned forward and set her mug down on the coffee table. "I appreciate where this opinion is coming from, Detective, but that wasn't our deal."

"And I appreciate your opinion on why you don't want him to know. But this latest note"—he pointed at his suit pocket—"and the fact it was left on your windshield while you were having dinner with his daughter and ex scared the shit out of you."

Felicity clenched her teeth and lifted her chin.

"You should be scared, too."

Princess Belle jumped into Felicity's lap.

"The notes are getting more threatening," he stated. "This person also knows where you live and work and is obviously following you—"

"I know all of that!" she snapped while picking up her dog. "But involving my brother won't solve this problem and will only cause him unnecessary worry."

A taut silence settled into Felicity's living room.

She looked away from Ian and hugged her dog to her chest.

"Felicity," Ian finally said, "I don't want to add to your fear. But Scott knowing wouldn't be unnecessary worry. You have to know by now this person isn't going away."

Lynn tilted her head and caught Felicity's gaze. "Maybe he's right. And you could think of it as another set of eyes watching out for you."

That was certainly fair. But Scott's idea of watching out for her would be calling and texting several times a day, and stopping by her house more frequently. He'd left his brief career in law enforcement without a backward glance years earlier and now, finally, had a life outside of being a college English instructor and single father.

"Believe me when I say I understand why you feel Scott should be told, but he can't know unless it's absolutely necessary." She eyed Lynn, then Ian. "You also said before you came over here that you'd find and stop this person."

Ian nodded.

"So go find and stop this person." She stood. "I'm tired and we have a huge wedding on Saturday that really starts tomorrow evening with the rehearsal."

Lynn also stood, followed by Ian.

He slid his hands into his pockets. "Since I can't talk you into telling your brother what's going on, can I talk you into doing something else for me and your safety?"

She continued to hug Princess Belle tight. "I'm listening."

He stepped back. "Invest in some mace and a whistle?"

She fought a grin while saying, "I can do that."

"And not just any whistle." He turned and headed for the door. "The kind that veteran PE teachers use to instantly silence a gym filled with thirty-plus kids playing dodgeball." To Lynn he said, "Finish having drinks and our conversation next week?"

She sent him an enormous smile. "Absolutely."

With a final, piercing glance at Felicity, Ian left.

Lynn released a quick breath. "Boy is that man a presence in a small space."

That did certainly describe the detective.

Lynn picked up her purse. "Try to get some rest and I'll see you in the morning."

Once alone with her dog and behind the locked front door, Felicity breathed deeply through her nose. She then once again recalled Ian's strongly spoken words.

I will find and stop whoever's doing this to you.

Despite the twinge of hopelessness she couldn't shake, she did believe and trust Ian would do everything in his power to make his statement come true.

That alone would help her sleep a bit easier.

LARRY FOCUSED on Ian after stopping at a red light. "So now you've gotta hard on for the friend and assistant?"

Ian smirked. "If by *hard on* you mean I don't trust her anymore, then yeah." He shook his head. "Her initial irritation when Felicity called me during our date is still bugging the shit out of me." At the same time, he hadn't seen anything but a concerned friend and employee after he'd walked back into the bar and told Lynn why Felicity had called.

The light turned green and Larry hit the accelerator.

"A jealous employee and friend whose sick of being in the shadows?"

Ian shrugged. "Unoriginal, but why not? Makes even more sense than some spoiled rich girl going after the so-called competition. From what I found, the Marsden woman's event-planning business is just as successful as Felicity's fancy-weddings-only biz."

Larry grunted before saying, "Potential for less *family* intervention if it's the friend, too."

Yeah. But if Ian's instincts ended up being right, what the hell would it do to Felicity? It didn't take a genius to see how much she trusted and relied on Lynn Delgado.

"I say start digging into the friend once we're done with this call," Larry added. "Hopefully it really ends up being an accident."

They'd been tasked with checking the scene of an elderly couple—the Zamoras—found deceased in their home in an old, worn out Denver neighborhood. On the surface it looked like they'd gone to bed and not woken up. In real life, there were only three possibilities for two people to die together in their sleep—carbon monoxide poisoning, suicide, or homicide. Working with CSI and the ME, it was his and Larry's job to figure out which one had happened.

With the exception of Felicity's harasser, this was Ian's first real case-mystery. Though he hated the fact it was a deceased elderly couple, he couldn't stop the adrenaline pumping through his veins… that intensified as Larry pulled up to the house surrounded by squad cars, the ME's van, and the CSI unit.

Ian heaved himself from the sedan.

To his left, across the street from the couple's home with chipped blue and white paint, their equally elderly neighbors had gathered in a small group while watching several uniformed officers mill about the property. Ian knew the uniforms were waiting further instruction, outside of keeping neighbors at bay, from the senior officer who happened to be Larry.

As he and his partner approached the house, Ian spotted a female officer to his far left speaking with a clearly distraught woman with short, dark hair and hugging her arms to her chest. They stood near the cracked driveway with a garage door that had the same chipping paint.

"Is she the one who found them?" Larry asked another officer stationed outside the front door.

"Yeah. Granddaughter. Think her name's Nicky or Nicole."

Larry glanced at Ian. "You wanna talk to her while I start inside?"

"Yeah." He strode toward her and the female officer.

Upon closer proximity, Ian noted the granddaughter looked to be thirty-ish, average height, and slim. Her eyes were damp with tears streaking her red cheeks.

"Hi." He nodded at the female officer he vaguely recognized. "I've got it. Thanks."

She returned his nod and left.

He held out his hand. "I'm Detective Ian Stafford. I'm sorry for your loss."

The woman barely grasped his hand, then went back to hugging her arms to her chest. "Nicole Zamora. They're my only grandparents—" Her voice hitched, followed by tears flowing from her blue eyes. "I just saw them yesterday." She looked at Ian. "They were fine."

Ian retrieved a small notepad and pen from his inside jacket pocket. "What time did you last see them?"

She nibbled her lower lip, sniffed, and said, "I left at five. That's the time I always leave after preparing their dinner. All my grandma has to do is warm it up." She leaned forward. "I swear everything was *fine*."

"It sounds like you were their caregiver?"

The woman swiped her nose with a tissue. "Part-time. I…do their grocery shopping, cleaning, laundry, some cooking. They're not invalids. Just…old." She cringed. "I don't mean that in a disrespectful way."

He gave her a warm smile. "You're fine. Were there some health problems?" And if so, it still wouldn't explain how they could have died together while sleeping.

"Um…they both had heart problems. And my grandpa recently had a stroke. But it didn't incapacitate him." She peered at him through bleary eyes. "Is that the right word?"

"It is." Ian hesitated before carefully asking, "Any history of mental problems?"

She stared at him.

"I'm sorry I have to ask that right now," he murmured. "But the fact they were found deceased together is highly unusual."

She sniffed twice. "Well, I have caught them mixing up their medications recently. Neither one of them could read the pill bottles without reading glasses." Her lower lip trembled. "But it seems they were always misplacing those."

Forgetfulness. Difficulty reading the small typeface on pill bottles. Could be a strong lean toward terrible accident.

Ian noted her statements, then asked, "How long have they lived in this house?"

"Since I was a kid. I spent so much time here I had my own

room. This was my home, too. And now…" She pressed her lips together.

"Thank you. That's all I have for now." He brought back his warm smile. "Is there anyone we can call on your behalf? You probably shouldn't be driving after what you've been through." In truth, she appeared on the verge of collapsing.

He fought the strong urge to grasp her elbow.

She vehemently shook her head. "No. I'm all they have." Tears filled her eyes once more. "They're all I have—" Her voice shattered as the dam fully broke.

Ian looked over his right shoulder, caught the female officer's gaze, and angled his head toward the sobbing woman.

The officer nearly sprinted toward them.

"Miss Zamora, I'm afraid I can't let you drive home like this." He glanced at the woman's name tag. "Officer McCurdy, can you make sure she gets home safely in her car? Have another officer follow you two and get back here as soon as you can."

"Yes, Sir."

He withdrew a business card from his notepad. "Here's my card in case you think of anything or need to reach me. I'll be touch when we have more info."

Officer McCurdy gently guided the devastated Nicole Zamora down the driveway.

With a heavy breath, he turned and walked toward the front door. But Larry striding out of the house while removing white latex gloves made him stop.

"How's the granddaughter?" his partner asked.

"A mess. I have a couple of uniforms taking her home." Ian eyed the house. "How's it look inside?"

"Like two old people went to sleep and never woke up."

"So carbon monoxide?" Ian frowned. "The granddaughter did mention health problems and that they'd been mixing up their meds recently."

"That could be helpful info." Larry lifted his shoulders.

"Regarding carbon monoxide, I didn't see any detectors and it's certainly not a new house. CSI's doing their thing. Won't know anything for certain until the ME's findings come back. And the lab work."

They fell into step beside each other.

"As of right now, cause of death is unknown," his partner added.

Ian paused beside the sedan, then glanced at the house and back at Larry. "Is it just me or does something about this not feel right? An elderly couple going to sleep and waking up everyday in a house they've lived in for years until last night?"

Larry opened the driver's side door. "Weird, for sure. But all we can do is wait until we know more."

Once they were settled into the sedan, Larry looked at Ian. "And it's not like you don't have enough to keep you busy right now, Hot Shot."

Ian fell silent while Larry carefully backed up and away from the house.

Yep. Lynn Delgado.

Regardless of digging into her background and his determination to fulfill the promise he'd made Felicity last night, Ian couldn't shake the strong hunch the death of the Zamoras would end up being far more than carbon monoxide poisoning. But Larry had been right. They couldn't do a damn thing until they had more info. In the meantime, he'd concentrate on getting to know Felicity's trusted assistant and friend much better.

But solely as a detective focused on a suspect.

Chapter Eight

FELICITY WALKED into The Halcyon Hotel's fireplace room and went straight for an empty spot on one of the two white sofas. The room with its roaring fire seemed quiet for a Saturday night. But it was right after eight p.m. Many guests had to be at dinner. Upstairs in the ballroom, however, a first-class reception filled with first-class decor and people was just getting started.

She removed her black heels and gently massaged her left foot.

Once the party aspect of wedding receptions began, Felicity always handed Lynn the reins and took her leave. She'd said her goodbyes before heading down to the lobby level, but her aching feet and trepidation had prompted her to prolong leaving. Though she had opted for valet parking when she arrived hours earlier.

She thoroughly despised the fact her harasser had her feeling so damn vulnerable. But how could she not feel that way? And, yes, she'd taken Ian's request to heart and purchased mace and a "professional" whistle, both currently tucked into her compact, crossbody purse. Investing in the items had done little to calm her nerves now running at a much higher frequency.

Her phone, also inside the purse, buzzed and dinged.

A grin replaced her frown since she knew who had texted.

How goes the latest wedding extravaganza?

She and Perry had been texting on and off throughout her busy day which had helped the long hours pass a bit more quickly.

The party has officially started and I'm headed home.

Just as soon as she leisurely finished massaging her feet.

"Excuse me, but you're Felicity Mayhew?"

She looked up from her phone and whipped her head left.

A pretty woman with shoulder-length blonde hair gave her a huge smile. Based on her pale-pink evening dress, strappy, high-heeled sandals, and glistening jewelry, Felicity felt certain the woman was a wedding guest.

"Yes, I'm Felicity."

The woman pointed at the empty spot beside Felicity on the couch. "Do you mind if I sit? I was so hoping to catch you before you left the reception." Her smile deepened. "I'm in need of the best wedding planner in Denver."

Felicity somehow managed to keep a sigh in check before saying, "Of course. Have a seat." Her phone lit up, and buzzed and dinged with Perry's reply, but she put her phone back inside her purse. She then retrieved a business card and handed it to the woman. "I'm actually getting ready to go home for the evening, but feel free to call my office Monday morning—"

"Oh, I definitely will." The woman leaned forward. "I'm a close friend of the bride's and recently became engaged." She, like so many brides Felicity had met and known, held out her left hand to show her bright, big, sparkling diamond engagement ring.

Felicity smiled. "Congratulations."

"Thank you." The woman lowered her hand. "And I certainly don't want to keep you. I'm sure you've had a very long day."

She kept her smile in place, but remained silent.

"I only wanted to introduce myself. And get a business card." She held it up and laughed. "I'm Emmy Swanson."

They shook hands.

Felicity couldn't help but grin at Emmy's extremely firm grip. It was a nice change from the brides-to-be who barely clasped her fingers before pulling their hands away.

"My fiancé is *kind of* a tech geek," Emmy continued. "Extremely successful, but doesn't understand how important a girl's wedding day is. I have no family here. Just a few friends." She placed her hand on Felicity's forearm. "That's why I need *the* Felicity Mayhew."

Felicity slipped her feet back into her heels which forced Emmy to remove her hand. "Then I'm looking forward to sitting down with you and your fiancé very soon." She stood.

"Honestly, I'm not sure how involved he'll be," Emmy said while also standing. "But you'll be hearing from me on Monday." She stepped back. "Have a nice weekend."

Emmy left, but instead of going to the elevators to rejoin the reception, she went toward the hotel's mains doors, walked outside, and disappeared from view.

Acquiring new clients at weddings had happened numerous times throughout Felicity's career, but occasionally it felt more like a hindrance than advantageous.

Lynn had told Felicity multiple times she needed to establish boundaries when it came to situations like the one with Emmy. At the same time, how could she turn a gushing, newly engaged young woman away? Even politely? She couldn't. It was that simple.

She retrieved her cell.

Perry had replied, *Let me know you got home safely.*

After sending him the smiling emoji, she followed the same path as Emmy.

While waiting for the attendant to return with her vehicle, a feeling she couldn't explain compelled her to choose another name in her contact list. Maybe because she needed to hear a familiar, strong male voice and didn't feel comfortable calling her brother under the current circumstances?

After only two rings, Ian answered, "Hi."

"Hi." She paused before saying, "It's Felicity."

Silence, then, "I know. Is everything okay?"

She cringed at the concern tinting his voice. "Yes." What the hell was she doing? "I just thought you'd like to know I did purchase mace and a whistle that cost more than a good bottle of wine."

He laughed, the deep, inviting sound making her smile.

The attendant pulled up in front of the hotel in her car.

"Good. I'm glad to hear it. So you're okay?" Ian asked again.

Felicity gave the attendant a tip and slid into the driver's seat. "I'm as okay as one can be having a stalker." Even saying the word caused her to shiver and she cranked the heat after driving away from the hotel.

"And I meant what I said the other night."

The corner of her mouth lifted in a soft grin. "I know you did, Detective."

"You mean *Ian*."

She sighed. "Fine."

"Don't get me wrong," he quickly added. "I like being called detective, but we might as well be family. I have known your brother for longer than either of us would like to admit. Your niece is also my goddaughter and calls me Uncle Ian."

She laughed softly. "Those are definitely valid points, *Ian*." Saying his name did sound and feel much better than the professional, yet highly impersonal "detective."

She had also heard his name multiple times the last ten-plus years.

"Keep agreeing with me and we'll continue to get along just fine."

She shook her head. "And I'll be sure to keep that in mind. You'll be speaking to Stacia Monday, right?" They needed to get back to why she'd called him.

But why had she really called him?

"That's the plan. I need to go. I'll be in touch next week."

Before Felicity could reply, the call ended.

She must have interrupted him, but he'd still answered. Then again, being a detective he was always on duty.

The only time her father hadn't been on duty was during family vacations. Until a few years before his death while on a call, those perfect moments had also been before cell phones. Nowadays, she couldn't help but think those in law enforcement were truly always on duty. Even while on vacation, they could be reached any day or time. Unless, of course, they turned off their phone. If her father had survived past the age of forty, he'd mostly likely be retired by now. But what would life—her mother's life—had looked like if he hadn't been taken so young?

Her parents had been in love and completely devoted to one another, but a constantly ringing cell phone would have driven her mother to insanity. The land line ringing with his work calls as much as it had when she and her siblings were children had sometimes been a point of contention. They'd always worked through the tension, though.

Felicity pulled into her driveway and waited for the garage to open.

Maybe that's the real reason she'd called Ian. She missed and wanted her dad, especially now. Retired or not and just like Ian, he'd be doing everything he could to find her harasser. He probably would have even tried to move in with her. Or have her move back home to Colorado Springs. She would not have agreed to either suggestion, but hearing the words from her overprotective, police officer dad would have been exactly what she needed to hear.

She parked in the garage as tears blurred her vision.

Losing him to a routine traffic stop that had resulted in gunfire because he and his partner had pulled over a violent criminal hadn't been fair. She and her siblings had lost out on so much growing up, and their mother had lost the love of her life. Now, when Felicity needed not only her dad but his detective mind, he wasn't there. She also still couldn't wrap her mind around why someone would bother harassing her, a mere workaholic wedding planner.

None of it made any damn sense.

She blinked her eyes clear, picked up her purse, and opened the car door.

With any luck, she'd have some answers before meeting Perry for dinner Monday evening. At least she had that to look forward to next week and she focused on his smiling, handsome face while walking into her house.

She had to stay focused on the positive or her harasser would in fact win, something she could never let happen.

"IS THERE anything you don't feed that dog?" Scott asked while Ian finished slicing up two recently off the grill hamburger patties. "I can't believe she doesn't get sick."

Stella, Ian's Bernese Mountain dog, licked her big mouth as she carefully watched him mix the meat into her dry dog food.

"It's freshly cooked beef with nothing added to it," Ian argued. "How could this be bad for her? Some so-called form of beef is supposedly in her dog food and treats."

Stella nearly knocked him over in her haste to beat him to where he kept her elevated feeder by the patio door to the right of the dining room. Before he could set her bowl in the feeder beside her water, she had her large head buried in the food.

Scott shook his head as Ian straddled a dining room table chair.

Stella's excited, sloppy munching filled the silence.

From his spot, Ian had a direct view into the living room that held nothing more than his navy-blue, sectional couch, glass-top coffee table, flat-screen television, and a few remaining unpacked moving boxes stacked in the left corner.

Getting truly settled into his rental home, located in an older Denver neighborhood, hadn't been at the top of his to-do list.

His buddy picked up his hamburger with every topping imaginable. "Thanks for cooking." He took an impressive bite.

"Thanks for inviting yourself over," Ian replied before taking his own bite. After swallowing, he asked, "Is Campbell feeling any better?"

Scott set his burger down and picked up his phone. "I don't know. I think she may already be out for the night since she hasn't replied to my text. I guess today's fairy tale, Felicity wedding was one of the biggest they've had in a while."

Ian nodded, recalling the fatigue he'd heard in Felicity's voice during their brief chat.

She'd happened to call while he'd been outside checking the burgers. Good timing. But the call had caught him off guard because it had seemed so...unnecessary. He was definitely relieved she'd taken his advice to buy mace and a whistle. Still, he couldn't shake the feeling that hadn't been the real reason she'd called him. On top of sounding tired, he'd heard something else. Something even more human. Like vulnerability. Not at all surprising she'd feel that way considering her situation. What surprised Ian was that she'd called *him*.

"Have you talked to Felicity lately?" he asked.

Scott swallowed a large bite before answering, "No. Not even in a text. It's weird. I know she's getting busier, but that's never stopped her in the past from calling and texting me all the time." He wiped his hands on the paper towel Ian had given him in lieu of a napkin. "She really hasn't been the same since she came back from her trip to Mexico, though she swore she had a great time."

Ian's brain latched onto that info.

During his initial meeting with Felicity and Lynn almost a week ago, she'd said the notes had started about a month earlier. Had they started after she'd returned from vacation? And if so, Lynn Delgado was looking like an even more viable person.

How the hell would the Marsden woman have known Felicity's schedule? She could have made a quick phone call, of course. Or had someone do it for her. But would an equally successful woman from a wealthy, influential family spend her spare time writing threatening notes that clearly had thought put into them, then find someone to deliver them?

Someone she trusted to *never* say a word to anyone.

None of that seemed remotely realistic to him.

Ian took an absent bite of his burger as he racked his brain for a logical way to start his questioning. Scott had known Lynn the same amount of time as Felicity and it happened to be one reason he'd let his good friend invite himself over tonight. That and the fact Scott had sounded pretty pathetic over his girlfriend bailing on their planned night together.

Stella turned from her feeder and plopped herself beside Ian's chair.

"Maybe your sister has backed off now that you have Campbell?" he offered.

Scott nodded and shrugged. "Makes sense." He picked up his beer. "Sorry there weren't any sparks between you and Lynn."

And there it was. The opening he'd hoped would happen after his Campbell comment.

He rubbed Stella's head. "I haven't completely given up."

Scott raised his eyebrows. "Really?" He laughed. "Is that the real reason you didn't get that woman's number last night?"

Right. The cute, curvy blonde who'd been out with her friends and drinking too much.

"Are you kidding me? You know she was wasted."

Ian had never understood guys, who weren't rapists, that picked up intoxicated women. How could that be fun for anyone at the night's end? When he was with a woman—though the list was extremely short—he wanted her to remember every damn thing during and after their intimate time together.

"She was having a good time with her fiends and I sure as shit didn't expect you to take her home," Scott tossed back. "A phone number. That's it."

"She probably wouldn't have remembered me. Anyway"—he grinned—"tell me what you know about Ms. Delgado." He'd discovered very little about her on his own and had to know everything Scott did since asking Felicity could never happen for obvious reasons.

"Seriously? You're that interested?"

Ian lifted his shoulders. "Why not? She's smart, independent, successful, attractive. What's not to like?"

Scott fell silent for several seconds, then said, "If that's really how you feel, I have to tell you that she and I went out on a date."

Ian froze.

"It was just once. And not too long after Felicity hired her."

Ian sure as hell hadn't expected Scott to say that. But in truth, it could end up being an even bigger plus for his investigation into the woman.

"How long ago was that?" Ian asked after taking a drink of his beer.

"A couple of years. At least." Scott frowned. "I think one of the reasons Felicity hired her and how they became close so quickly was because Lynn had been in a pretty messed up relationship, too. Before she moved to Colorado."

Ian knew next to nothing about Felicity's marriage to the British guy, outside of what little she'd said about him during their initial meeting and what little he'd heard from Scott. Regardless, it didn't sound like it had been a happy union. His research into Lynn hadn't uncovered an ugly marriage, which made him ask, "Was it a boyfriend?"

"Yeah. And one of the reasons she left Wisconsin."

Madison, Wisconsin to be exact. Born and raised in the midwest. Her family, that consisted of her dad and an older brother, still lived there. Mom had passed away from cancer a couple of years before Lynn moved to Colorado.

"This is going to make me sound like a shit bag," Scott added. "But between Felicity finally being away from that worthless piece of crap and Peyton being so young and coming off of the long relationship with Shannon, Lynn had more going on than I could deal with at the time." He took another swig of beer. "I think she was more interested in me than I was in her."

Ian winced, but said, "It happens. And you're not a shit bag for doing what was right for you and her in the long run." As interesting as this info on Lynn happened to be, though, he hadn't learned anything giving him insight into Lynn's relationship with Felicity.

Okay. They'd long since bonded over being with and leaving assholes. But two years had passed, and he hadn't misread Lynn's irritation at Felicity calling him during their date.

"That's all I know about Ms. Delgado," Scott continued, "outside of she works very closely with my sister on a daily basis. They're a workaholic team."

Ian narrowed his eyes. "Except when Felicity goes on vacation." Leaving Lynn behind to do a two-person job.

Scott laughed. "Her trip to Mexico in February shocked the shit out of everyone."

It didn't take a genius to understand what his buddy had inferred.

Scott finished his beer and stood. "Do you want another beer?"

"I'm good. Thanks."

Ian stared at his unfinished burger that now had to be cold.

Maybe he was grasping at the Lynn straw since the common sense side of him didn't want to tangle with the Marsden family unless absolutely necessary. Still, what if feelings of resentment and jealousy had developed over the years on Lynn's part when it came to her boss?

Felicity Mayhew qualified as an unmistakable presence in any space she occupied. A force to be reckoned with. Her name meant something to the Denver area VIPs with daughters who'd always dreamed of their weddings as if royalty. On the other hand, did anyone in that circle ever notice her assistant? Not to say Lynn could be considered invisible. Not even a little bit. But she sure as hell wasn't a woman with fiery hair, razor-sharp, light-brown eyes, and a sassy mouth.

He fought a grin at recalling the way Felicity defiantly lifted her chin—followed quickly by the image of pressing his mouth to hers, silencing her instantly.

Ian shifted in the chair at his purely physical response to that vision filling his head.

Shit, where had that come from? And with her brother standing steps away while vigorously petting Stella sprawled on the kitchen floor.

He gave his head a hard shake, then finished his beer.

Perhaps he should have gotten the blonde's number last night. He hadn't been with a woman since January. A much-needed escape from his life in Grand Junction that had crumbled around him. Unfortunately, she'd wanted to go on an actual date after their night together which had left him no choice but to tell her, as nicely as possible, thanks but no thanks.

It had not been received well, and he'd decided soon thereafter he had no business being with a woman in any way, shape, or form. Now, nearly three months later, maybe he needed to rethink that position. In any case, he no longer trusted Lynn Delgado and would have to figure out another way of discovering the ins and outs of her relationship with Felicity without her boss knowing. He couldn't jeopardize the trust he and Felicity were establishing.

And for reasons that went beyond finding and stopping her stalker.

Chapter Nine

THE BELLS over the door of Daisy's Bouquets tinkled as Felicity entered the shop decorated for the approaching Easter holiday. Fragrant lilies had been set in various spots on the counter that lined the shop's left wall. The women of the flower shop had also placed white and pink stuffed bunnies of varying sizes beside the lilies, as well as throughout the cozy space filled with a myriad of flowers and lush plants.

To Felicity's right sat their wedding consultation table, a place she'd spent much time due to particularly difficult brides and mothers.

Alyson Preston's Siberian Husky, Thatcher, trotted toward her from the direction of the backroom located straight ahead from where Felicity stood.

She rubbed his head. "Hello, Handsome. Can you sit for me?"

His butt went to the floor, and she fed him a dog treat.

She'd long since put a stash of treats in her glove box since this had, at some point, become their little ritual.

"Hi. This is a nice surprise."

Felicity looked up at the sound of Campbell Grey's warm

greeting and returned her smile while the woman emerged from the backroom.

"Good morning." She met Campbell at the counter. "Have all of you recovered from last week and Saturday?"

Alyson, a co-owner of the flower shop, joined Campbell near the register. "Barely."

Campbell laughed. "I was so exhausted I had to cancel my plans with Scott, then crashed and burned when I got home. But he ended up at Ian's place, so it worked out."

Scott had been at Ian's place Saturday night. Could that have been the real reason Ian had rushed off the phone? Not that it mattered, of course. It's not like she'd expected him to stay on the phone with her indefinitely.

Felicity shoved thoughts of Ian and why she'd called him Saturday night to the back of her mind. She'd stopped by the shop for a very important reason. "Are Jillian and Hayley not here? I wanted to thank all of you for your hard work on that wedding."

"Jillian's out on a delivery right now," Alyson stated, "and Hayley's off on Mondays."

"Well…*dammit*."

The two women laughed.

"I was hoping all of you would be here. I guess I should have called first." Felicity shook her head. "You'll just have to pass on my thanks to them." She sighed. "The bride and her mother weren't the easiest clients."

Campbell and Alyson exchanged a quick grimace.

"The wedding was also quite large and expectations were incredibly high." She gave them warm smiles. "But the flowers turned out beautifully. My clients were extremely satisfied."

In truth, most of Felicity's clients walked away satisfied with her vendors' work, especially Daisy's Bouquets.

Alyson returned her smile. "That's always nice to hear. But you didn't have to stop by to tell us that. I'm sure you have much better things to do on a Monday morning."

"Actually"—Felicity reached into her purse and withdrew an envelope—"I did need to stop by. I had to give you this." She handed Alyson the envelope. "We've officially been working together for over a year and you've never let Felicitous Wedding Creations down, despite the elaborate, sometimes enormous weddings and difficult clients."

The two looked at each other and back at Felicity.

"It's a token of my deep appreciation for the last year and especially this last week."

They continued to stare at her.

She pointed at the envelope. "You can open it."

Alyson dragged her gaze from Felicity's. A few seconds later, she and Campbell were staring, wide-eyed, at the check.

"Oh, my God," Campbell murmured.

Alyson lifted her gaze back to Felicity's…then burst into tears.

Felicity halted.

Campbell removed the envelope and check from Alyson's hand and gave her the nearby box of tissues.

"I'm…so sorry." Alyson swiped a tissue. "This has nothing to do with you. I mean"—she wiped her nose—"it does. But it's not what you think."

Felicity peered at her. "I'm not sure what to think." She glanced at Campbell focused on her boss. "I certainly didn't mean to make you cry."

She released a quick laugh. "I know. My emotions…are all over the place right now." She wiped her cheeks, sniffed, and smiled. "I just found out last week that David and I are pregnant."

Felicity's mouth dropped open as she glanced at Campbell who lifted her shoulders.

"She told us the news on Friday."

Alyson giggled. "It caught us a little off guard since we haven't been really trying. But we're still so excited."

Felicity laughed with her and Campbell. She then walked behind the counter and gave Alyson a tight hug. "I'm so happy for you two."

She released the now glowing woman and stepped back. "How far along are you?"

"About six weeks. We'll be a family of three when the holidays arrive." She continued her giggling. "Four counting Thatcher. I can't *believe* it."

Felicity opened her mouth to respond, but something about Alyson's glow and giddy laughter caused her to stop. A thick, almost overwhelming sense of sadness shrouded her.

She was a thirty-seven-year old single, workaholic dog mom. But she'd wanted much more for herself and life when she'd been Alyson's age a handful of years ago. A bad choice in a husband and uprooting her life to live with him in London had absolutely sealed her late twenties and early thirties. She'd happily returned to Colorado and had done a damn good job rebuilding her life in her native state. What did she have to show for it, though, outside of the superficial?

Yes. She had her adorable Princess Belle, family, and a few close friends.

A mere two months earlier that had been enough.

"Felicity, you have no idea how much we appreciate this." Alyson's eyes became wet once more. "How much we appreciate you. And that you took a chance on us a year ago."

A mere two months earlier she hadn't been receiving threatening notes.

"Thank *you*," Alyson added and she wiped the tissue under her eyes.

Having one's life and safety threatened certainly had a way of making a person take a long, hard look at their life. Now, however, wasn't the time for such a thing.

"Each one of you earned what was in the envelope. Please don't thank me." Felicity leaned forward. "I also command you this instant to stop crying."

Alyson and Campbell laughed.

Felicity's phone started to ring inside her purse.

It could be Ian with an update so she stepped from behind the counter.

"Please tell your handsome hubby how excited I am for you both." She turned and headed for the door. "I'll see you later this week."

Once outside she retrieved her phone, but her shoulders fell at the unknown number.

Keeping a heavy sigh in check, she answered, "This is Felicity Mayhew."

"Hello! It's Emmy Swanson. From Saturday night?"

Felicity briefly closed her eyes at the woman's chipper greeting.

She really wasn't in the mood for a gushing bride-to-be, much less *this* bride-to-be. But guilt swiftly replaced her crabbiness. Giving excited brides exactly what they wanted on their wedding days was her livelihood. An ungrateful attitude would not serve her well right now.

"Good morning, Emmy. I'm so happy to hear from you." She turned right and walked toward her vehicle. "Let's figure out a day and time for you to meet with me and my assistant."

Hopefully, Ian would call soon about his meeting with Stacia Marsden.

Considering her revelations from just now in the shop, she wasn't certain how much longer she would last before her patience and sanity snapped in half.

IAN RELEASED a low whistle as he and Larry entered the Ritz-Carlton in downtown Denver. "Must be nice living indefinitely in a place like this." Still, something about the opulence and stench of money made his blood go cold.

Why did luxury always equal a black-and-gray color scheme and furniture that wouldn't be comfortable to sit in for longer than five minutes?

Larry grunted, then said, "Setting their money on fire, if you ask me."

Right. But Stacia Marsden happened to be from the kind of family who could afford to stay in a suite in a hotel like this while her condo was being renovated.

"Where does this woman actually live?"

His partner frowned. "Some high rise around here—oh, shit. Here we go."

Two men and a woman approached them from the right.

Formal business suits. Expressions set in unhappiness. The leader carried a briefcase.

He and Larry slowed to a stop at the same time the lawyer threesome arrived.

Ian grinned and looked at his partner. "Wow. All of this for *us*?" He focused on the leader, a white-haired guy about his height and size, but minus a sense of humor and soul. "I can't tell you how flattered we are."

All three remained unsmiling while white-haired lawyer handed Larry an envelope.

"Ms. Marsden's official statement about Ms. Mayhew's accusations."

Ian narrowed his eyes.

He still couldn't figure out how the hell the Marsdens had learned about any of this.

Larry eyed the envelope he held, then the lawyer. "This must mean Ms. Marsden is unavailable to answer a few questions after all? Her assistant *did* say this would be a good time."

But Ian knew as well as Larry did that this had been the Marsden's plan all along.

"As you are well aware, Ms. Marsden has recently returned from a long, overseas trip and is quite jet lagged. She also has much work to catch up on." White-haired guy pointed at the envelope. "I've included my business card. If you have further concerns on this matter, you can call my office and leave a message with my assistant. I'll return calls as quickly as possible."

Ian smirked. "Gee, that's awfully generous of you."

The three turned their unsmiling faces on Ian before walking around them to leave.

"Can't say I'm surprised by any of this," Larry grumbled. "Still pisses me off, though."

Ian hitched his chin at the envelope. "So what did her royal highness have to say?"

"You mean what her lawyers came up with?"

Ian fell silent while Larry removed the letter.

"*Ms. Felicity Mayhew and I had a pleasant and professional working relationship for two years*—blah, blah, blah—*mutually went our separate ways last year*—blah, blah—*I've only ever wished her the utmost success…* Yeah," Larry breathed the word. He then folded the paper back up and shoved it inside the envelope. "I hate to tell you this, Hot Shot, but unless something comes back from the lab, we've taken this as far as we can."

They turned and headed out of the hotel.

The gray, chilly, early April weather matched the vibe in the upscale hotel.

Ian shoved his hands into his trench coat's pockets. "Larry, I honestly don't think the Marsden woman is the one harassing Felicity."

"I've been gathering that."

When they reached the sedan, Ian paused at the passenger side and decided to tell his partner another idea that had crossed his mind yesterday while walking Stella. "But what if Lynn Delgado was the one who gave the Marsdens the heads up on Felicity's claim?"

Larry's thick eyebrows shot skyward. "You've really got a bad feeling about this friend-assistant and it's not based on much."

Ian leaned forward. "Who else could it have been? Realistically?" He couldn't and wouldn't think about the Marsdens having a close *friend* on the force.

Something about it felt too…cinematic.

"Okay. Fair enough." Larry shook his head. "But the woman's clean. And have you considered that maybe she'd had a bad day with her boss and just wanted to be off the clock on a Thursday night?"

Fine. He hadn't considered that. Still, his instincts about Lynn wouldn't leave him alone.

"If it isn't the Marsden woman," Ian persisted, "and not Lynn, who else do we have?"

They slid into the vehicle.

After Larry started the engine, he eyed Ian. "You're not going to like me saying this about your friend's sister, but could she possibly be sending them to herself? A desperate plea for attention or some shit like that?"

Ian angled his head back. "You can't be serious."

His partner lifted his shoulders. "It's not unheard of. And how well do you actually know this woman?"

Ian grabbed his seat belt. "Maybe I don't know her very well, but I do know her family." He belted himself in and locked gazes with Larry. "Trust me when I say she'd never do such a thing. She's also scared. I've heard it in her voice and seen it firsthand. She's a wedding planner, Larry. Not an award-winning actress."

"Alright." He faced forward. "I believe you. But I don't know where that leaves us."

Ian stared out the windshield. "I haven't given up on Lynn Delgado." With that thought, he reached into his inside coat pocket and withdrew his cell—

He halted at seeing a number he'd long since deleted but still recognized.

She'd had the audacity to leave him a voicemail, too.

He gritted his teeth while going into his contacts.

A part of him wanted to delete the message without listening to it, but the curious, detective side of him had to know why the hell she'd called.

Sending his sonofabitch, ex-partner to the hospital with a black eye and split lip had been Ian's last word on what they'd done to him and Maren.

"Well, hello there," came Lynn's almost purred greeting. "I was just thinking about you."

Ian frowned and glanced at Larry, watching him closely while they sat at a red light.

Okay. He hadn't been out in the dating world for a long time. Her greeting, however, seemed a bit too intimate for having only been on one date that had ended early.

"I'm really glad to hear you say that," he somehow pulled out of his ass. "I know it's Monday, but feel like trying again this evening? Maybe a different place this time?"

She laughed. "I do know a place closer to your work, if that would be helpful?"

He smiled at Larry and said into his phone, "I'd appreciate that. And hopefully my partner won't stick me with a crap load of paperwork tonight."

Larry fought a grin while hitting the gas pedal.

"Maybe we could hit the happy hour a little earlier?" Lynn asked. "Felicity also has a date this evening, so we're closing the office sooner than usual."

Ian gripped his phone.

Felicity had a date? With who?

"I thought you both told me she wasn't seeing anyone."

Larry caught his gaze and also frowned.

"Oh, it's nothing serious. He doesn't even live in Colorado."

Lynn's response caught Ian's attention for two reasons. One, the fact the guy lived out of state. Two, the slight disdain that had been mingled with Lynn's words.

"Must be somewhat serious," Ian slowly continued, "if he's come to Colorado to see her." Where exactly did the guy live and how the hell had he met Felicity?

"He's here for some week-long conference at the convention center. She's simply a bonus. Anyway, how does five sound?"

"That'll work."

He didn't like Lynn's tone. Or the fact Felicity would be on a date tonight with some guy who didn't even live in the state. And not just because she had a stalker out there, watching her every move. Unfortunately, he didn't know what to do with that knowledge.

"I'll text you the name of the place."

"Sounds good." He hung up and looked at Larry. "There is a guy."

"Got that much. But he doesn't live here?"

"No." Ian stared blankly at his phone. "I'll get to the bottom of it, though."

Larry sighed. "I'm sure it's nothing. But I know that's not going to stop you."

His partner was probably right, too, as was Lynn who'd definitely made it sound like Felicity and this guy were no more than a fling. Which didn't sit right with Ian, either.

Nothing about the Marsdens and Lynn's behavior and this strange guy from another state sat right with him. He also had to do something with the voicemail from his ex. Listen to the message, then delete it or just delete it, followed by her number. But this time he'd block it first.

He placed his phone back inside his coat pocket. He'd face his ex's call later.

"I plan on having a nice, long chat with Ms. Delgado this evening."

Maybe his instincts were working in overdrive. Still, he had a job to do and had made a promise. Unlike many people, though, promises and loyalty meant something significant to Ian.

Chapter Ten

PERRY SAT BACK AND LAUGHED. "God, you look great. It is so good to see you again."

Felicity managed a soft smile before taking a sip of white wine.

Perry Cantrell, software engineer from San Jose, California also looked great, but less tan and he'd grown a goatee. His thick, dark, wavy hair streaked with gray complemented his facial hair. His bright eyes, focused on her, were as blue as she remembered, too.

"Thank you," she murmured. "This is a nice change from how I normally spend my Monday evenings."

His smile deepened as he picked up his glass of wine.

Despite his good looks and easygoing smile and personality, Felicity couldn't get on the same enthusiastic page as her *friend* from Cancún. A trip that now seemed like a lifetime ago.

"And how does the great and powerful Felicity Mayhew normally spend her Monday evenings?"

She sipped more wine before answering, "Typically on the couch in my pajamas with my dog, laptop, and work notes."

When Perry had called last week to tell her his travel plans, she'd been excited and had looked forward to, perhaps, picking up where they'd left off in Mexico, if only for this week. A much-needed and deserved distraction. Based on his warm, inviting smiles and never taking his eyes off of her, Felicity knew he had to be thinking that way.

"I'll bet you look just as good like that as you do now," he said with a wink.

But she'd been a different person in February, especially while on her tropical vacation.

Now, all she really wanted was to be at home in her locked house with the alarm set and wearing her pajamas while she worked on the couch with Princess Belle cuddled beside her.

She glanced over her left shoulder, then her right. Something she caught herself doing more often than not since she'd received the latest note last Thursday night. Notes that, according to Ian's voice-mail from earlier in the day, were probably *never* going to be linked to Stacia Marsden who had, with the help of her father, lawyered up. Of course, hearing that hadn't been a huge surprise. It didn't change the fact Felicity felt more exposed and vulnerable than ever.

Even in a busy, upscale restaurant in LoDo sitting across the table from a tall, strong man couldn't settle her feelings of unease.

She once more glanced all around at her surroundings.

"Felicity?"

She whipped her head forward and met Perry's inquisitive stare.

"Is everything okay tonight?" His grin slipped. "You seem to be somewhere else."

No. Everything was certainly not okay. But she wasn't about to tell Perry, whom she didn't know that well, anything about her harasser.

"I'm fine." She forced her mouth into a smile. "I thought I saw someone I knew. Tell me how the conference went today."

Felicity tried to focus on his words, but fighting the urge to continue looking over her shoulder consumed her mind.

Her flesh rose while she imagined a faceless person following her and was now somewhere nearby, watching her closely. It had probably happened before, too.

Perhaps numerous times.

Had the person been watching her talk and laugh and eat with Shannon and Peyton last Thursday, then left the note on her windshield? If so, how long had he-she been observing her?

A chill slithered up her spine and settled onto her shoulders which made her shiver.

She was being watched, and she again looked over her shoulders but didn't recognize one face in the restaurant. In addition to the fact everyone seemed absorbed in their dates and conversations and meals.

"Felicity, where are you right now?"

She jumped at Perry's question filled with perplexity before refocusing on him, staring at her with wide, wary eyes.

In that moment it hit—in spite of her determination to not let it happen, her harasser had officially gotten into her mind and soul. Because of that, there was only one person she wanted at this precise moment as another truth hit.

This particular person made her feel safe and not just because he was a detective.

"Maybe meeting up wasn't such a good idea after all." Perry picked up his wine glass. "I get this isn't like being on a tropical vacation. It's reality."

She released a heavy sigh. "Perry, I'm so sorry." She sat back. "The timing is just really…off." Nothing but the truth, too, as well as a complete understatement. "I have so much on my mind right now." Also nothing but the truth. She cracked a smile. "Would you believe me if I said being back in Cancún sounds absolutely idyllic at this moment?" More truth, only another handsome man's face drifted through her weary mind.

Maybe she was now feeling drawn to Ian for all the wrong reasons, but something about him relaxed and smiling and wearing nothing but swim shorts while lounging by a pool in Cancún, Mexico replaced some of her chill.

Perry leaned forward. "Oh, I'm right there with you. Believe me." He grinned. "How about we finish our wine and call it an early night? It's been a long day for me, too."

She returned his smile. "That sounds perfect. Thank you."

Several minutes later, and once outside the restaurant, Perry wrapped her in a hug.

He did happen to be a wonderful hugger. It still didn't stop her from imagining a different man's arms holding her tight. And, *dammit*, where were these feelings coming from all of a sudden?

"Would you be interested in meeting up for lunch this week? I have a lighter day on Thursday. Or dinner any night will work." Perry released her. "I leave Friday evening."

Felicity heard the disappointment in his voice. Probably over the fact tonight—his week in Denver so far—wasn't going the way he'd wanted when it came to them. This hadn't been what she'd pictured last week, either. But he'd called before note four.

She buttoned her coat up to her neck. "I'd like that." She slid her gaze right and left. No one obvious appeared to be watching her. Them. Then again, a harasser wouldn't be obvious. "Maybe we can touch base on Wednesday? See how the week is going?"

He stepped back and nodded, though remaining traces of hope in his eyes had vanished. "Would you like me to walk you to your car? I don't mind."

She did want him to walk her to her car. She didn't, however, want to face the possibility of a kiss goodnight or avoiding one altogether. They'd done their fair share of kissing and so much more while in Cancún. Shutting him down would equal additional disappointment and confusion she saw in his dimmed blue eyes.

"Thank you for the offer." She stepped backward. "But I'm parked just around the corner." The closest spot she'd been able to get to the restaurant.

"Then text me when you get home?"

"I will do that." With a final, quick smile, Felicity headed right.

The dark, damp, cold early spring air surrounded her while she reached into her purse and removed the mace that she gripped in her right hand.

Her breath came out in bursts of white puffs with each rapid step she took. No matter her walking speed and the mace she clenched, the chill—not from the weather—returned and wound up her spine.

The chill from the feeling of being carefully followed and watched.

She half expected to see a white envelope placed under the windshield wipers as she approached her vehicle. Not seeing one did little to ease her trepidation, however.

Felicity wasted no time climbing into the driver's seat and locking herself inside.

Her breath continued to come out in swift, white puffs as she started the engine. She then carefully loosened her grip on the mace and placed it in the passenger seat. Seconds later, she nearly sped in the direction of home, all while fighting another strong urge.

If not for the fact Ian happened to be on a second date with her closest friend and assistant at this very moment, nothing would have stopped her from calling him.

Oh, God. *Lynn.*

Felicity's heart almost stopped at the image of the woman's glowing face when it came to Ian. She could never get in the middle of what might be developing between the two. Nor could she jeopardize her close relationship with Lynn, meaning Ian Stafford could never be anything more than her brother's best friend and detective working to find her harasser.

Her brother's best friend.

She'd never before responded this way to any of Scott's close friends, and not only because she happened to be three years older than him. She simply hadn't viewed them as anything more than having other younger brothers. Scott being so amiable and having nice men as friends meant he probably wouldn't have cared one bit if something had ever happened between one of his friends and sisters. Thinking of his immediate and intense dislike for her ex,

Scott most likely would have preferred such a thing to happen. But it hadn't.

Until now.

Felicity didn't truly understand why she was thinking of Ian in any other way, either. Head-turning good looks and occasional charm aside, he was a *detective*. And arrogant. Though now that she'd spent a bit more time with him, the arrogance seemed more playful than true self-absorption. None of it changed the truth he was in law enforcement. That's what she needed to focus on when it came to Ian. As her headlights illuminated her garage door, however, her mind went blank at seeing something familiar.

She hit the brake pedal, then stared at the white envelope taped to the door.

The engine quietly humming filled the silence; the headlights putting a spotlight on what undoubtedly had to be note number five.

Tears blurred her vision for mere seconds before her dam shattered.

▭

"THIS NIGHT IS DEFINITELY SURPASSING THURSDAY." Lynn raised her wine glass and tipped it toward Ian's tumbler of bourbon. "A toast to that."

He returned her grin while they tapped glasses. After taking a quick drink, he set the glass on the table.

Okay. They'd covered "safe" topics such as the weather and the best things to do in Denver this time of year and touched on their families. Everything she'd told him about hers he'd already known, but he'd put on an award-winning performance when it come to acting interested and asking questions. But now he needed to steer the chitchat in another direction.

"What kind of wedding do you have this Saturday?" He forked a stuffed mushroom. "I can't imagine doing what you do for a living." He popped the mushroom into his mouth.

Her flirtatious grin slipped.

Shit, he'd already hit a nerve? Which only fueled his distrust for Lynn Delgado.

"The wedding this weekend isn't nearly as grand as last Saturday's. Thank God," she added under her breath. "Sometimes being a wedding planner is very satisfying. It is nice to watch a bride's vision come to life and see the look on her face."

He leaned forward. "But…"

Her gaze caught his. "Most of the time it's exhausting and frustrating and maddening because of how *those* types of people treat us." She paused before adding, "Me, mostly."

And there it was. The opening he'd been wanting.

"I'm sorry." She picked up her glass. "I shouldn't have said that." She took a long drink. "We're getting into wedding season and I think it's going to be longer than usual."

"Don't apologize." He gave her what he hoped was his most charming smile. "I don't know how you two can work with people who are demanding and entitled, more often than not."

Lynn frowned. "Felicity is a very special type of wedding planner."

Very special in general. But Ian stayed silent.

"She's amazing to watch," Lynn quietly continued. "I've learned a lot from her."

Ian tilted his head left to catch her gaze. "So you seem to like working for her."

Lynn's dark eyes flashed with indignation, no doubt at his deliberate phrasing.

"I like to think I work *with* Felicity. And I know if she were here, she'd say the same thing." Lynn finished her wine. "But most of her —our—clients don't seem to think that way."

"I'm sorry to hear that."

She sent him a ghost of a smile. "Felicity's earned every thing she has and is the hardest worker I've ever known."

"I'm starting to see that." He frowned. "But she's made an enemy."

Lynn stared at him. "Do you really believe that?"

Ian froze.

Had she just implied what Larry said that morning?

"Ian, you and I know that someone like Stacia Marsden would never lower herself to petty threats while risking her business and family's name."

Petty threats?

He eyed Lynn whose expression had transformed into exasperation.

"You can tell me the truth." She sighed. "If I know for a fact what I already suspect, I can sit down with Felicity, as a friend, and figure out how to help her. Get her family involved, too."

Help her?

His frown deepened. "You think she's sending the notes to herself."

Lynn turned her exasperation on him. "Of course she's sending them to herself. There's no one else it could possibly be and you have to know that, as well."

When Larry had tried this theory on him, Ian had come back with the argument of knowing the Mayhews very well. And that Felicity couldn't be that good of an actress. So hearing Felicity's closest friend and assistant—who had to know exactly what Ian knew about her and more—basically throw her and her sanity under the bus slashed his insides.

He managed to simply narrow his eyes and ask, "Is there a legitimate reason you think this of your friend and *boss*?"

Indignation returned to Lynn's eyes. "An unhealthy and desperate need for attention now that she's the only one of her siblings who's alone."

Ian kept what he called his cop face, but wanted to laugh at such a ludicrous idea.

How was it possible he knew Felicity Mayhew better than this woman sitting across from him who'd worked closely beside her for two years?

"Interesting." He watched her closely while adding, "But your theory doesn't seem very kind or sympathetic or loyal. Unless, of course, you can back up this claim with evidence?"

She looked away. "I can't. And do you think I'm enjoying having this conversation with you?" She slid her gaze back to him. "After racking my brain for over a month, I can't come up with anyone in her past or present who could be sending the notes."

Except you. But Ian said, "What about this out-of-state guy she's on a date with?"

She peered at him. "What about him? He's no one. They met in Cancún."

Ian's mind seized her statements.

"They were staying at the same resort."

His memory rewound to Saturday night while talking to Scott who'd mentioned Felicity hadn't been the same since returning from her trip.

"When did she receive the first note? I need a date."

Lynn blinked a few times, then her eyes widened. "Two days after she came back from Cancún. It was late February." She reached for her purse. "I can look on the calendar and give you the actual date."

"No. That's good enough," he answered while his brain started to churn.

Felicity takes herself on a rare vacation to a resort in Cancún, Mexico, hits it off with some guy, they obviously grow *close*, then part ways. She returns home and two days later she receives the first threatening note of four from someone who has to know her on some level. Several weeks later, Cancún guy shows up in Denver for a conference and to probably reconnect with Felicity.

"Ian, it has to be a coincidence."

Lynn's voice broke through his thoughts, and he caught her wide-eyed gaze.

"This guy's a nobody from California."

"And when you're a cop, there's no such thing as coincidences." Though nothing but the truth, he wouldn't let go of his Lynn suspicions. Especially after tonight. And Cancún guy from California could be a nobody, but it didn't stop Ian from asking, "Do you know his name?"

She fell silent until, "I only know his first name. Perry. I think Felicity said something about him being in computer software."

A guy named *Perry* from California who happened to work in the computer industry? Yeah. This wouldn't be hard at all. Unless he planned another long, friendly chat with a different woman first thing tomorrow morning. A conversation that might not go too well when he considered the woman. Still, he had no choice but to put aside his confusing and unexpected pull toward Ms. Felicity Mayhew.

He finished his drink and stood. "I'm afraid I'm going to have to call it an early night."

Lynn released a humorless laugh. "Of course you are." She also stood. "You don't like what I said about Felicity, but I was simply being honest."

Ian tossed forty bucks on the table and faced her. "And I don't think your loyalty is where it should be right now." He slid his hands into his pockets. "If what you said is really what you think of Felicity, maybe you should consider finding a different job."

Lynn's eyes hardened.

"It doesn't sound like you know a damn thing about who Felicity Mayhew is or her family." He leaned forward. "Because if you did, you wouldn't believe what you think. And you sure as hell wouldn't have said it out loud." He straightened and stepped aside. "After you."

Ian didn't particularly like Lynn Delgado at this moment, but he'd been raised right.

"I need to use the restroom." She turned from him. "Goodnight, Detective."

He shook his head while striding from the restaurant.

Perhaps he'd been a little harsh. But *shit*. From what he knew and had seen, Felicity had done nothing to deserve someone she loved and trusted betraying her like that.

His steps slowed when Candace and his ex-partner's faces filled his head.

Betrayal and disloyalty. Yep. Highly touchy topics in his world, for sure. The fact Felicity had no idea how Lynn really felt about her only added to his outrage.

He tightened his hands into fists inside his pockets.

Thinking of Candace, though, reminded him of her call he still hadn't faced. At the same time, there was no rush since a huge part of him could give a shit less about anything she had to say. Could be she'd only called to tell him the "good" news, probably hoping to beat Maren.

Ian climbed into his SUV and slammed the door.

This had been far from a good day and he needed it to end. After taking Stella on a long walk, he'd scrape some kind of dinner together, grab a beer, and plant himself on his couch.

That damn good vision grew in strength the closer he got to his rental house. But when he caught sight of a familiar, bright-white SUV parked outside his home, his pulse accelerated.

He pulled into his driveway, parked, killed the engine, and rushed to the driver's side of the SUV.

Felicity opened the door, and Ian halted at the sight of her tear-soaked face while she sniffed and clutched her little dog. She continued to cry while handing him an envelope.

He gently grasped her forearm, helped her from the vehicle, then wrapped her and her dog in his arms and tightly held her trembling body.

Chapter Eleven

IAN PAUSED outside the door that led from the garage into the house. "I'm not sure you can answer this, but did you happen to notice if anyone followed you here?"

Felicity sniffed. "No. I was looking, too." Glancing nearly nonstop in the rearview mirror…and over her shoulder like she had in the restaurant.

He gave Felicity a tight smile.

On the other side, the distinct sounds of his large animal's excitement her human had finally returned home barely registered in Felicity's emotionally and mentally drained mind. Princess Belle, on the other hand, had started to tremble.

"I know you and Stella got off on the wrong foot—paw?—when you first met."

Felicity released a soft laugh.

"But I swear," Ian continued, "the worst thing she'll do is sniff you to death." Their gazes snapped together. "And I promise I won't let her eat your dog."

She managed a weary smile. "Princess Belle and I would appreciate that."

"Your dog's name is Princess Belle?" Ian asked as he opened the door.

Stella nearly knocked him sideways in her enthusiasm, then turned it on Felicity.

Princess Belle began her frenetic, high-pitched barking while Stella did in fact sniff Felicity up and down before shoving her huge nose between Felicity's legs.

"Stella, no!" Ian grabbed her thick collar and pulled her backward. "Knock it off."

Princess Belle's yapping filled the space until Ian looked at her and said, "You, too."

Silence descended.

Stella sat, her enormous mouth hanging open in heavy panting.

Ian raised his eyebrows. "Princess Belle? Really?"

Felicity hugged her dog to her chest. "I let Peyton name her."

His face relaxed into a grin.

His rather disarming grin.

"Now it makes perfect sense." He released Stella's collar. "The living room's this way."

She followed him down a short hallway, went right and into the living room where she halted at the sight.

Ian tossed his trench coat over the back of the navy-blue, sectional sofa. "I apologize for the mess. I—we—weren't expecting company."

Felicity eyed the coffee table in front of the couch covered with some crumpled napkins, an empty beer bottle, and half-full glasses of what looked like water. The couch itself had an oversized gray blanket draped over one end. Based on the amount of dog hair the blanket held, it clearly had to be Stella's spot.

"You can put the princess down." Ian rubbed Stella's head. "She's really a great dog and won't hurt her."

Felicity hesitated before bending down and gently placing her dog on the floor. Princess Belle immediately trotted toward Stella… where they did the normal sniffing-of-butts greeting.

She straightened and caught Ian watching her closely.

So closely it seemed as if he were trying to see straight into her mind.

"Would you like a drink?" He shrugged out of his suit jacket, revealing his holster that held his gun. "I can offer you beer or bourbon." He paused before adding, "Or water."

She sniffed a couple of times. "I do believe it's been a bourbon kind of day." Her voice cracked on the last word when the latest note's message appeared in her mind once more.

Bold, black letters bearing another ugly threat again left at her home, the one place on this planet she should feel *safe*.

"I'll find a box of tissues, too. Make yourself at home." He walked past his dining room table, covered with papers and files, and disappeared behind a wall.

Make yourself at home.

While removing her coat, she took in the chaos of a single man who worked atypical hours and the few, still unpacked moving boxes. He'd hung nothing on the beige walls and had placed very little on the built-in bookcases that flanked a narrow wall where he'd hung a modest flatscreen television. He'd strategically situated his massive sofa and the coffee table near the entertainment spot where he clearly spent most of his time when he was here. But it appeared Ian Stafford had barely made himself at home here in the weeks he'd lived in Denver.

Princess Belle started yipping at Stella playfully bumping her with her nose. The two then took off in the direction Ian had gone.

The corner of Felicity's mouth lifted in a slight smile.

Despite the chaos in Ian's living space, something she wasn't accustomed to in her life, a sense of calm settled around her for the first time that day. And safety.

She closed her eyes and deeply breathed the feelings into her mind and soul.

After pulling the latest note from her garage door and reading it, she'd wasted no time or thought grabbing Princess Belle and heading straight to Ian's place. She hadn't known how he'd react to finding her at his place, but she had known he wouldn't turn her away.

Ian strode back into the great room with the dogs at his heels. He now held her drink and a beat-up box of tissues instead of his suit jacket. He'd also removed his tie and holster, and unbuttoned his shirt to the center of his broad chest.

He took her coat, and she grasped the glass, followed by the box which really had seen better days.

"Stella got a hold of the tissues." He glanced at his dog gently batting Princess Belle on her rear end. "Every now and then she reverts to being a puppy." He shook his head. "Never really know what I'll be walking into when I get home from work."

Felicity took a long drink of the bourbon, then cleared her throat at the slight burn.

"Better or worse?" he asked, back to watching her closely.

"Better. Definitely." She stared into the glass. "Thank you. This is above and beyond your job as a detective."

"Most days I'm more than a detective." He placed his hand on the small of her back and guided her toward the couch.

Perry had touched her a few times the same way in Cancún, but something about Ian's hand in that spot felt decidedly more…soothing. Familiar, too, though she didn't know why.

They sat in the area of the couch not belonging to Stella.

The dogs continued their playing behind where they sat, filling the silence between them.

Felicity finished her drink and placed the glass on the cluttered coffee table. She then grabbed a tissue from the box and wiped her nose. When her gaze settled again on his unpacked moving boxes, she asked, "No time to finish unpacking?"

He shrugged. "That and lack of real ambition."

She focused on him, focused on her. "You didn't really want to move here. Did you?"

Something resembling anger briefly flashed through his dark eyes. "Yes and no."

Remembering what little Scott had told her about Ian's break-up caused her to say, "I loved living in London. But the price was entirely too high to stay there." A painful truth.

His mouth eased into that disarming grin of his. "The British accent comes through every now and then. How long did you live there?"

"Seven years."

His eyes widened. "Well, that explains the accent hanging on for so long." He shifted right to fully face her. "How'd you meet Mr. London?"

She sat back and stared at a clear spot on his table. "I was there on vacation with my mom and sister. He and I met in a pub, and I fell embarrassingly hard soon thereafter." She eyed Ian. "The rest falls into the category of a forgettable time in my history."

Ian nodded. "From the way Scott talks about him, he sounds like a real piece of shit."

"A narcissistic, abusive *wanker*."

His forehead formed a deep frown. "Physically abusive?"

Felicity's face became warm.

Talking about her ex still brought on feelings of shame that she'd not only fallen for his charming, good-man act, but stayed with him for so damn long.

"I'm sorry," Ian murmured. "It's none of my business."

"It was mostly emotional, but he did grab my arm once during a stupid argument while we were in a store." She cringed at the memory of the action hurting and being horribly humiliating. "His grip had been so strong he left a substantial bruise on my upper arm."

Silence, outside of the dogs still scuffling, fell once more. Until Ian said, "Tell me that's when you left the sonofabitch."

She cracked a smile. "Without a backward glance. And one of the best days of my life."

His face relaxed. "Good." He pointed at her empty glass. "Another drink?"

She shook her head. "I'm good. *Better*. The one helped immensely." As had the company and fact he was being a friend right now instead of a detective. She shifted onto her left side. "From what Scott has told me, you went through a bad break-up before moving here."

Ian smirked. "It seems Scott has a pretty damn big mouth." He sighed. "Candace and I were high school sweethearts and supposedly getting married. But we weren't on the same page and hadn't been for a long time." He paused, then added, "We'd also stopped *really* talking." The anger returned to his eyes. "But I still never expected she and my partner with the Grand Junction PD to take me and his wife out to dinner one night and tell us they'd been screwing around for months. They then stated they were leaving *us* to be together."

Felicity's mouth inched open.

"Now she's pregnant and they're going to Hawaii to get married." His eyes hardened. "I recently found that out from my ex-partner's ex-wife, Maren."

Felicity stared at him. "You two are good friends?"

"Since he and I first became partners five years ago." Their gazes locked. "That bastard, who I considered a brother, broke Maren in half. She would have done anything for him."

Felicity hesitated before asking, "And what did all of that do to you?" It clearly had to be the main reason he'd left Grand Junction, but that couldn't be the whole ugly story.

"I got hammered that night and stayed that way." His eyes slid sideways. "Until a few days later when I marched into the precinct, hunted the asshole down, and…" He refocused on Felicity. "I got in a couple of damn good punches, giving him a black eye and split lip."

She couldn't imagine this man sitting beside her, who'd gently pulled her and her dog into his arms and held her tight while she sobbed into his chest, being that angry with another human being. But it's not like his ex-partner hadn't crossed an immensely personal line.

"The bastard had slight seniority over me, too." He shook his head. "Needless to say that pretty much ended my career with the Grand Junction PD."

She remained silent.

"But my captain saved my career as a cop."

"He helped you get the job on the Denver police force?"

Ian slowly nodded. "Yep. I'd just made detective grade in Grand Junction. So one might say the timing couldn't have been more perfect for a big change."

She reached out, hesitated, then clasped his right hand and squeezed.

His dark eyes met hers.

"I'm terribly sorry about what they did to you two." She frowned. "I can't imagine ever going through that kind of betrayal. And by *two* people close to me?" She again squeezed his hand without breaking their eye contact.

Ian opened his mouth, clearly on the verge of saying something, but straightened and pulled his hand free. "Speaking of betrayal, we need to talk about this latest note."

Felicity faced forward. "I know." But it was the absolute last thing she wanted to do at this moment.

"And the fact you may no longer be safe at home."

She whipped her head in his direction. "What are you suggesting?"

He rubbed his eyes. "Felicity, I respect the fact you're an independent, strong woman who can take of herself. You are, after all, a Mayhew." He settled his bleary gaze on her. "But we're up to five threatening notes, two of which have been left at your home. Do I really need to walk you through the what if this person decides to follow through on the five threats?" He angled his head in the direction of where Princess Belle and Stella were lounging. "Your dog qualifies as an ankle biter. Not a fierce protector."

She lifted her chin. "I understand that."

"You probably don't own a gun."

She narrowed her eyes. "Up until several weeks ago I haven't needed one."

"So be honest with me." He leaned forward. "Do you feel safe at home?"

The nasty messages in the five notes swirled through Felicity's exhausted mind, two of which had been left at her home and one on her windshield.

Her lower lip trembled as her eyes once more turned wet. "No," she whispered. "I don't."

Ian scooted closer, wrapped his arm around her shoulder, and hugged her to his side. "Then you and the princess will stay with us tonight since you're already here."

Felicity relaxed into his warm, strong arm, too weary to put up a fight. In fact, she couldn't escape the feeling of relief Ian, who she trusted with her life, was taking charge.

All sense of control over her life had left upon finding and reading the latest note.

"We also need to figure out your next steps." He gave her a quick squeeze before gently releasing her and stood. "I'm guessing you'll want something more comfortable to sleep in than a business suit?"

She glanced at her dark-blue power suit now wrinkled and her matching heels. "Yes." She then eyed Ian and found him giving her what could only be described as a look of affection. Remembering he'd been on a second date with Lynn, Felicity tore her gaze from him and focused on the floor. "Would staying with Lynn work?" The fact of the matter was that she only had Lynn because she'd kept her family out of this horrible mess to not cause them worry. "But I guess that would put us both at risk." And with that said, Felicity wasn't certain she could continue keeping everything from her family.

"Yeah. It would. I also have another idea."

She looked up.

Ian's eyes flashed with an emotion she couldn't quite decipher.

"Take a sick day tomorrow and stay here."

She vehemently shook her head. "Ian, I can't—"

"Yes, you can. It's only one day. I'm sure Lynn can handle it."

Something about the way he'd said Lynn's name hit Felicity sideways.

He stepped backward. "Call her in the morning. Tell her you're sick. That's it."

She returned his frown. "Why the hell would I lie to her all of a sudden?" Unease crept up Felicity's back and settled onto her shoulders. "What's going on? I thought you liked her."

His face transformed into an emotionless mask. "It turns out we have very little in common." He sighed. "Felicity, I need you to trust me and do what I asked. Please?"

Despite the sense of foreboding now surrounding her, she nodded.

He couldn't possibly think Lynn had anything to do with the notes.

Or did he? It made no sense whatsoever, though.

"Thank you. I'll be back with something for you to change into." He started to leave, but stopped and added, "We're also going to talk about Perry."

She froze as he left the room.

Lynn must have told Ian about Perry, but why would he want to talk about a man who didn't even live in Colorado? And what the hell had happened between Ian and Lynn tonight? A huge part of her wanted to shoot Lynn a quick text, but Felicity had agreed to Ian's odd request.

She reached up and released her hair from the tight bun. As she ran her hand through the thick locks, one question landed in her mind.

When had her pretty structured life become so unstructured and unrecognizable?

But it's not like the answer was terribly difficult to reach.

Chapter Twelve

IAN WAITED until Felicity closed the guest bathroom door down the hall before retrieving note five from his coat pocket, as well as his cell. He then walked into his bedroom, closed the door, and chose an all-too familiar name in his list of contacts.

He'd promised Felicity he wouldn't get her brother involved, but that time had officially passed. Someone in her family needed to know what the hell was happening, especially now that she couldn't be at home alone and he didn't trust Lynn.

"Hey," Scott answered. "How'd date two go?"

"Yeah, we need to talk about that and a few other things. When is your break tomorrow?"

A long pause fell on his buddy's end, followed by, "First thing in the morning and early afternoon. What the hell's going on?"

"So will nine work? Your office?"

"Sure. But should I be—"

"I'll see you then." Ian ended the call.

He tossed his phone onto his bed, lowered himself to the edge, and stared at the envelope.

Note number five taped to Felicity's garage door. He-she had wanted to make sure she got it right away.

He once again removed the white paper and read the words that had led her to his house.

ENJOYMENT IS TAKING PLEASURE IN SOMETHING.

I WILL ENJOY OUR FIRST AND LAST MEETING.

SOON.

Ian focused on the second sentence and gritted his teeth.

A first meeting seemed to heavily imply Felicity and this person had never met. Unless, of course, it had been said with the intent to look that way. No matter if was Lynn or not, he would *enjoy* putting the person into cuffs and leading them to a jail cell.

He put the note back inside the envelope and tossed it beside his phone.

Lynn supposedly had been racking her brain for a person in Felicity's life who could despise her this much, but had reached the conclusion it could only be Felicity. Recalling her wet face when she'd opened the car door while hugging her little dog, then sobbing into his chest, Ian could only reach one thought.

Even if Lynn wasn't Felicity's tormentor, she obviously didn't respect or like her. At least, not anymore. So why continue to work for and with her? What the hell could Lynn be getting out of the deal? She'd told him with zero hesitation she rarely received the respect from clients Felicity did. It didn't even sound like she genuinely enjoyed wedding planning. His instincts were screaming something wasn't right with this woman, but what? He also needed to get the facts on the Perry guy.

Okay. Maybe Ian was again grasping at what few straws he had when it came to Felicity's stalker. Still, the notes had started once she returned from the trip where she'd met this guy. With Stacia Marsden hiding behind her dad and fancy lawyers, who else did he have but Lynn and Cancún guy? The notes were getting closer together, too.

A distinct sign he-she had to be losing patience. Getting antsy. Preparing to strike.

Soon.

He couldn't keep Felicity safe and find this piece of shit at the same time. Though all he wanted to do was keep her by his side until he did catch the person.

And he would catch them.

On that thought, Ian stood and went to his dresser. Once he'd swapped his dress shirt and suit pants for a pair of basketball shorts and sweatshirt, he strode from his bedroom. At the sight of Stella sprawled in her spot on the couch and head resting in Felicity's lap, he stopped.

He couldn't help but smile at Felicity gently petting his dog's head and neck while mumbling something to her. The princess had plastered herself to Felicity's left side.

"It seems you've made a new friend."

Felicity glanced his way and grinned softly. Which caused his mind to go blank. That and the sight of her wearing one of his U.S. Army sweatshirts and sweatpants that had to be ten times more than her actual size and length. She'd also pulled her hair into a loose knot at the back of her neck. Thin, red hairs framed her face no longer tear-stained and less red from emotion.

She always looked damn good in her high-dollar suits and heels. But like this happened to be his definition of perfect.

Holy shit, he was officially in trouble. Especially if that British accent came through.

"You're right." Her grin deepened. "Stella's a sweetheart."

He cleared his throat and said the first thing that came to mind. "Told you so." He then fought the overwhelming urge to cringe.

Told you so? Wow. He definitely needed to work on the witty comebacks.

Her grin slipped. "I feel I should apologize for that night we met at Scott's place."

Ian stepped forward. "Water under the bridge as far as I'm concerned."

"No. You were there helping Campbell and my brother, and I acted atrociously."

Of course there was the hint of British accent.

Maybe it was his turn for a shot of bourbon.

"I'd had a lousy day and had been very worried about Scott." She lifted her shoulders. "I lashed into you and Stella." She scratched his dog's face. "I don't normally like big dogs, either, but she's an absolute lover."

"Just like her dad."

A round of silence followed his words that had tumbled out before they registered in his brain. But the fact Felicity seemed to be fighting a smile did ease some of his embarrassment.

Yeah. He'd been out of the game for a long-ass time. Still, what the hell was wrong with him? They needed to get back to the reason she was here to begin with.

"I'm going to get a drink. When I come back, we're going to talk about Perry."

Her smile vanished. "Ian, he has nothing to do with this. He doesn't even live here." She lifted her chin. "It's also none of your business."

Damn him if she didn't look even more appealing with her chin raised in that familiar defiance. He managed to say, "And believe me I don't want to know anymore than what I need to when it comes to this guy. But I can't ignore the fact you started receiving the notes right after you returned from your trip where you met him. Lynn gave me the time frame."

Felicity's eyes widened like Lynn's had earlier when he'd mentioned the "coincidence."

"I'll be right back."

After pouring himself a healthy shot, Ian released a quick breath.

He needed to focus. And not on how good she looked and sounded.

Following another breath, he picked up his glass and walked back into the living room.

"Okay," he said after dropping onto the lounger section of his couch. "Let's start with his full name and where he lives in California."

She narrowed her eyes. "Why? Sounds like Lynn already told you everything."

"If that were actually the case, I can promise we wouldn't be having this conversation." He swigged some bourbon. "*Perry* must have a last name."

She stayed silent.

Ian returned her hard stare. "Please tell me you know his last name." An uncomfortable thought suddenly occurred to him which promoted him to ask, "Or did you two make one of those no-full-name and no-real-personal-details pacts while in Mexico?"

He couldn't imagine Ms. Felicity Mayhew, who projected nothing but a need for order and control, agreeing to such a thing. Then again, he'd witnessed the fire inside of her that couldn't be contained. But that realization caused a spark of envy toward Cancún guy for obviously having seen her fire in a completely different way.

Ian finished his drink in one swallow.

"No," she enunciated. "We did not make such a pact." She gently scooted out from underneath Stella's massive head. "Cantrell." She stood. "Perry Cantrell. Satisfied?"

Perry Cantrell.

Ian filed away the much-needed info. Now he only needed a few more details.

"Where in California does computer, Cancún guy live?"

Felicity stared at him. "I'm being perfectly serious when I ask what *didn't* Lynn tell you?"

He grinned. "I'm being perfectly serious when I say please answer the question."

She turned, marched toward his dining area, then veered right, into the kitchen.

Ian looked at Stella and the princess, staring at him. "This might be a long night."

"Where's your trash can?" Felicity asked in a raised voice.

He frowned. "Under the sink."

A couple of seconds later, she marched back into the living room with the can. She set it beside the coffee table and began throwing away the few crumpled napkins.

"I don't understand why you're so interested in Perry." She dropped the empty beer bottle into the can. "He's a software engineer from San Jose, California who, like me, desperately needed a vacation and decided on a trip to Cancún."

Perry Cantrell, software engineer from San Jose.

"He's here for a computer conference and is leaving Friday evening." She picked up a half-full glass sitting on his coffee table and took a tentative sniff. "I'm assuming this is water?"

"Yeah." He sighed. "Please stop cleaning up after me and sit down."

She pointed at the other two glasses. "How many glasses of water do you need?"

Ian stared into the empty glass he held, willing another shot of bourbon to appear. "Felicity, I'm just doing my job."

"And I'm telling you he has nothing to do with this!" she snapped. "We're two single adults who happened to meet while vacationing at the same resort. *That's it*." She grabbed the trash can and stalked back into the kitchen.

Needing another drink and struck by what she'd said, Ian followed her.

She dumped the water into the sink and nearly slammed the glass down on the counter. But he couldn't and wouldn't back down.

"How exactly do you know he's single?"

She halted while putting the trash can away.

"He was in Cancún by himself and I have to assume not wearing a ring. But none of that means he is in fact single."

Felicity slowly closed the cabinet door and faced him with wide eyes. "I have no reason not to believe him." She gestured at herself. "I'm single and was there alone."

He leaned against the counter, almost hating himself for where he'd taken the conversation based on her deer-caught-in-headlights expression. Which made it clear she'd never once considered the possibility the guy had lied and was still lying.

"You know firsthand some guys can be real shit bags."

She crossed her arms and looked at the floor.

"I'm not saying he is," Ian quietly continued. "But what do you really know about him? Outside of whatever he's told you."

She lifted her head, and their gazes collided.

"Ian, it goes both ways. And our interactions, even before he arrived in Denver, have been exactly the same."

"Okay." He leaned forward. "But he's not the one receiving threatening notes."

Larry's initial reaction after reading the messages again landed in Ian's mind.

This stinks of a jealous woman.

At the same time, Perry Cantrell lived in California. If the guy had lied about being single, it had to mean the possible woman also lived there.

Two straws barely visible enough to grasp? Probably. He still had to say, "Can you manage to stay away from the guy until I've had a chance to check him out?"

If Perry Cantrell happened to be completely on the level, Ian would have no choice but to send Felicity back into the guy's wide open and ready arms. But what could he do about it?

Except pour himself another shot of bourbon to help eradicate the image.

"We decided to see how the week goes before meeting up again." She straightened. "So to answer your question, yes. But I positively believe you'll be wasting your time on him."

Ian grasped the bottle of liquor. "Your opinion has been duly noted. Are you hungry?"

"No. I want to talk about Lynn."

He shook his head while pouring himself another stiff shot. "I can't comment on her at this moment. I know it'll be hard for you, but you have to trust me." He held up the bottle. "You sure you don't want another drink?"

She lifted her chin as fire flashed through her light-brown eyes.

A different kind of flame ignited his insides.

What the hell was it about this woman, his good buddy's *sister*, that suddenly made him want to argue with her, then hold her in his arms, then kiss her until they couldn't breathe?

"Dammit, Ian. I'm tired of answering your questions and not getting answers to mine."

He twisted the cap back on the bottle and put it inside the cabinet by his head. "That's what happens when I'm the cop and you're the lady in distress. Are you sure you're not hungry?" He grinned. "I have leftover pizza and don't mind sharing."

Her mouth inched open, but in a different way than when he'd spilled the entire, ugly Candace-and-his-ex-partner story. An action that had been surprisingly easy, considering it still haunted him daily. Though uprooting his life to Denver had helped ease the haunting's intensity.

"How do you do that?"

He squinted at her. "Eat leftovers?"

"Go from infuriating to charming in zero point five seconds?"

The question dangled between them for several seconds before he brought back his grin.

"You think I'm charming?"

Her face turned a rather enticing shade of pink. "I'm not answering any more of your questions tonight, *Detective*." She paused, then added, "Except that yes, I'll have another drink. And yes, a slice of pizza does sound quite good."

His smile deepened.

"Where do you keep your cleaning products?" She looked around his cluttered kitchen. "Or do you even possess such items?"

His smile transitioned into a frown. "As a matter of fact I do, *Ms. Mayhew*. But I don't need or want you to clean my house."

"I find cleaning to be calming. And I don't plan on cleaning your house." She gestured toward the living room. "Just the coffee table."

How the hell could he argue with that?

"Then by all means"—he swallowed some bourbon—"clean away. You'll find everything you need under the sink."

She was about to leave the kitchen with paper towels and glass cleaner when the memory of her parked outside his house hit, followed by another question.

"I know you declared you aren't answering any more of my questions, but how did you get my address?"

She obviously hadn't reached out to Scott, and Shannon had no idea where Ian lived. Those two were their only personal connections, outside of Peyton.

Felicity cracked a smile. "The day you moved in here I dropped off Scott to help you because his car was in the shop."

Ian nodded when the vague memory returned.

"Google Maps remembered your address." She disappeared from view.

He expelled a long, slow breath.

Yep. It would definitely be a long night. But the most important fact was that she was here with him and safe where he could keep her that way. Tomorrow, however, would be a challenging day for many reasons, starting with his conversation with Scott...who wouldn't react well to anything Ian told him. Still, that fell into the category of tomorrow along with everything else on his must-do list. In the meantime, he'd give Felicity whatever else she needed to stay "calm" while he tried extremely hard not to dwell on the realization he wanted her the way a single man desired a curvy, sassy, single, smart woman with fire in her hair.

And maybe even wanted more than that.

Unfortunately, he had no idea what to do with *that* knowledge, either.

Chapter Thirteen

FELICITY ROLLED onto her side and nestled her head deeper into—
her eyes popped open. She blinked until the fatigue cleared…then
froze at being curled against Ian Stafford on his couch.

His head, propped up on a couch cushion, had tilted slightly left
and his arm securely held her to his warm side.

She stared at his handsome face, relaxed in deep sleep.

Black, thick morning scruff enhanced the hair he didn't shave on
a daily basis, but clearly kept trimmed. The extra morning hair
accentuated his defined cheekbones and jawline. Being this up close
and personal to him, she noticed his long eyelashes.

The man undeniably qualified as beautiful.

Remembering his awful ex-girlfriend story, Felicity couldn't
ignore one question.

What the hell had that Candace woman been thinking giving up
this man who was not only head-turning handsome, but the definition
of a military and everyday hero.

Yes. There were always two sides to every story. No doubt her
delightful ex-husband had his own version of how their relationship
had gone and ended. But what on earth could that woman have

needed and wanted that Ian hadn't been providing? It's not like his career in law enforcement had been the issue since she'd left him for his partner.

She frowned, unable to wrap her mind around what had obviously been a heart-wrenching betrayal. From what she remembered of the few partners her father had during his career, they'd been like his brothers, especially his last partner who'd barely survived the shooting that had taken *him*.

She reached out and lightly placed her hand on Ian's cheek. That's when she noticed Stella stretched out in her spot with her head against his right thigh. Princess Belle had buried herself beside Felicity and underneath the blanket he must have placed over her at some point. She couldn't remember a thing after eating a slice of warmed pizza and the second glass of bourbon. The night had certainly gone in a direction she'd never expected. Considering how warm and safe she still felt at that moment, and had definitely experienced last night, she had no regrets over driving to his place.

She definitely hadn't liked him doing his job or him avoiding her Lynn questions. But it didn't change the fact she did trust him. Implicitly. If she continued being honest with herself, she liked *this*. Being curled into his side on the couch with their dogs sleeping with them.

Ian suddenly shifted onto his left side, facing her, and placed his hand over hers. He then grasped her fingers, brought her hand to his mouth…and gently kissed her palm.

Her breath stalled at the intimate action, her eyes never leaving his face.

He had to be dreaming. Or maybe it was something he'd done with Candace?

Felicity started to pull her hand free, but his grip tightened.

"Ian," she whispered. "It's Felicity."

He nestled his head deeper into the couch cushion and continued to hold her and her hand. "I know," he mumbled with his eyes still closed. "What time is it?"

She again tried to tug her hand free. "You just kissed my palm. Wake up."

His eyelids fluttered open.

Their gazes connected.

"I know that, too."

They silently stared at one another.

She cleared her throat. "Why did you do that?"

He gave her a sleepy smile. "Felt like the right thing to do."

Between his deep voice, smile that could almost be defined as sexy, and his reply, Felicity somehow fought what she wanted to do at that moment.

Press her lips to his, then lose herself in all things Detective Ian Stafford.

"What time is it?" he asked again around a full-body yawn.

She remained still, unable to change the direction her thoughts had taken. But Ian slowly untangling himself from her and the blanket forced her to sit upright. That, in turn, caused Princess Belle to wiggle out from under the blanket while Stella also sat up.

Ian grabbed his phone off of the coffee table. "I have to get ready for work." He faced her. "Can I trust you to call Lynn and simply tell her you're sick?"

All thoughts of getting lost in him fled Felicity's mind. Reality had returned and she had no choice but to face it.

"Yes," she murmured. "But you owe me an explanation, Detective."

"And I promise I'll give it to you as soon as I can." He hesitated for a few seconds, concentrating on her as a smile teased the corner of his mouth. "You look pretty damn good in the morning, Ms. Mayhew." He stood and headed in the direction of his bedroom.

Stella jumped off the couch and followed him.

Felicity sat back and released the breath she'd unknowingly been holding in her lungs.

He looked just as good in the morning, if not better.

She sighed and flung the blanket aside.

Princess Belle followed her to where she'd set her purse last night after changing into Ian's oversized sweats. She had no idea what to expect from this day, but no matter what, she needed to return home at some point to get her own clothing.

She stared at her phone as questions swirled through her mind.

Why would Ian suddenly be so wary of Lynn? What in the world could have happened between them last night? It sounded as if Lynn had done nothing but give Ian what he wanted, namely Perry Cantrell. Doing his job or not, Felicity still couldn't get on board with any suspicions Ian had about her Cancún *friend*. Just like how he now felt about Lynn, it made no sense. All she could do, though, was trust he'd explain himself soon.

"Hi," Lynn answered. "I'm headed to the gym. Is this an emergency?"

Felicity frowned at the woman's distant, almost cold tone.

Something big had definitely happened between Ian and Lynn.

"I'm...quite sick this morning." She focused on her bare feet. "Something I must have eaten last night. Can you move my appointment and have office calls forwarded to your cell?"

Silence fell before, "Of course. I believe your only appointment was with Emmy Swanson. What day and time would you like me to reschedule it?"

Felicity pictured her calendar for the rest of the week and said, "Thursday afternoon. And please feel free to work from home today. If anything pressing comes up, let me know and I'll get back to you as soon as I can."

A wave of nausea hit, but not at all due to anything she'd eaten.

Why were she and Lynn talking to each other as if they were strangers?

"Okay." Another round of silence fell until, "Have you, by chance, talked to Ian?"

Felicity slid her gaze down the hall to his closed bedroom door. "No. But that reminds me, how was your date last night?" Slight break in her promise to him.

What the detective didn't know, however, wouldn't hurt him in the slightest.

"No connection there after all." Lynn laughed, but there was absolutely no humor behind it. "It happens. I hope you feel better. Let me know if you need anything."

The line went dead before Felicity lowered her phone from her ear.

What the hell had just happened? Lynn had never hung up on her. In fact, the Lynn she'd known for the last two years would have been shocked at Felicity calling out sick, on top of making doubly certain there wasn't anything she could do to help because they'd been, almost from the beginning, friends. But there had been nothing friendly or warm about their brief chat.

Felicity raised her chin, turned, and marched toward Ian's bedroom.

He would answer her questions about Lynn whether he wanted to or not.

She opened the door without knocking, stepped inside—and stopped at the sight of him shirtless, wearing only dark-gray suit pants and loafers.

Her gaze landed on his dark, smooth, defined chest and she lost her breath. The scent of his masculine soap from his shower permeated the room and filled her head, causing it to turn steamy. Like his bathroom.

"Was there something you needed?"

She glanced up to find him closely watching her…barely fighting that grin of his.

Though her face became uncomfortably warm, she said, "Yes. I want to know what the hell happened between you and Lynn last night."

He turned and swiped a bright-white dress shirt off of his bed that had been inches from where Stella happened to be lounging. "This is starting to feel like déjà vu."

She walked toward him at the same time he began buttoning his shirt. "I just had the most uncomfortable conversation with her which has never happened until she went on a second date with you." She stared up at him. "I'm not leaving or letting you leave until you answer my question, *Detective*."

Ian roughly tucked in his shirt, then grabbed his belt. "And has it once occurred to you, *Ms. Mayhew*, that I'm protecting you." He buckled the belt and next grabbed a light-gray tie.

"From Lynn?" She crossed her arms. "You cannot be serious."

He hooked the tie around his neck. "If you'll trust me to do my job, I swear you'll get all the answers you want and need."

"No," she ground out. "That's not good enough. I've also known Lynn much longer than I've known you. Up until moments ago, she hasn't done a thing to warrant me not trusting her."

Their gazes remained locked. Until Ian picked up his nearby holster and shrugged into the straps. He next put on his suit jacket and closed the small gap between them. Without breaking their eye contact, he reached up and gently cupped her face.

Felicity became still as his dark eyes—now smoldering—stared into her hers.

"It's getting harder and harder to not kiss you when you look like you do right now."

Her lips parted.

He glanced at her mouth and a slight grin replaced his frown. "All fired up with passion and loyalty and strength." He barely touched his lips to hers. "It's a massive turn on."

Based on *him* pressed against her mid-section, that was a massive understatement.

She breathed in his delicious scent while he nuzzled her nose.

"But I'm not one to start something I can't finish."

She peered at him.

Not finish? Him?

"And I sure as hell don't mean like that." He just as gently removed his hands from her face. "I have to get to work." He sighed.

"Felicity, all I can say about Lynn is that you need to be careful until I say otherwise."

She stayed silent while her mind absorbed his latest Lynn statement…as well as what would have surely been a perfect and delectable first kiss.

"I know it will be difficult for you"—he opened his nightstand drawer and removed his gun—"but try to relax and stay put." He placed the weapon inside his holster and headed for his bedroom door. "I'll check in with you later."

Suddenly remembering she wanted her clothing, she turned and asked, "Do I have permission to go home and change into my own clothes?"

He grinned. "Why would you want to do that since you look so damn good in mine?"

A soft laugh escaped before she could stop it.

"How about we meet at your house later? I'll text you when I'm leaving work."

"What if you indefinitely get stuck at work?" Another aspect of law enforcement life.

As irresistible as Ian had become, he was a detective.

The long, abnormal hours.

Interruptions that could happen at any hour of the day.

The never knowing if he'd arrive home safe and sound.

So what the hell was she doing almost kissing him and desiring him to kiss her?

And more.

"Then I guess you'll indefinitely be stuck in my clothes." With that he left his room.

Her shoulders fell forward and she closed her eyes.

Something Lynn had said about Ian last week appeared in her mind as if a neon sign.

That man is a presence in a small space.

Felicity could still feel all of him around her, as well as the heat from his lips barely touching hers while he held her face.

She released a slow breath and opened her eyes. That's when she noticed his bedroom seemed no more moved into than his living room.

Disheveled king-sized bed on a frame with a headboard that matched his nightstand and dresser, both of which looked like his coffee table had last night before she'd cleaned it off. Nothing on the walls. One oversized window with closed white blinds. Two moving boxes stacked in the corner between his closet and bathroom door.

Her heart splintered at once more recalling why he'd really moved to Denver in February. A move that hadn't necessarily been wanted, but definitely needed for many reasons.

Stella rolled upright, stretched, and climbed off of her human's bed. She then stared up at Felicity while wagging her thick, fluffy tail. Princess Belle had probably jumped back on the couch and buried herself in the blanket.

Felicity scratched Stella's head. "Looks like it'll just be the three of us today." She frowned when she realized Ian had left without telling her where he kept the dog food. Or anything else about what Stella might need.

Then again, it did sound like his dog was used to being home alone all day.

"Let's go find your food." Food she'd also have to give her dog.

When she rounded the corner into the kitchen, though, she stopped and shook her head.

There was no way in hell she could function in such a cluttered, chaotic space for an entire day. She also had every intention of grabbing her traveling office out of her vehicle and getting some work done. Without question, she would need a clear space.

But he did—thank God—have a coffee maker.

She glanced at Stella watching her while panting. "First feed you two, followed by coffee, then we'll clean. Sound good?"

Stella continued to pant, but wagged her tail.

All of those activities would keep her busy and mind off of her harasser, Perry, Lynn, and wanting so much more than protection from Ian Stafford.

▭

SCOTT NARROWED HIS EYES. "The only reason I'm not tearing your head off your shoulders right now is because I know how stubborn my sister is."

Ian stayed silent since he'd expected this reaction from his long-time friend who, like Ian, had a fiercely protective side when it came to those closest to him, specifically family.

Scott ran a hand through his hair while shaking his head. "Now that I've said that and understand her distant behavior since she came back from her trip, what do you need from me? I'm sure Felicity has no idea you're here telling me everything."

Ian winced. "*Hell*, no. I can't take on that kind of wrath right now." He sat back. "I also need her to trust me because I've put doubt in her head when it comes to Lynn and Cancún guy."

His buddy frowned. "I have no idea who he is, so I can't comment on him. I also don't want to think about my sister having a fling with some random guy in Mexico."

Yeah. Ian didn't want that image in his head, either, but for entirely different reasons.

"But Lynn…" Scott's voice trailed into silence. "She really said she thinks Felicity is sending the threatening notes to *herself* for attention?"

Ian slowly nodded. "If she's not sending them, there's still something going on there."

Scott's eyes hardened. "Felicity trusts and loves her like she's family. We all do. Did," he swiftly corrected under his breath.

Which happened to be one reason why Ian didn't want to tell Felicity about Lynn until absolutely necessary. He couldn't stand the thought of hurting her. He also couldn't ignore the feeling there was more going on with Lynn than now disliking her boss. Her being the note writer or not, he needed to be armed with the facts when he had the conversation with Felicity.

"So what's the plan? Outside of keeping my sister—the most headstrong person I've ever known—under house arrest. For lack of a better phrase."

This happened to be the part of the conversation Ian had struggled with the most during his drive to Jefferson County Community College. But replaying the rather hot moment with his good friend's hot sister before Ian left his house had complicated the obvious answer.

"She can't be at home because of this person," Scott continued. "She can't stay with Lynn. She can't stay with me because I'm not supposed to know any of this. I also have Peyton this week." His frown deepened. "Even if I did tell my sister tough shit about me knowing and make her stay with me, her suddenly living at my house would cause a lot of questions."

"Which would piss her off even more."

"Yep."

They fell silent.

Ian couldn't help but think their imaginations had gone in the same direction.

Scott focused on him. "I guess that leaves you, Detective. And you two apparently didn't kill each other last night. I'd say that's a good sign."

Ian's memory went to this morning, waking up beside Felicity on his couch.

Kissing her warm palm. Her thick, deep red hair framing her face. Her eyes bright with confusion and apprehension mingling with need. Her storming into his bedroom while crackling with irritation and passion. Then with zero hesitation she'd checked him out.

How he'd possessed the self-control to not start and finish what his mind and body had desperately wanted still eluded him.

"Hey."

Scott's voice broke through Ian's inappropriate thoughts, then scattered. At least, his thoughts were inappropriate considering the person sitting across from him. Still, Ian had a strong suspicion if he and Felicity did end up truly *connecting*, Scott wouldn't blink an eye.

"What are you going to do?"

Ian pushed the thoughts aside and straightened. "Keep an eye on her when I can. I want you to check in with her, too. But don't overdo it," he added. "I'm also going to try my damndest to talk her into working from home and away from Lynn until I can put more of the pieces together." Unfortunately, he seemed days from finishing what felt like a thousand-piece puzzle.

"And Cancún guy, as you call him?"

Ian stood. "Felicity and I have already reached an agreement when it comes to him."

After Ian's two unforgettable moments with her this morning, he couldn't help but think Perry Cantrell from San Jose, California wouldn't be too hard for Felicity to walk away from, whether or not he somehow, someway, fit into the puzzle.

Scott concentrated on him. "My stubborn sister not only went to your place last night and stayed with you, but also agreed to call in sick to keep her distance from Lynn *and* made another agreement with you with regards to this guy she met in Mexico?"

Ian grinned. "What can I say? I can be pretty damn persuasive when I need to be."

His buddy's eyes widened. "Holy shit. You two actually like each other."

That was Ian's cue to get the hell out of Scott's office before he said anything else that might incriminate himself and Felicity.

He also had yet to fully absorb the fact he did like her. A lot. And wanted her. A lot.

"Give Peyton a hug from her Uncle Ian." He turned and headed for Scott's closed office door. "Remember what I said about not overdoing it when checking in with your sister. I'll be in touch soon." At that moment, his phone started to ring.

"You're lucky I need to get ready for class and that your phone is ringing," Scott stated as Ian left his office. "But I know my sister will be safe with you."

Ian closed the door behind him, then retrieved his phone.

"Hi," he said to Larry. "I had to make a stop, but I'm on my way." He turned right and quickly strode down the hallway, passing other offices in the school's English department.

"Tox reports came back on our elderly Zamoras," Larry replied. "It wasn't carbon monoxide poisoning."

Ian punched the down elevator button with his index finger. "Drugs?" The only other thing it could be when he thought about how the elderly couple had looked while still in bed.

"An opioid. Probably the hydrocodone prescribed for Mr. Zamora."

Ian stepped into the elevator. "So suicide?"

"Or something far worse."

He frowned.

"We need to get the granddaughter in here as soon as possible and have a chat."

"Okay." The doors opened and Ian veered left. "Felicity received another note last night. It was taped to her garage door and it's the most threatening one yet."

"Well, *shit*," Larry muttered. "So much for a quiet Tuesday."

"I'll be there soon."

"You should be the one to call the granddaughter," Larry added, "and talk to her when she gets here since she already knows you."

"Right." Ian ended the call and walked outside into the dreary, wet air.

So much for a quiet Tuesday.

Yeah. He might actually get stuck at work, too.

Hopefully Felicity would stay put at his house with his big, over-protective dog. He also had no choice but to believe her stalker hadn't followed her last night to his place. There'd been no evidence of it when Ian had inspected her SUV before leaving, but that didn't mean shit.

Scott had said Felicity would be safe with Ian. The truth, too. But only if she continued to listen to and trust him. Recalling her streaks of stubbornness and fierce independence, however, there were no guarantees the lady would indefinitely remain cooperative.

Chapter Fourteen

MISS EMMY SWANSON. *June ninth of next year. Marrying Mr. Jason McAvoy at the JW Marriott in Cherry Creek.*

Felicity rubbed her tired eyes.

She'd spent the day doing her least favorite part of the job—writing contracts. She'd been terribly behind on it, though, and being stuck inside had given her a reason to finish them.

Miss Emmy Swanson and Mr. Jason McAvoy.

Yet another couple—bride—who wanted nothing but the finest. The best. The most expensive. As did the daughter of the state representative and the young socialite marrying the son of a prominent Denver family who owned half of a local, professional sports team. Of course, the women all wanted to be June brides. Felicity couldn't believe she already had three enormous weddings on her schedule for next June. Two of those weddings would definitely get mentions in Denver's monthly magazine that featured the best of the city, which meant exposure for Felicitous Wedding Creations.

She stared blankly at her laptop monitor, unable to work up any excitement at the thought. Her memory then drifted to Alyson glowing from pregnancy and love for her husband, David, and their New Year's Eve wedding.

Felicity had only seen pictures, but the house on Lake Estes had been elegantly decorated by the couple's friends and family; no wedding planner required. But even couples who wanted small weddings still hired planners. That's exactly how Felicity had started.

When had she lost planning intimate, romantic affairs that were about genuine *love*?

As lucrative as the grand weddings were for her business bottom line, Felicity couldn't help but miss the Alysons and Davids. Couples who were in love and only cared about marrying each other while surrounded by their family and closest friends. One of Felicity's favorite wedding spots before becoming the *fairy tale* wedding planner of Denver had been the Boettcher Mansion in Golden. A beautiful, peaceful, elegant place perfect for small, romantic weddings with stunning views of Denver as a backdrop.

Now, she spent almost every Saturday of the year in ballrooms of four-and-five-star hotels around the city, especially this time of year. The summer months that were fast approaching did include many outdoor ceremonies—quite a lovely change—but the receptions were, more often than not, inside due to Colorado's monsoon weather that literally blew into the city in the late afternoons and early evenings.

She focused on the contract filling her computer screen and a realization filled her head.

The Miss Emmy Swansons and Mr. Jason McAvoys were no longer all she wanted.

When she'd moved her business from London to Denver, she'd needed and wanted the wealthy, prominent families. But now she craved more balance. Maybe there was a way she could do grand *and* intimate weddings? Two cozy affairs for every elaborate one?

She straightened and closed her laptop.

If something didn't change soon, she'd do something horribly drastic. Like run away to Cancún or some other tropical place and stay there indefinitely.

Indefinitely.

Ian's rather disarming grin appeared in her mind, followed by his deep, soothing voice.

Then I guess you'll indefinitely be stuck in my clothes.

The corner of her mouth lifted in a smile while she gave herself a quick glance.

She couldn't remember the last time she'd worn a man's clothing for so long. Probably during the initial good days with her ex…that had turned dark not too long after their wedding. But she sure as hell did not want to think of him right now or ever again, for that matter. Thinking of her ex, however, caused her to think of Ian's.

Felicity stood from the dining room table she'd managed to clear without disturbing too many of his files and papers.

What she was about to do unquestionably qualified as snooping. But while tidying…cleaning…his living room earlier she'd noticed one of the unpacked moving boxes had the word "photos" scrawled on the side. The chances of Ian having kept pictures of his ex were nonexistent. Perhaps others would still provide some insight into the detective's life?

Princess Belle and Stella, curled up on the couch together, lifted their heads as Felicity crept by—she stopped and shook her head at her ridiculousness.

She and the dogs were the only ones in the house and it's not like they could tattle on her.

Once she reached the stacked boxes, she opened the flaps of the top box that held the photos and paused at seeing several frames haphazardly stacked on top of each other.

Either the man didn't know how to properly pack delicate items or he'd been through the box since moving into the house.

She reached for the frames and withdrew a stack of four in various sizes. She then backed up and sat on the edge of his couch's lounger.

Felicity smiled at the first frame holding a picture that she happened to recognize since Scott had the same one in his house; her brother and Ian looking like mere boys with their shaved heads while wearing white T-shirts, army fatigue pants, and dog tags. Her smile slipped, though, when imagining what the two had seen and experienced while in Afghanistan.

She put the frame aside and cleared her mind of those dismal thoughts.

The next frame held a picture of Ian with a man who had to be his brother, based on the strong family resemblance. Like the photo of him and Scott, the two had their arms hooked loosely over each others shoulders as they smiled at the camera. But their backdrop happened to be a large, elaborately decorated Christmas tree instead of desert. The two also wore the ugliest Christmas sweaters she'd ever seen which made her laugh.

Frame three, larger than the last two, contained a family photo taken years ago since Ian and his brother were boys. Ian appeared to be the eldest, too, since his brother looked like Peyton's age, maybe a tad older. What really caught her attention was their striking parents —their father with his thick brown hair, blue eyes, and disarming grin, and mother with her rich, dark skin, equally dark eyes, and distinct cheekbones. Her black hair was piled on her head in an elaborate and elegant up-do. A multi-colored headband complemented her hairstyle.

Ian's mother was absolutely stunning, and Felicity couldn't help but wonder where she was from and how his parents had met. Though Ian and his brother had inherited their dad's strong jawline and that familiar grin, they mostly favored their exotic mother.

It certainly explained Ian's head-turning handsome good looks.

She carefully set the frame beside her and concentrated on the last one.

Her eyes widened.

A part of her had been hoping to find a picture like this, but hadn't been confident she would when she remembered the ugly story. But there it was. There *they* were.

An attractive brunette sitting beside Ian and next to another man with a pretty blonde sitting beside him. It had to be Ian and Candace with the ex-partner and the man's ex-wife, all of them wearing huge smiles and elegantly dressed, as if they were at a wedding or holiday party.

She narrowed her eyes while staring at Candace and the ex-partner.

Had their affair already begun when this photo had been taken? If so, there seemed to be no signs of guilt or deception. Just a photo of two beautiful couples clearly enjoying an evening together. Maybe that's why Ian had kept the photo?

Could this night out have meant something significant?

Knowing what she now knew, there had to be a reason he'd not only kept the picture but hadn't removed it from the frame.

Her phone, inside a pocket of the oversized sweatpants, started to vibrate and ring.

She set the frame down and stood. When she saw who was calling, however, she cringed and stared at the photo of him kissing Peyton's pink cheek while she laughed.

Felicity had taken the picture of Scott and Peyton this past Christmas when they'd all been together for the holidays. Something else that now felt eons ago.

After another second of hesitation, she answered, "Hi. Are you done for the day?"

"Teaching? Yes," Scott replied. "Grading? Just getting started."

She lowered herself once more to the lounger. "I don't envy you one bit."

"And I'll take grading essays over dealing with bridezillas any day."

She laughed, savoring the release and hearing her younger brother's voice.

"So how come we're not friends anymore?"

Her humor slowly disappeared while she had no choice but to say, "What do you mean?" Guilt then shrouded her as if it were a thick, heavy, black blanket.

He sighed. "Felicity, before your trip to Mexico I had to sometimes avoid your calls."

She frowned. "Really? I was that obnoxious?"

"That's not at all what I'm saying. It's who you are. And Mom and Leann have called me, also wondering why they've stopping hearing from you."

Her eyes became damp while the guilt weighed her shoulders down even more.

"You're the one who consistently calls and checks in on everyone and keeps us connected when life gets nuts and…stops by with your dog without warning."

She released a quick laugh.

"If there's something going on with you," he added, "you know you can talk to me. I'm not that distracted and busy with work and Peyton and Campbell."

Something about Scott calling and saying this right now tugged at Felicity's insides.

Could it be Ian had broken his promise? Could he have done the one thing she'd asked him not to do just last week?

Just last week.

Oh, God. Only a week had passed since she and Lynn, who Ian no longer trusted, had walked into the police admin building to meet with him.

"Felicity, what's going on with you?"

A huge part of her wanted to let go and tell her protective little brother *everything*. As such, she opened her mouth, the entire story sitting on the edge of her voice. Then her gaze landed on Ian's photos and her surroundings.

Telling Scott everything would include explaining being at Ian's house. She'd come here last night needing refuge. Ian had certainly provided it and so much more. Scott would never in a million years criticize her decision. But now she wanted more than refuge from Ian and based on his actions that morning, he felt the same way about her.

Though Felicity couldn't imagine Scott criticizing her and Ian exploring the possibilities, she still didn't feel remotely close to facing any of those realizations for several reasons.

"Are you there?"

"Yes." She cleared her throat. "I'm sorry if I've been distant the last several weeks." Remembering where her thoughts had gone before deciding to snoop through Ian's photo box, she said, "I'm thinking about making some big changes in the business." She cracked a smile. "I was at Daisy's Bouquets yesterday morning and Alyson announced she and David are pregnant."

A long silence fell on Scott's end before, "Yeah. Campbell told me their good news. She also told me about that bonus you gave them which was really generous of you."

"They more than earned it," she murmured.

"So what do Alyson and David have to do with making changes to your business?"

She slid her gaze to Ian's family photo. "True love and romance and intimate weddings."

"Okay," Scott slowly said. "Can you be more specific?"

"No." She lifted her chin. "At least, not right now. I have many things I need to work out and through until I can really focus on my newest plans for Felicitous Wedding Creations." Relief at telling Scott that truth replaced some guilt. "But I kind of love you for calling me."

"And I kind of love you back." He paused, then added, "I still feel there's something you're not telling me."

It wasn't out of Scott's character—the Mayhew blood, in general —to be persistent. The fact she'd shown up here at Ian's in a mess of tears and fear and defeat due to finding another threatening note at her home still fueled her suspicion the detective had broken his promise.

Could she really hold it against him? Blame him, even? She had agreed that if the notes started to go in an "ugly direction" she'd tell her brother.

Would it be so bad if Ian had taken it upon himself to tell Scott everything?

She still replied, "I'm fine. Truly." At this precise moment in time, she did feel that way. "I'll call Mom and Leann later."

More silence until, "Then I won't push. Talk soon?"

"I promise." She ended the call and stared at her phone.

Dammit. All she wanted and needed was to get her life back. Maybe not the same life she'd lived before her trip to Cancún. She no longer felt like that woman. Right now she'd take being at home in her own clothes, and feeling safe and secure within her hard-earned walls.

Safe and secure in her home.

Something she would never again take advantage of when the darkness lifted.

"THANKS FOR COMING IN." Ian sat across from Nicole Zamora. "Sorry to keep you waiting."

The young woman's gaze swept the brightly lit beige room that felt like being in a box with a cheap table, uncomfortable chairs, and a "window" where he knew Larry was carefully watching and listening to everything being said. The room also contained a video camera.

"I don't understand why we're talking in here." She hugged her arms to her chest. "Am I going to be arrested? I didn't do anything. My grandparents were *fine* when I left them."

Ian flashed her a warm smile. "We're just talking Miss Zamora. Can I get you anything?"

She shook her head. "No. I want to get this over with. I also have to be at work by five."

He'd read in the notes she waited tables at some restaurant along 16th Street, the pedestrian mall that happened to be a quick walk from the police admin building.

Ian observed the young woman's Arizona Diamondbacks baseball hat and heavy sweatshirt. Dark circles had developed under her blue eyes since he'd seen her on Friday.

Losing her grandparents had hit her hard or more was going on with Miss Nicole Zamora. Based on what he'd found in his research on her and in the notes, he didn't have a feel for her or her backstory. None of which settled right with him.

"You must like baseball." He pointed at her hat. "You're from Arizona, too."

Her eyes widened for a second, then she said, "I do. And I'm from Scottsdale."

He opened the file folder he'd brought into the room with him. "You've also lived all over California, and in Las Vegas and Colorado."

She stared at him as irritation flashed across her face. "I know where I've lived, Detective. What do you want from me?"

Attitude. *Fantastic.* Always made this part of the job so much more fun.

He sat back and continued to smile. "Tell me what brought you back to Denver."

She frowned. "Taking care of my grandparents. Didn't I tell you this on Friday?"

"No. It's interesting you say that, though." He watched her closely while adding, "A neighbor and close friend of your grandmother's made a statement to one of our officers that your grandparents hadn't seen you in years. That you simply"—he looked down at the notes—"showed up on their doorstep a couple of months ago or so."

Her face transformed into an emotionless mask. "My grandmother's friend must have misunderstood what was said."

He nodded. "Right." Now for the full unveiling. "The reason we needed you to come in here, Miss Zamora, is that the toxicology reports already came back on your grandparents."

Their gazes locked.

"Lethal amounts of hydrocodone were found in both of them. A common opioid?"

Her face remained emotionless. "I told you on Friday they both suffered from various ailments that included terrible arthritis. But the arthritis affected my grandfather more."

"Of course. That would explain the prescription being his. We also have calls in to their doctors about these ailments." He tilted his head right. "You admitted to me you were at their home Thursday night."

"Yes." She leaned forward. "But as I've told you—*twice*—they were fine when I left."

"Well, that's the thing." He also leaned forward. "According to that same neighbor, who lives right across the street, she only saw you over there during the day."

The young woman's eyes became slits. "That woman can't see two feet in front of her while *wearing* her glasses."

Ian had read that somewhere in the notes, but said, "Between her statements and the fact you were with them Thursday night—the last time they were known to be alive and well—I'm afraid that currently leaves you in a pretty tenuous situation." Though fingerprints and DNA from the Zamora home had yet to come back from the lab. "But we will be talking to their doctors about their mental health, too." They did have to explore every possibility.

She released a heavy sigh.

He fell silent, waiting.

"Detective, I understand you're doing your job," she calmly stated, "but regardless of what the old *bat* across the street is saying about me, I loved my grandparents and they needed me. We needed each other. It's the only reason I came back to Denver."

He let those strong statements settle for several seconds.

"I also told you that I'd recently caught them mixing up their medications."

Yeah. She'd mentioned that. But he had no way of knowing for certain if that had actually happened. And in truth, what they had at this moment on Nicole was circumstantial. They had a she-said-she-said situation with the neighbor and no solid motive.

Larry had found out the Zamoras only left their granddaughter the house. Considering its overall age and disrepair and location, it wasn't worth much. Even in the competitive Denver housing market.

Still, Ian persisted with, "Miss Zamora, do you really believe your grandparents could have *accidentally* consumed lethal amounts of hydrocodone after you left them Thursday night?" Because he sure as shit didn't, allegedly mixing up their meds or not.

"Yes," she enunciated. "Their eyesight was no better than that woman's who lives across the street. And like I also told you on Friday, they were constantly losing their reading glasses."

Yep. She'd mentioned that, too.

Ian kept his own sigh in check, then stood and picked up the file folder. "I'll be right back. Are you sure you don't want anything?"

She stared up at him. "I want to go home and get ready for work."

He grinned. "And I will make that happen as soon as I possibly can."

Her stare transitioned into a glare so cold Ian had to consciously stop himself from cringing before he turned from her and left the room.

He closed the door behind him and met Larry a few steps down the hallway.

"I can't figure her out," Ian muttered. "A hot, weepy mess on Friday. Now, a few days later, emotionless as a Michael Myers mask even after finding out how her grandparents died."

"Could be nerves," Larry offered. "No one—guilty or not—likes being called into a police station, put into an interrogation room, and questioned."

"Yeah." Ian glanced at the closed door and back at his partner. "You're the veteran detective. What do you think?"

Larry rubbed his goatee. "I think drugging your sick, elderly grandparents for nothing more than an old house in an old neighborhood is twisted, illogical shit."

A complete and enormous understatement.

"That house was all the Zamoras had. And what's inside of it," Larry swiftly added. "Very little in life insurance. No retirement funds. Only had social security."

"I know it's a weak motive," Ian argued. "But the only other possibility is suicide." Recalling something he'd read in the notes made him say, "The nosy neighbor disputed the Zamoras possibly being suicidal and had zero nice things to say about Nicole."

"I don't like a lot of people, either. But it's my *opinion* of them." Larry lifted his shoulders. "The truth is that the Zamoras were sick, probably in constant pain, living in a house as old as them, had little in the way of income, and a bottle of Vicodin sitting on the nightstand."

Ian processed his partner's statements that were the facts.

"We'll know more once the reports come back on what was found at the house and after talking to their docs. But we have nothing to keep her here." Larry pointed at the closed door.

"I'll let her loose." Because that's all he could do.

Ian opened the door and grinned. "Thank you, Miss Zamora, for coming here and chatting with me. I appreciate it."

She eyed him warily. "Does that mean we're finished?"

His grin deepened. "For now." He stood aside. "I hope you have a good night at work."

"Thank you," she murmured while walking past him.

"I'll be touch in soon."

Once he returned to his cubicle, he dropped the file folder onto his desk and sat.

Because of the Zamoras, he'd had zero time to research Perry Cantrell. Now with the elderly couple's case temporarily on hold, he could focus on Felicity's case.

Case. For some reason, he'd never thought of it that way until now. Thinking of her, and how damn good she'd looked before he'd left his house that morning, caused him to remember their deal to meet up at her house so she could get her own clothing. But it was already mid-afternoon and he refused to leave this building until he had info on Cancún guy.

Ian retrieved his cell and chose the lady's name.

"Hello," Felicity answered. "I know why you're calling."

Of course she did. But he said, "I'd be more than happy to loan you another set of my sweats since you do look so good in them."

She sighed. "Cute. But I like my clothing. And how I look in my clothing."

He sat back, not able to argue with those declarations. Especially the last one since he, too, happened to like how she looked in her clothing.

"How late do you plan on being? We could still meet at my house since I'd also like to collect some bathroom items."

"I don't know. But it'll probably be dark and I don't like the thought of you out there by yourself. Not after last night," he quietly added. "Felicity, I'll make it up to you."

A long pause, followed by, "I know you will."

He fought a grin while asking, "How's your day going? You haven't done anything crazy have you? Like clean my house out of sheer boredom?"

Another pause, then, "My day hasn't been too bad. I've actually been able to get quite a bit of work done. Your day?"

Asking about each other's days. An entirely different type of intimate.

"Busy." He straightened. "I have to go. I'll see you tonight." He ended the call.

He'd asked the question without any forethought. It had been natural. Easy. Like falling asleep with her on his couch while surrounded by their dogs. And holding her close last night and in his bedroom this morning. That had particularly felt natural and easy, and he wanted more.

Holy shit, he had to be insane. Remembering how easily Felicity had responded to him, though, they both had to be insane.

His phone started to vibrate and ring, but he halted at the familiar, yet unsaved number.

He'd forgotten all about Candace. She'd called him yesterday and left a message…for some reason. And now she was calling him again?

He silenced the call and put his phone aside, still having zero interest in wasting his time on her and whatever she had to say.

A woman with her hair pulled up into a tight bun appeared in his cubicle's opening. "Results from testing on those letters." She held up the folder. "No unknown prints or DNA. Sorry, Detective."

He grasped the file and gave her a tight smile. "Thanks. But not surprising."

Ian stared at the folder, that also held the first three notes, for a handful of seconds before tossing it onto his desk, as well.

Damn, he really needed to catch a break on Felicity's stalker.

He faced his computer.

If Perry Cantrell checked out, Ian had no idea where he'd go next with fulfilling his promise to Felicity which now meant even more than it had last week.

Chapter Fifteen

STELLA BARKED, followed by Princess Belle, while Felicity poured a second glass of wine.

She looked at the dogs watching her every move. "Don't either of you look at me like that. I've more than earned this."

They wagged their tails as her phone buzzed and dinged with a text.

It could very well be Ian telling her he'd be even later.

Her thoughts went directly into the past and hearing their household landline often ringing at about this time—dinnertime in many households—and her mother sighing before answering. It had always been her father calling to say he'd be late.

Interruptions that could happen at any hour of the day.

She walked toward Ian's dining room table where she'd left her phone beside her laptop.

And here she stood in a home belonging to a new detective with the Denver police department. A handsome, occasionally charming detective who she couldn't stop thinking about. She also couldn't stop imagining picking up where they'd left off that morning in his bedroom.

She'd clearly lost her mind because of the harasser turmoil.

How's it going with Cancún Perry?

Felicity frowned at Shannon's message. At least it wasn't Ian saying he'd be even later. However, she didn't quite know how to reply.

Ian had, without question, turned her life inside out with his suspicions about Perry and Lynn. Her life had already been turned upside down due to the harasser and now?

People she'd trusted might as well have gigantic question marks over their heads.

She typed, *Had dinner last night, but the sparks seem to be gone.*

The truth, too, meaning no added guilt to her shoulders also heavy with confusion.

She walked back into the kitchen for her glass of wine. At that moment, the faint sound of a garage door opening filtered into the kitchen.

Stella came to attention and started whining and wagging her tail while trotting toward the door that led to the garage. Princess Belle followed her new best friend.

Despite the dogs' excitement, Felicity heard her phone go off again.

She headed back to the table.

What a bummer. And Lynn and Ian?

The garage door started to close. A millisecond later the door into the house flew open.

Stella *and* Princess Belle went back on their hind legs as Ian walked inside, both whining their frenetic greeting.

Ian vigorously rubbed Stella's head and even squatted to give her dog a quick pat.

Felicity couldn't help but grin softly.

He carefully moved around the dogs, stepped into the kitchen, and their gazes met.

His eyes went directly to her head with her wet hair wrapped in one of his towels and he smiled. But then he glanced at the kitchen sink and countertops.

His grin vanished. "You did clean."

"You're welcome."

He walked deeper into the kitchen with the dogs right at his feet. "You did say you got a lot of work done today." He winced when he focused on the dining room table. "Felicity, some of those are case files."

She lifted her chin. "I simply moved them out of my way so I could work at the table."

Her phone again went off in her hand. "I didn't look inside them."

As Ian approached her, she replied to Shannon, *No sparks there, either.*

She set her phone down.

He stopped touching distance from her. It was at that moment she realized he held a bag.

His disarming grin slowly reappeared.

Felicity's skin became warm beneath his sweats she'd had no choice but to put back on after her shower.

No sparks between Ian and Lynn for reasons that included his unexplained suspicions. But there seemed to be fireworks between herself and the detective.

"I have something for you." He handed her the bag. "I hope I chose well."

She grasped the bag and peered inside. She then laughed at the sight of what appeared to be a black pajama set, in addition to a toothbrush, shampoo, conditioner, and body wash.

"But it looks like you made do with what's in my shower."

She lifted her gaze which connected with his. "I did. But thank you for all of this."

"I told you I'd make it up to you."

Yes. He certainly had said those words.

He shrugged out of this trench coat, then his suit jacket. He dropped both on the now clear and clean countertop, then stopped. "Where'd the wine come from?" His forehead formed a deep frown.

"Ian, relax." She set the bag down and picked up her glass. "I had it delivered."

His face relaxed. Until he focused on something behind her.

He narrowed his eyes. "You went through my moving boxes, too?"

She didn't have to look over her shoulder to know what he was asking since she'd placed three of the four frames on one of the built-in bookcases.

"You were busy today," he muttered before striding into the living room.

She sighed and followed him. "Yes. I was curious about the box labeled photos."

Ian stopped in front of the bookcase. "Curious is a nice way of saying nosy." He smirked. "What the hell else did you do around here, *Ms. Mayhew*?"

"Those are lovely photos and should be out, *Detective*."

He fell silent while staring at the pictures.

"Your mother is absolutely beautiful." She paused before asking, "Where's she from?"

"Cape Town, South Africa." He smiled. "My dad went there with some friends the summer before his last year of college, met my mom while she was working at a restaurant they went to, and he knew. *They* knew," he quickly added.

Felicity smiled. "Sounds terribly romantic."

"She moved to Colorado not too long after he returned from the trip, they got married, and she never looked back."

Her smile slipped. "It sounds like she's not close to her family."

He faced Felicity. "No. They disowned her for choosing my dad who was not only American, but…" His eyes hardened.

"White?" she quietly offered.

He nodded. "The not-so romantic part of their story. But my dad's parents—my grandparents—fell in love with her and made her a part of the Stafford clan. She also became a U.S. citizen years ago."

He brought back his grin. "Now my mom is the first lady of Grand Junction for the second time."

Felicity's mouth inched open. "Your dad's the mayor of Grand Junction?"

He laughed. "Hard to believe when you're around me, right?" He leaned forward. "My little brother has always technically been the *good kid.*"

She stared into his dark eyes and said, "Knowing what I do about you, I find that extremely hard to believe."

Darkness flashed across his face as he straightened. "Sending my ex-partner to the hospital with a black eye and split lip didn't go over so well with my very important parents." He slid his hands into his pockets. "They're still pretty pissed off at me. I've only talked to them a couple of times since I left Grand Junction."

She frowned. "But they do know why it happened?" She'd never condone violence, but it's not like Ian hadn't been in his own turmoil when he'd made such a choice.

"Yeah," he murmured. "But for them it was still no excuse." He slid his gaze to the photos. "I can't say I blame them, either. I'm really damn lucky my ex-partner didn't press assault charges against me. And that my former captain is a good man."

She tilted her head right to catch Ian's eyes. "Could it be not pressing charges was your ex-partner's last true act of loyalty after what he'd done to you and his wife?"

Ian lifted his shoulders. "Maybe. I don't know." He stepped back and removed his gun from the holster. "I need to change and take Stella for a walk."

"I also saw the picture of the four of you. All dressed up at some event?"

He stared at her. "You really can't be left alone for an entire day. And I would much rather talk about Cancún guy."

She sipped more wine, then said, "Would you please stop calling him that?"

"Only if you promise to stay out of my stuff when I leave you here tomorrow."

Her eyes widened. "Another day? You cannot be serious. I have a job."

He grinned. "That you can easily do from here."

She raised her chin. "Dammit, Ian Stafford. Tell me what the hell is going on or I will take my dog and walk out your front door."

He set the gun on the coffee table and shrugged out of his holster. "Did you know *Perry* is recently divorced?"

Felicity briefly closed her eyes, counted to five, then said, "Of course I do. The divorce happened in November and it's now April."

"But it was February when you two met." He dropped the holster on the table. "You didn't think to give me that info last night when I asked about him?"

She clenched her teeth. "Almost everyone is divorced nowadays. It didn't seem terribly important or relevant." She stepped toward him. "Why are you so determined to make him the bad guy? He's done absolutely nothing wrong."

He expelled a frustrated sigh. "I'm not saying *he's* the bad guy. But it's too much of a coincidence you started receiving threatening notes after you returned from that trip. And now there's an ex-wife." He caught her gaze. "My partner—a veteran detective—said from the start the notes sound like a jealous woman." He stepped toward her. "Felicity, I don't have all the pieces to this puzzle, but none of this is sitting right with me."

Her shoulders dropped and she sat on the edge of the couch. "Perry made it sound like the divorce was mutual. I had no reason not to believe him." She glanced up at Ian, of course watching her closely and something she was getting quite used to seeing. "We spent one week together at a resort in Cancún. I didn't hear from him again until last week about his trip to Denver for a conference." She leaned forward. "Ian, I honestly don't understand how he could be connected to any of this. He doesn't even live here. And I'm almost positive he told me he gave his ex-wife the house in the divorce which has to mean *she* doesn't live here."

Perry being involved in any way simply made no sense.

Silence descended in the living room.

Princess Belle suddenly jumped into Felicity's lap as Stella dropped at Ian's feet.

Felicity set her wine glass on the table, away from Ian's holster and gun.

"Okay. Fine."

She removed the towel from her head which made her damp hair fall to her shoulders.

"I'm waiting for some info to come back on *Perry*," Ian said. "I would still prefer you continue to keep your distance from him until I know for a fact he's not at the heart of this."

She opened her mouth to reply, but Ian lowering himself to make them eye level caused her mind to go blank.

He tentatively reached out and gently tucked a strand of her damp hair behind her right ear. "I've been avoiding telling you the truth about Lynn because I hate the thought of hurting you. But if it's the only way I can keep you away from her, I guess I have no choice."

Felicity's breath stalled in her chest.

"She thinks you're sending the notes to yourself for attention now that you're the only one of your siblings who's single."

Another round of silence descended as Felicity processed Ian's statement.

Sending the notes to herself? Why on earth would Lynn think such a horrible thing?

"There's a clear lack of loyalty going on there," he softly continued, "that's making me suspicious and uncomfortable."

Felicity hugged Princess Belle to her chest. "Lynn said that? To you?" She vehemently shook her head. "No. It doesn't make sense. Why would she say that?"

"That's what I'm trying to figure out."

She peered at him. "Do you think Lynn might be sending…" A

round of nausea like the one from this morning nearly knocked her sideways at where her thoughts had gone.

"I can't rule it out." Ian frowned. "Especially since she threw *you* under the bus."

Everything Ian had just told her had to be the reason Lynn had sounded so cold and distant this morning on the phone. The fact Felicity hadn't heard from Lynn at all the rest of the day happened to be another glaring signal something had shifted between herself and Lynn, and not because of anything Felicity had recently done.

Lynn Delgado. A woman who'd become a close friend not long after Felicity had hired her as an assistant. A woman she'd always treated like family. A woman she'd trusted with her business, her secrets, her ambitions…her actual, physical life.

Ian angled his head down to catch her gaze. "Felicity, I need to know if anything unusual happened between you and Lynn before you left for your trip or after you returned." He paused before adding, "Or did something happen while you were gone?"

She tried to focus on Ian while saying, "I don't remember." She set Princess Belle beside her on the couch. "I need a moment… alone." She started to stand which forced him up and out of her way. "I don't understand. Why would Lynn turn on me like this?"

Her ex had definitely betrayed her trust in numerous ways, but this kind coming from a close friend and confidante, someone she'd also allowed into her family, sliced her insides.

Ian cupped her face. "Tell me what you need right now."

She turned from him, forcing him to lower his hands. "Just to be alone." She darted in the direction of the guest bathroom where she closed the door.

Each threatening message drifted through her mind, as did the fact Lynn had been present when Felicity had received two of them and had appeared to be nothing but concerned. And supportive. She'd seemed that way for each note except number five. She didn't know *it* existed.

But the whole time Lynn had been harboring the opinion Felicity had sent them to herself out of what would have to be a desperate and pathetic need for attention?

Tears she was beyond tired of shedding turned the guest bathroom into a hazy blur.

And what about Perry Cantrell? Had she foolishly trusted him, too? Timing aside, him being somehow connected to the notes didn't click in her non-detective mind. Ian, on the other hand, refused to let it go until he knew for certain Perry was innocent. If that more than likely happened, only one logical person would be left. Ian had said almost as much.

A couple of tears slid from Felicity's eyes which she roughly wiped away.

She'd told Ian just last night she couldn't fathom the level of betrayal he'd experienced at the hands of his ex-girlfriend and partner.

More tears fell as she caught a glimpse of herself in the medicine cabinet mirror.

A face flushed yet again with emotion and wet from tears.

An image she was sick of seeing.

She'd give herself this moment to accept what Ian had told her about Lynn. She'd work from here tomorrow since he did have her best interests at heart. But she had to physically return to work on Thursday for reasons that now included doing her own detective work in her soon-to-be *former* assistant and close friend's office since Felicity had a sudden suspicion of her own.

Chapter Sixteen

DICKHEAD. The only word to describe him at this moment.

Ian picked up his gun and holster, then headed for his bedroom.

Still, Felicity had really given him no choice but to tell her the truth about Lynn. The only other way he would have been able to keep the stubborn lady from going into her office tomorrow would have been handcuffing her to a dining room chair.

He opened the nightstand drawer, placed his gun inside, and dropped his holster in its spot on the still cluttered piece of furniture. It appeared Felicity had limited her cleaning spree to the kitchen, and dining and living rooms.

Stella wandered into the room with the princess trotting underneath her.

Ian lowered himself to his bed's edge and absently rubbed his dog's face. The princess leapt up and settled herself beside him.

Holy shit, this week was not going the way he thought it would.

He eyed the princess staring up at him, her eyes wide with expectation. She probably wanted him to give her the same attention he happened to be giving his dog.

Ian had never in his life liked little dogs, much less miniature poodles named Princess Belle. Though he couldn't fault the name considering it had come from his adorable goddaughter who loved all things Disney, specifically the princesses.

He gave this princess a quick rub around her ears. But the memory of Felicity hugging her dog to her chest while he'd told her about Lynn filled his already jam-packed brain.

She'd fled the living room, wanting to be alone to most likely process what he'd said.

After Candace and his ex-partner had dropped their nuclear bomb, he'd fled the restaurant, stopped at a liquor store to buy a bottle of bourbon, then checked himself into a hotel and proceeded to get drunk. He'd stayed that way until his brother found him two days later, hauled him into the shower, and turned the water all the way to cold.

Utter betrayal. The feeling a bitch of an experience and something Ian wouldn't wish on anyone…accept Candace and his ex-partner. But he couldn't—wouldn't—think about them or their actions. Not when he had a woman closed up in the guest bathroom down the hall, distraught over the fact someone she implicitly trusted had betrayed her.

The one question that remained was how far did Lynn's betrayal go?

Yeah. He couldn't shake *Perry* somehow being at the heart of all this bullshit, but Lynn Delgado being behind it made more sense. She lived here. She knew Felicity's life, inside and out. She also had a clear problem with her boss. But what, exactly?

This stinks of a jealous woman.

Jealous of Felicity's respect in the wedding world? Success? Being close to her family? Her looks? Or maybe all of the above?

He frowned while staring blankly at Stella nudging his hand for more attention.

Perhaps it was time to haul another woman into the station for a chat while in the waiting line when it came to the Zamoras and Cancún guy.

The sound of cabinets opening and loudly closing reached him in his bedroom.

Felicity had obviously emerged from the bathroom and was now in his kitchen.

With a sigh, Ian stood and headed for his dresser.

He still needed to change and take Stella for a walk. And maybe the princess.

Minutes later, he walked into the kitchen but stopped at the sight of Felicity standing in front of an open cabinet and staring at the contents. Or lack thereof.

"What are you looking for?" he calmly asked.

"Something to make for dinner. But you don't have much to choose from, Detective."

He strolled toward her. "I have nothing to choose from." He stopped at her left side. "I'll have to order something."

She went up on her tiptoes, continuing to peer inside. "I see a box of pasta. I can do something with that." She looked at him from the corner of her eyes. "How is it you look the way you do when you apparently eat nothing but junk?"

He grinned. "Is that way your way of saying you think I look good?"

"Please stop grinning at me like that." She reached up and grasped the box. "I'd rather make something than have anything delivered."

On a deep breath, Ian placed his hand over hers now holding the box. "And I need you to stop whatever *this* is." He closed the cabinet door and tugged the pasta from her fingers.

"Ian, I have to do something right now." She lifted her chin. "Because if I don't, I'll drive myself crazy thinking of that phony, manipulative—" The familiar fire flashed through her eyes.

Ian set the box on the counter.

He'd definitely take this Felicity Mayhew over the defeated woman who'd been crying inside her SUV with her dog while she waited for him to arrive home.

"I get it. Believe me." He stepped closer. "But you need to take a breath. Or several."

Their gazes snapped together.

The anger in her eyes transformed into a completely different heated emotion that caused something deep inside of Ian to awaken. And for the first time in…forever.

"Felicity, I didn't tell you any of that to hurt you."

She nodded. "I know."

He gently brushed loose hair off of her now pink cheek. "So you trust me?"

Her lips parted. "Yes," came out a bit breathless. "Absolutely."

He cupped her face. "I will do everything in my power to keep you safe." He paused before murmuring, "And not just because your Scott's sister."

"I know that, too," she whispered as he brushed his lips against hers.

"Are we insane for doing this?"

Her eyes drifted shut. "Certifiably."

Ian pressed his lips to hers, sealing their agreement and so much more.

Her mouth opened easily against his, and he deepened the kiss, savoring her warmth and softness and taste. White wine, but mixed with the salt from her tears she must have released while alone in the bathroom. That thought prompted him to slide his hands from her face, down her body, and he slipped his arms around her waist, hugging her tightly to him.

Like he should have done before she'd run into the bathroom.

Felicity's muffled moan penetrated his cloudy head while she hooked her arms behind his neck, bringing their bodies as close as they possibly could be in this moment.

Her mouth moved perfectly with his, matching his level of clear need and desire.

He stepped forward, positioning her snugly between himself and the counter.

Another moan escaped her, and he grinned between a kiss. He then lowered his hands even farther, cupped her fine ass, and pressed her against him.

She gasped, though her arms tightened around his neck.

He was about to lift her onto the counter, but his back jeans pocket started to buzz.

They gradually brought their kiss to an end, each catching their breath.

"You're vibrating," she whispered against his mouth while still locked in his arms.

He nuzzled her nose with his, unwilling to release her curvy, pliant body.

Until he suddenly remembered what he did for a living.

"*Shit*," he muttered. "I have to see who it is." He reluctantly released her.

"I know." She slowly lowered her arms. "It's fine, Ian."

"No, it sure as hell isn't," he replied, reaching into his pocket. "Hopefully it's no one important." Like her brother.

But wouldn't that be seriously messed up timing if it did happen to be Scott?

Ian glanced at the screen and froze.

A northern California number.

He lifted his gaze to Felicity and stepped backward. "I have to take this."

She smoothed her fiery hair and sent him a weak smile. "I understand. Probably good timing, too."

He stared at her. "I call bullshit, Ms. Mayhew." He turned and headed for his bedroom. "I'll be right back. And I'm really hoping we can continue our insanity."

Before he closed the door, he answered, "Detective Ian Stafford."

"Hi. It's Clara Cantrell. You're the one who called me earlier?"

Clara Cantrell. Also known as *Perry's* ex-wife who did in fact still live in the San Jose area. It didn't make her a viable person of interest in Felicity's case, but chatting with the ex could never be considered a bad idea in a situation like this.

"Yes." Ian walked toward his bed where Stella and the princess happened to be sleeping. "Thank you for calling me back."

"I apologize for the later hour on your end, but I'm leaving early tomorrow morning for a business trip to Boston and figured this couldn't wait."

"I appreciate it. And I'll make this as quick as possible. The reason I called—"

"Is because of my relationship with my ex-husband, Perry. You said that in your message. But I'm not the person you should be talking to or concerned with."

He frowned. "Can you be more specific, Ms. Cantrell?"

The woman's heavy sigh reached him through the phone.

"Contrary to most divorce situations, Perry and I parted as friends. *Good* friends."

Felicity had told Ian the guy stated it had been a mutual divorce. Unless the ex-wife was also lying, it appeared to be the truth.

"We simply no longer worked as a couple and decided it would be best to go our own ways before either of us made really bad decisions."

They'd acted like adults instead of hooking up with other people.

He looked down at the floor while shaking his head.

What a damn concept.

"I know Perry is currently out in Denver for a work conference," Clara Cantrell continued. "I also know he met a woman from Denver while on vacation in Cancún who he was very interested in seeing again."

Shit, the ex spouses clearly were still in close contact with one another.

Ian's suspicions that Perry was somehow part of the stalking mess started to collapse around him. Which would in fact leave—

"I honestly could care less about who Perry dates. But you need to know about Nicola."

Ian lifted his head with such force his neck popped.

"He met her through one of those dating apps right around Christmas. According to what he told me, he'd wanted a date for his company's holiday party."

Ian held his breath, silent, waiting for her to continue.

"They went on an initial date and hit it off so he asked her to the party. I certainly didn't need or want any details after that."

"Of course." His frown deepened. "So they began dating after the party?"

"They had one more date after that night. New Year's Eve."

"But…" Ian's voice trailed into silence.

"She had decided they were in a relationship on date three which made Perry uncomfortable since they'd never had that conversation. He told me he tried to discuss it with her, but she wouldn't listen so he ended things." A pause fell on her end, followed by, "That's when this woman completely lost her mind and started stalking him. He eventually had to get a restraining order. It was another reason he went to Cancún for a week."

Lost her mind. Stalking. Restraining order. Nicola also happened to be damn-near the same name of another woman under suspicion in Denver for the death of her grandparents.

This stinks of a jealous woman.

"As crazy as it may sound, if Perry has ended up in some kind of trouble while in Denver, it's because of that woman. Restraining orders might as well be a joke, no offense to your profession," she added. "But if Perry's still being harassed by this woman, he hasn't told me."

Ian absently nodded while asking, "Nicola, correct?"

"Yes. I guess she went by Nicole, too."

He gripped his phone.

And there it was.

Could Nicola and Nicole Zamora actually be one and the same? If so, how the hell could she have found out about Felicity? And what had really brought the young woman to Colorado?

He managed to calmly ask, "Do you happen to know her last name?"

"I'm sorry, I don't."

Right. But *Perry* would know her last name. There was also a restraining order Ian would easily be able to track down.

"Perry's okay, right? Should I be worried?"

At this point, the only way Ian could answer her question was, "As far as I know, he's fine." He would, however, have to ask Felicity to shoot the guy a quick text just to make sure.

"Please let me know if anything changes? We didn't work anymore as a couple, but I still care for him deeply and Nicola's behavior...unnerved him."

"I understand. I'll be in touch if anything should change. Thank you again for calling."

Because Clara Cantrell, ex-wife of Perry, may have stopped even more wreckage.

Ian looked at the dogs, watching him, and tried to slow his brain now in overdrive.

Larry. He needed to talk this through with his veteran detective partner.

He had his thumb over Larry's name when his bedroom door popped open.

Felicity, still looking so damn irresistible and flushed and enticing, leaned against the door frame. "What's going on?"

Ian faced her. "Did Perry ever mention a woman named Nicole Zamora? Or Nicola?"

She pursed lips, then said, "No." She pointed at his phone. "Who were you talking to?"

"Clara Cantrell, Perry's ex-wife." He walked toward Felicity.

Her mouth inched open.

"Turns out the divorce was extremely mutual." He stopped, again with touching distance of her. So close he could feel her warmth. "It seems your Cancún guy *was* honest with you."

Of course the guy wouldn't volunteer seeing an unhinged woman from a dating app.

Felicity raised her chin. "I asked you to stop calling him that." She angled her head toward his phone. "What else did she have to say? Who's Nicole Zamora?"

He reached up and rubbed his thumb against her lower lip. "Your possible stalker."

Her eyes widened. "Ian, I swear I've never heard that name."

He slid his hand to the back of her neck and guided her toward him. "I believe you. But I have to call my partner and figure out next steps." He gently kissed her forehead. "I have to go back into work, too." And only because the Zamora file happened to still be on his desk.

She slid her arms around his waist and rested her head on his chest. "I know that, too."

Nicole Zamora. Wow. His instincts had been right about her, as well as Perry being at the center of this crap. But the pieces of the massive puzzle had only doubled in size and amount. He couldn't even be certain Nicole and Nicola were the same. At least, not at this moment in time.

He leaned back, causing Felicity to lift her head. "Can you send Perry a check-in text?"

A deep frown settled onto her flawless features. "Why? What the hell's going on?"

"I can't answer that right now." Mostly because he didn't even know. He kissed her forehead once more, then stepped back. "Please shoot him a text and let me know what he says?"

Chances were Perry was fine since the wrath had always been directed at Felicity. He still had to make sure without *unnerving* the guy even more. Not until Ian knew what the hell was going on here. That meant not only leaving the lady, but postponing their insanity.

"Felicity, I hate that I have to leave, but I swear I'll make it up to you."

She cracked a smile. "I know you will." She headed left and out of view.

Ian chose Larry's name.

As he waited for his partner to answer, adrenaline surged through his blood at finally getting the much-needed break in this mystery going in a highly unexpected direction.

Chapter Seventeen

FELICITY PACED the length of Ian's dining room.

She'd texted *and* called Perry over an hour earlier and had yet to hear from him. The fact Ian had specifically asked her to reach out to him had to mean something huge. Perry had never gone this long without replying to her, either. And who in the world was this Nicole Zamora?

A foreign name to Felicity, but who might have some connection to Perry.

She sat in the dining room chair in front of her laptop.

How in the hell could a vacation fling from weeks ago in a different country have placed her where she currently sat? Literally.

She slid her gaze left and heat shrouded her at the memory of being nearly wrapped around Ian while they stood in his kitchen, their mouths moving in sync in an unforgettable and delectable first kiss. Just like she knew it would be when they'd almost kissed that morning.

That morning.

How could it still only be Tuesday? It felt as though a lifetime had passed since she'd pulled into her driveway last night to be greeted by the nastiest message of them all; the reason she'd ended up Ian's house. Now, a little over twenty-four hours later, she'd agreed to work remotely once more, still wore Ian's sweats, had learned a great deal about his life, and had practically melted in his warm, strong arms during the hottest kiss she'd ever experienced.

Her face became the temperature of a sunny, humid day beside the pool in Cancún.

If not for Perry's ex-wife interrupting them, ironically enough, Felicity knew she and Ian would be in his bed right now instead of the dogs and wrapped around one another.

Without their clothing.

The thought caused her entire body to flush.

It had to be truly serendipitous they'd been interrupted due to his work.

But something about Detective Ian Stafford made Felicity want to forget the vow she'd made as a teenager on the heels of losing her father…and give Ian every part of herself.

However, despite their growing and mind-blurring attraction to one another it seemed quite clear he could in no way be considered ready for any kind of emotional commitment. The pain and anger that had flashed through his eyes and across his face while telling her about Candace and his ex-partner's betrayal couldn't be ignored. It also hadn't been that long since his world imploded, ultimately forcing him to move to Denver and start over.

She sighed and shook her head.

On the surface, they seemed doomed for anything beyond the physical. Regardless of her fling with Perry in Cancún, she'd never been one for casual intimacy with a man. She also couldn't help but feel one night in Ian's bed would never be enough. Between his emotional unavailability, her trepidation when it came to his career, *and* the fact someone out there wanted to hurt her, Felicity couldn't at all be certain where that left them.

Her phone inside a pocket of the sweatpants vibrated and dinged with a text.

It had to be Perry. But when she saw another familiar name, she narrowed her eyes.

Will you be back in the office tomorrow?

Lynn Delgado, the unexpected enemy who had emerged due to Felicity's harasser.

She'd confessed to Ian at needing something to occupy her mind instead of Lynn's betrayal. He certainly hadn't disappointed her, either. Then he'd received the call from Perry's ex-wife which seemed to have breathed new life into him and his partner tracking down this person who now, possibly, had a face and name.

A face and name not belonging to Lynn.

She still couldn't fathom that Lynn had actually told Ian during their "date" more than twenty-four hours earlier she felt Felicity was sending the notes to herself for no reason beyond needing attention.

Felicity clenched her teeth as memories inundated her overwhelmed mind.

She remembered the day she'd hired Lynn, no longer able to handle her swiftly expanding business on her own. The woman had just moved to Denver from Madison, Wisconsin, and on the heels of a terrible break-up with an equally terrible man. A story Felicity had known and understood firsthand. Lynn had also chosen Denver because she'd visited once and fallen in love with the city.

The day she and Lynn had moved into the office right off of 16th Street. Felicity had bought the finest champagne, Lynn had provided a set of beautiful flutes, and they'd toasted the business and each other, namely their *friendship*.

Mental snapshots from grand weddings—the best to the worst— they'd handled together appeared in Felicity's mind as if a slideshow.

Inviting Lynn into her mother's house, also Felicity's childhood home, for holidays with the Mayhews the few times the woman hadn't traveled home to Madison.

Felicity glared at her *assistant's* message.

What could she have done to Lynn to warrant her saying such a horrible thing?

Outside of Felicity's family, Lynn knew her the best. Her shoulders fell, however, when the mere suspicion that hit while crying in the bathroom suddenly became a stark realization.

Lynn Delgado had proven without a doubt she could no longer be trusted and her loyalties laid elsewhere. But for how long and with whom? Or could she be planning something bigger? Maybe leaving Felicitous Wedding Creations to start her own company? If that did happen to be the case, how long had Lynn been planning such a thing?

At that moment, an entirely different memory presented itself. A memory having to do with Felicity's initial suspicion that Stacia Marsden was behind the threatening messages. The thought then reminded her she had access to Lynn's work e-mail as the owner and administrator.

That meant she didn't need to be at the office to do this particular detective work.

She replied to Lynn's text with, *I'm afraid not. This stomach thing has hit me hard. Please feel free to work remotely again tomorrow. I'll let you know about Thursday.*

Felicity put her phone down and opened her laptop.

Ian was currently following up on an entirely different and unknown woman possibly being her harasser. It certainly didn't make Lynn Delgado innocent.

Her phone buzzed and dinged with Lynn's reply, but Felicity stayed focused on getting to the bottom of her soon-to-be *former* assistant's baffling and shocking behavior. And hopefully she'd hear from Perry before the night ended. Several minutes later, however, her breath became lodged in her chest at the series of e-mails between Lynn and another woman. At seeing a message with the subject line of URGENT dated Tuesday of last week, the nausea returned with so much force her vision blurred.

It happened to be the day Felicity had given Ian a specific name as her harasser; the name belonging to a wealthy, entitled, well-connected woman who was the daughter of the devil.

With a shaky breath and trembling hand, Felicity opened the e-mail and started to read.

———

"*SHIT,*" Ian muttered. "Why can't I find the restraining order?"

Larry's head appeared over the cubicle's partition. "Maybe Mr. Cantrell lied to the former Mrs. Cantrell?"

Ian sat back and rubbed his eyes. Once his vision cleared, he focused on Larry. "Why would he lie about something like that to his ex-wife?" Not tracking down the alleged restraining order would leave them no other choice but to track down Perry tomorrow.

And why the hell hadn't Ian heard from Felicity yet about the guy?

Larry lifted his shoulders. "Why would those two get divorced, but remain so close?" He grunted. "Makes no sense to me. But I am a romantic at heart."

Ian smirked. "Right. A true sap." He hitched his chin in the direction of his partner's computer. "What'd you find out?"

"A whole lot of nothing and nothing important." He sighed. "Crickets when I searched for a Nicola Zamora. Our Nicole Zamora is on social media, but overall doesn't seem too active. I can't really see her face page—guess we need to be friends?—and her last post on that tweeter site was a week ago, before her grandparents' untimely passing. It had something to do with people not tipping well. The post before that was two weeks ago. Nothing else came up on her."

Ian fought a grin while he asked, "Do you mean Facebook and *Twitter*?"

Larry waved his hand. "I hate that social media crap. Tess and the kids post pictures here, there, and everywhere. I think it's a bunch of nonsense and a waste of a person's valuable time." He shook his head. "Anyway, you know we're going to have to talk to this Perry Cantrell, right?"

Ian nodded. "Hopefully it won't be too hard to find him tomorrow at that conference."

"Does your lady friend by chance have a picture of him?" Larry paused, then said, "If not, we could always get a copy of his California driver's license."

Did Felicity have a picture of Cancún guy? A damn good question and something Ian hadn't even thought of for numerous reasons. But now he had to ask.

"How's she doing, by the way?"

When Ian had left her, she'd already been on her phone, texting Perry. Minutes before, however, she'd been locked in his arms, her mouth as hungry and greedy as his had been.

"She's okay." He cleared his throat. "Hurt and angry over what Lynn said."

"I'll bet," Larry murmured. "But I said the same thing, too."

Ian pointed at him. "You were doing your job and don't know her like Lynn does. In any case, Felicity's been keeping a low profile, per my request." He lifted his gaze to Larry. "That last note scared the shit out of her."

Dammit, he'd been on fire on his drive over here and not because of lingering desire from his moment with Felicity in the kitchen. He'd had a solid lead on finding out for certain who Perry had the misfortune of meeting on a dating app—the restraining order.

Perry must have lied to his ex-wife about it, but why? It didn't make any sense. Another thing that didn't seem terribly normal was something Larry had said about Nicole Zamora.

"How old is Nicole?" Ian asked. "She's relatively young, right?"

Larry disappeared from view for a few seconds before reappearing with the Zamora file. "Twenty-nine so, yeah. Certainly much younger than me." He frowned. "Why?"

Ian concentrated on his monitor. "My brother's thirty and damn-near addicted to social media. So is his girlfriend and every girl he's dated the last few years his age and younger."

Larry raised his eyebrows. "Your point being…?"

"Nicole's lack of presence on social media." He looked up at his partner, watching him expectantly. "Most people her age, especially women, are on *all* the big platforms and posting daily. Sometimes several times a day. But she's only on Facebook and Twitter, and barely posts anything?"

"Well, she did lose her grandparents suddenly. Make her even more suspicious if she was posting as if nothing happened."

"Yeah. But you just said she's on these sites, but not too active *overall*. It's not normal for a woman her age." Ian straightened. "Now I want to see her Facebook page." He also couldn't help but wonder if Nicole's lack of online presence was intentional.

Staying on the sweet spot of where visible met invisibility?

"And maybe she feels the same way about social media that I do."

The laughed escaped before Ian could stop it.

His partner glared at him. "Alright, Hot Shot. Maybe that's even less normal."

Ian remained silent.

"We'll talk to the boss tomorrow morning about getting into her face page."

Ian shook his head while Larry glanced at his watch.

"As much fun as this has been"—he handed Ian the Zamora file —"you called right before Tess was finishing up dinner." Larry smiled. "Fried chicken night. Care to join?"

Under pre-Felicity-being-at-his-house circumstances, Ian wouldn't have hesitated saying yes to a home cooked meal with his partner and family. Especially with the meal being fried chicken. But that reminded him of Felicity's sassy question that he still felt was a compliment.

How is it you look the way you do when you eat nothing but junk?

That memory, however, led him directly to his hot kiss with her, a *smokin'* hot redhead he officially wanted more of now and in the immediate future. Unfortunately, Ian couldn't shake what he'd left behind in Grand Junction.

"I'm good. Thanks for the invite, though. Tell Tess I said hi. And that I appreciate her letting you loose to help me tonight."

Would it be fair to the lady, who he liked and respected and happened to be the *sister* of his closest friend, to pursue something when he could offer her very little right now?

"You're lucky Tess likes you." Larry stepped back. "She's still nagging me about setting you up with that yoga friend of hers. Yay or nay so I can get her off my back."

Ian released a quick laugh, then had no choice but to say, "Nay. But tell her I'll let her know if that changes." Though he already knew it wouldn't since he wanted someone else.

A woman with fire in hair and heart and who tasted as good as she looked.

Yep. He was definitely in *a lot* of trouble.

"Get out of here, will ya?" Larry shrugged into his jacket. "Our Miss Zamora and Mr. Cantrell will still be here tomorrow morning. And you said yourself your lady friend is a-okay."

More than a-okay. But Ian said, "I'm right behind you."

Miss Zamora and Mr. Cantrell.

Nicole and Nicola.

Nicole Zamora's suddenly deceased grandparents.

The timing of the notes.

The timing of Nicole's return to Denver—Ian's eyes widened.

The chatty, nosy neighbor. The officer who'd talked to her had been savvy enough to get the woman's phone number.

Ian would add her to tomorrow's talk-to list. But he, too, was hungry and needed to head home. The fact a beautiful, feisty woman with a little dog happened to be there with Stella only added to his urgency to leave.

He didn't bother to fight an altogether different grin at the image.

Chapter Eighteen

THE DOGS LEAPT off of the couch at Ian again walking into the house.

Felicity continued to sip her wine while watching a movie she'd found on a streaming app. For the life of her, however, she couldn't make sense of the characters or plot.

Due to nearly finishing the bottle of wine, she couldn't make sense of much accept the cold, bitter taste of breath-stealing betrayal.

The dogs reappeared at the couch, followed by Ian.

She sipped more wine.

"So did you ever hear from *Perry*?"

"Yes. He's fine. And please stop saying his name like that."

Silence, followed by, "You were supposed to let me know he's okay."

She slid her gaze to Ian, standing on the other side of the couch's nearest arm. "He just texted me back. He was out having a *wonderful* time with some colleagues." She narrowed her eyes. "Lucky him, right? Being able to enjoy an evening out with people he trusts?"

Ian raised his eyebrows before walking around Stella and the couch. He sat close beside Felicity, then glanced at the near-empty wine bottle sitting on his coffee table. "Apparently something happened while I was gone." He tilted his head right to catch her eyes. "Talk to me."

The dogs settled themselves at their feet as she lifted her chin.

"I found out what that sneaky bitch has been up to behind my back."

E-mail after e-mail after e-mail. Short, damning messages between Lynn and the most deplorable woman in Denver. The most deplorable woman on the planet.

Ian remained silent.

Felicity finished her wine. "My soon-to-be former assistant and friend has been in almost constant contact since I was in Cancún with the *lovely*—"

"Stacia Marsden?"

Of course this didn't seem to surprise Detective Ian Stafford.

Her lower lip trembled as e-mail after e-mail after e-mail sifted through her mind. "In the latest message dated just yesterday, Stacia made Lynn an offer she didn't refuse." Felicity leaned forward, picked up the wine bottle, and poured the remaining contents into her glass.

"How did you find this out?"

She sat back. "I have access to her work e-mail since it's my company." Before today, she'd never had any reason to go into Lynn's Felicitous Wedding Creations account because Felicity had implicitly trusted the woman. "And her accepting Stacia's generous job offer was just the tip of the betrayal iceberg."

Ian released a heavy sigh. "Lynn was the one who tipped her off to your accusation."

She angled her wine glass in his direction, then took a long drink.

"What else did she do?"

Felicity lazily lifted her shoulders. "Gave Stacia everything she wanted when it came to all of her questions about *my* business that I started from *nothing* when I lived in London." Tears tried to fill her eyes, but she furiously blinked them away.

She would not shed one more damn tear over someone like Lynn Delgado.

Ian placed his left arm around Felicity's shoulders and hugged her to his side. "What are you going to do next?"

She gritted her teeth. "Fire her before she can quit. That's all I can do."

She couldn't even refuse giving the woman a reference since she already had a cozy spot with Stacia's company that would provide her with more than enough financial security.

The long-ago, broken woman from a modest family in Madison, Wisconsin, who'd decided to start over in Denver, had been bought by the devil's daughter. But why Lynn had never gone to Felicity about wanting to make their working relationship a partnership eluded her.

Trusting and loving Lynn like Felicity had, she would have seriously considered the idea.

How could Lynn not have known that?

She focused on Ian. "I don't understand what I did to make her turn on me like this."

After reading through every single sickening e-mail, she'd filled up her wine glass and scoured her brain trying to recall a moment or situation or *something* she could have said or done in the last several weeks to cause Lynn's startling change.

"It seems so incredibly sudden, too."

Ian hugged her tighter. "That's how betrayal works. You never see it coming," he quietly added. "And I have a feeling you did absolutely nothing wrong." Their gazes connected. "Whatever's going on with Lynn Delgado could have been brewing for months. Maybe longer."

Knowing he spoke from experience prompted her to ask, "Do you know why Candace did what she did to you? And her friend, your ex-partner's ex-wife?"

He sat back into the couch cushions, bringing her with him. "Boredom, I'm sure." He rolled his head slightly left. "What they did to us *hurt*." He paused before saying, "But I can now say Candace and I stayed together way longer than we should have. My ex-partner, on the other hand, had a wandering eye."

Felicity winced.

"Maren never took it seriously, that's how devoted she was to the bastard." Ian frowned. "I never in a million years thought his eye would wander to Candace."

Felicity clasped his left hand and squeezed.

"I'm not sure why she and I stayed together for so long," he continued. "The fifteen months in Afghanistan changed me. Nothing looked or felt the same when I came back. Including Candace." He stared at their joined hands. "I was a mess." The corner of his mouth lifted in a slight grin. "Scott and I talked a lot during that time."

"I know," she murmured. "I remember that's when I first heard your name." In truth she'd been relieved, as had her mom and sister, that Scott had developed such a close friendship with Ian, the two having been through hell together and managed to come back safely and unharmed. Other soldiers in their unit hadn't been so lucky. "I'm really happy that you two had each other then."

"Me, too." He rested his head on a cushion. "Candace and I never came back from that time. We should have been adult enough to see all of that and end things years ago." He eyed Felicity. "I guess both of us got too comfortable with being *okay*. If that makes any sense."

"Settling." She nodded. "I think that's what happens with too many couples. I certainly settled for my ex-husband." She'd also gotten caught up in his looks and accent and living abroad.

"You had the sense to get away from him." Ian sighed. "I know I shouldn't give a shit—and a huge part of me doesn't—but my ex-partner will probably break Candace in half. Just like he did to Maren." He focused on Felicity. "What is it about smart women and bad boys?"

She sipped some wine before answering, "My ex wasn't a bad boy. He's British."

Ian rolled his eyes. "Right. Pompous but with an accent."

"And I've never been into bad boys, so I can't help you with that." Though something about Detective Ian Stafford gave off the occasional bad boy vibe. She instead said, "I truly believe the Candaces and Lynns and Stacias and assholes of this world eventually get back the ugliness they put out." She frowned at her glass. "I only wish the people they crush could see it when it happens."

"It's interesting you say that."

She lifted her gaze that locked with his.

"Candace has called me twice in the last day and left a message."

Felicity stared at him while her mouth slowly opened.

"But I haven't listened to it. Or called her back."

She understood those two decisions. It didn't stop her from asking, "Don't you want to know why she's calling you?"

"No." He broke their eye contact. "Not one bit."

Felicity sipped her wine.

"It may not show," he softly stated, "but I've come a long way since where I was before leaving Grand Junction." He eyed her. "Listening to Candace's message or calling her would only set me back." He squeezed her hand. "And I'm determined to keep moving forward."

His strong, honest statement settled between them.

A twinge of hope ignited inside of Felicity and she gave him a soft smile, though they did have to be insane to pursue any type of relationship being the definition of opposites attracting.

She couldn't be certain as to what they did have in common, outside of Scott, Peyton, drinking bourbon, owning dogs, and thoroughly enjoying kissing each other while in a kitchen.

And experiencing betrayal by people incredibly close to them.

They definitely had that in common.

"I'm sorry about Lynn."

Ian's deep voice interrupted her thoughts, and she looked up to find him watching her closely.

"I know this is easier said than done"—he shifted onto his left side to face her—"but I need you to keep your fire in check until

Larry and I find your stalker." He leaned forward. "Felicity, we're close. I can feel it. But you're not safe until we do that."

She shook her head. "What do you expect me to do?" She gestured toward his living room. "Hide in your house until that day comes? I can't and won't do that." She narrowed her eyes. "Lynn Delgado is going to face me and her extremely bad choices before this week is up." Tomorrow morning, as a matter of fact. But what Ian didn't know wouldn't hurt him.

"I also have a client meeting on Thursday I can't reschedule again." With Miss Emmy Swanson who was marrying Mr. Jason McAvoy, also known as the last extravagant wedding she'd be putting on her schedule for a while.

Lynn wanted the world of Stacia and so many of Felicity's previous and current clients. Now all Felicity wanted was to attain balance in her business.

Two intimate weddings for every elaborate one sounded quite perfect.

"I had a feeling you'd say that," Ian muttered. "Larry and I hit a road block tonight with a person of interest which means we have to talk to Cancún—Perry—tomorrow."

No doubt the person had to be the mysterious Nicole Zamora.

Felicity finished her wine in one swallow.

This had officially turned into a nightmare.

"That being said, do you happen to have a picture of him?"

Felicity burst into laughter.

Ian's dark eyes widened. Eyes that looked perfect while smoldering and focused on her.

"Of course you want a picture of him." She continued to laugh while setting her glass next to the wine bottle on the table. "It's just my personal life."

"Felicity, I sure as hell don't *want* a picture of him," Ian clarified. "I need it if you have one so Larry and I can find him tomorrow at that conference."

Still laughing, she picked up her phone beside her on the couch.

"You're in luck, Detective, because it just so happens I have one." She went into her phone. "It's actually a lovely selfie of the two of us near the swim-up pool bar. Would you like me to text it to you?"

"Yeah. That'll work, Ms. Mayhew. And to be clear," he added, leaning forward, "I'm not doing any of this because I want to immerse myself in your fling with Cancún guy."

She sent him the picture.

"Larry and I won't be asking him questions specifically about the two of you."

She dropped her phone on the couch, then rubbed her eyes that had become heavy and tired. "I just can't believe that hooking up with him in Mexico is why any of this is happening." The unmitigated truth, too.

"I can't believe you, Felicity Mayhew, just said the phrase 'hooking up.'"

She cracked a smile. "Or that I clearly lost my senses while on vacation?" Something she would never do again, but for reasons that went beyond the consequences she currently faced.

Surprisingly, Ian gave her his rather enticing grin. "You were on vacation, alone, and were probably looking damn fine in a bikini." His grin deepened. "It's not like I can blame the guy for setting his sights on you. Or blame you, a workaholic, for letting yourself have fun."

She released a soft laugh. "Thank you for understanding and not judging me considering that choice may have led to this dark path I've found myself on the last several weeks."

At the same time, that choice had also put this loyal, determined, terribly handsome man with integrity to spare right next to her on this couch.

Ian reached out and gently cupped the left side of her face.

She closed her eyes, took a deep breath—and released a noisy, full-body yawn.

He laughed. "Good to know I have that effect on you, too."

She tried to smile. "It's been a long day and I think the wine is starting to hit." She was about to curl into the couch cushions when Ian wiggled his arms underneath her and stood.

Picking her up as if she weighed no more than Stella's blanket.

"What are you doing?"

"I need my bed tonight and so do you." He began walking toward his room.

Heat consumed her face. "Ian, I don't think—"

"As *hard* as it will be, I'll be a perfect gentleman."

She fought a smile while asking, "What about the dogs?"

He strode into his room and set her on his unkempt bed. "Stella may try to kick you and the princess out, but I think you can take her." He then brushed his lips against hers. "I need to turn everything off and lock up. I'll be right back." He gave her a quick kiss and left.

Felicity curled onto her side and hugged the pillow covered in his masculine scent.

Tomorrow would bring facing the person behind betrayal she'd never seen coming, possibly even more heartache. She also had to face more of the unknown when it came to whomever was harassing her and the fact it could have something to do with her choices while in Mexico…unbelievably. But right now all she wanted was to fall asleep beside one of the few people in her life who made her feel safe and secure and as if nothing would ever harm her.

Ian's enticing grin drifted through her mind before it went blank.

Chapter Nineteen

"I THINK we have our winner heading this way." Ian showed Larry the pic of Felicity, looking damn fine in a red bikini, black sunglasses, and hair piled on her head, sitting beside a guy with dark hair streaked with gray. "Do we have a match?"

Larry squinted at the photo for a few seconds, then focused on an approaching man wearing khakis and a windbreaker with a laptop bag slung over his shoulder. He was striding toward where they stood outside the main entrance of the convention center.

"Sunglasses seem to be the same. But his goatee is throwing me off." Larry straightened. "Only one way to find out for sure." The possible Perry Cantrell was about to open the door when Larry said, "Excuse me?"

The guy stopped and focused on Larry and Ian.

"Are you Perry Cantrell?"

A hesitant smile settled onto his mouth before, "Yeah. Do we know each other?"

Ian exchanged a quick glance with his partner at the same time his phone started to ring.

"We just need a few minutes of your time, Mr. Cantrell." Larry headed toward Perry.

Ian retrieved his phone. "I'll be there in a sec."

Larry nodded and gestured for Perry to walk ahead of him, into the massive lobby.

"Detective Ian Stafford," he answered.

"I got Walsh's message," their captain replied. "You've gone from the daughter of King Marsden to chasing down a woman who might have a connection to a guy your girl screwed around with while on vacation *and* who you think lethally drugged her grandparents?"

Though not at all comfortable with the image of Felicity screwing around with Cancún guy now standing on the other side of the glass, Ian said, "Yes."

Captain Alan Gellar released a quick laugh which sounded like a Stella bark. "You've been busy. Where are you two?"

"At the convention center. The guy—Perry Cantrell—is here from California for a work conference. We've already found him." Because of Larry's suggestion they get there well before the conference started for the day, plant themselves at the entrance, and hope for the best.

"The guy doesn't even live here?"

Ian hesitated before saying, "No."

Gellar's deep sigh reached Ian through the phone. "You're going to have to talk me through what you two are thinking."

As quickly as possible, Ian gave his captain a highly abridged version of what he and Larry had uncovered in the last twenty-four or so hours with Felicity's case and the Zamoras.

"You have got to be shitting me," the man muttered. "You and Walsh have to realize this sounds like fiction."

Ian rubbed his eyes. "And maybe it is. That's why we need to talk to Cantrell and show him a picture of Nicole Zamora."

"Fine. Let me know what he says. *If* this Zamora woman has brought her crazy to Denver, then we'll get into the Facebook page. That's the best I can do right now."

"Alright. I'll let Larry know." Ian ended the call and headed inside.

Larry and Perry stood several steps from the doors. Based on Cancún guy's round eyes, Larry had started the conversation.

Perry turned his wide-eyed gaze on Ian as Larry faced him.

"Turns out you couldn't find a restraining order because there isn't one."

Right. Not a huge a surprise. Ian still felt the need to ask, "Why did you lie to your ex-wife about it?"

Perry ran a hand through his thick hair. "To appease her because she was convinced Nicola was crazy. And, yeah, she did some spooky shit, but I never thought she was *dangerous*."

Silence, outside of the lobby becoming busy with conference goers, fell between them.

"And," Larry suddenly continued, "Mr. Cantrell's Nicola has the last name of Oliver."

Ian somehow managed not to grit his teeth in frustration.

"That's what she told me, anyway." Perry focused on Ian. "Your partner said you've been the one in constant contact with Felicity?"

Ian's mind went to again waking beside her, only in his bed, and her curled into a tight ball against him with their dogs surrounding them. "Yes."

After what she'd told him about Lynn Delgado last night, leaving her while she slept had been the hardest thing he'd done in recent memory. And not just because he wanted more than sleeping next to her and being the definition of a gentleman.

Lynn's betrayal had knocked her sideways and down, and he'd hated seeing it written all over her beautiful face. A feeling no one should ever experience.

"The notes." Perry shook his head. "It explains why she was acting like she did Monday night while we were at dinner. Well"—he sighed—"it was drinks. We ended the night early."

The guy's tone alone made it clear it's not how he'd expected the evening to go, either.

Ian pushed that thought aside to focus on Perry's relationship with Nicola Oliver. Something about all of this refused to release his instincts.

"You met Nicola on a dating app?"

Cancún guy huffed. "Yeah. And after escaping her crazy train and being questioned by cops in Denver about her possibly stalking someone else here, I'm going to seriously rethink dating apps moving forward."

Larry half grunted, half laughed.

Ian persisted with, "Did she by chance ever mention having a connection to Colorado?"

The man frowned. "I don't remember."

Shit.

"But she did say something about living all over the place."

Ian exchanged a quick glance with his partner.

Nicole Zamora had in fact lived in many places.

Larry asked, "When was the last time you saw her?"

Perry stared at the floor for several seconds. "At a coffee joint near my office before my trip to Cancún. So early February." He frowned. "I had to get firm with her, too. I threatened getting a restraining order to scare her and it seemed to have worked. She walked away, and I haven't heard from her since. It's another reason I didn't actually get one."

February seemed to be the key month. A mere eight weeks ago.

Larry looked at Ian and lifted his shoulders.

They only had one more chance in hell here, and Ian reached into his pocket.

"I know the last names aren't the same," he said, handing Perry a clear photo copy of Nicole Zamora's Nevada driver's license, "but can you take a look at this photo?"

"Of course." Perry took the paper and peered at the young woman's picture.

Ian held his breath—until Perry shook his head while handing over the paper.

This time Ian couldn't stop himself from gritting his teeth while glancing at Larry.

"The eyes are familiar, but this woman is a brunette with short hair," Perry stated. "Nicola's almost a platinum blonde and her hair goes to her shoulders."

Between the different last names and hairstyles and Perry not making a match, they'd officially taken this lead as far as they possibly could—

An idea landed in Ian's head. Not a hugely far-fetched idea, either. But surely Perry would have mentioned if Nicola's platinum blonde hair had been a wig.

Clara Cantrell had implied Perry and Nicola had been *together*.

"I'd like to see Felicity before I leave Denver. That'll be okay, right?"

At Perry's question, Ian kept a sigh in check and said, "She's under advisement to keep a very low profile for obvious reasons. I'm sure you can understand why?"

Hope fled Perry's face, but he nodded.

Okay. Ian had successfully cut that cord, but now what? This had been his last, viable hope…outside of Lynn Delgado. Based on what Felicity had told him, the woman would have to be dumber than a box of rocks to jeopardize the career-making deal she'd made with Stacia Marsden by sending the threatening notes.

His promise to Felicity seemed to be on the verge of breaking into a million pieces. Unless, of course, Nicola had been wearing a wig, meaning she and Perry were never intimate.

"I hope you find who's harassing her." Perry stepped back. "She's quite a woman and doesn't deserve it. I was also really hoping to reconnect with her while I was here, but it appears to be extremely bad timing."

Larry leaned forward. "Thank you for your time, Mr. Cantrell."

"Actually," Ian interjected, "I have one more question." He felt his partner's piercing stare while he asked, "Were you and Nicola Oliver ever intimate?"

Perry's eyes widened as he angled his head back.

The noise in the lobby seemed to have gone up several notches while Ian waited for Perry's reply to the extremely personal question.

"No. Absolutely not. We went on three dates and her crazy came out on date three."

And there it was. His ex-wife must have simply made a huge assumption.

Ian shot Larry a quick grin before once again handing Perry the copy of Nicole's driver's license. "Can you take a look at this again, but this time imagine her with the blonde hair?"

Perry unfolded it, peered closely at the pic—and tapped a spot. "It is her. And not just because of picturing her with blonde hair. The tattoo." He held out the paper while still pointing at a spot. "On the front of her right shoulder? I didn't look at the picture close enough earlier to see it."

Ian and Larry leaned in to better see the photo.

Nicole had been wearing a thin-strapped top when the photo had been taken. Under the black strap was a tattoo, no bigger than a quarter, of the yin and yang symbol.

"The woman I know as Nicola Oliver has the same tattoo in the same place."

Ian again lifted his head with enough force that his neck popped.

"She wore some red, strappy dress to my company's Christmas party," Perry added. "That's when I saw it. I remember now asking her why she chose the symbol and placement." He looked at Ian. "Right, front shoulder? Not a real popular place for a tattoo."

Adrenaline spread through Ian as he asked, "What did she say?"

"Something about how she thought the symbol best represented her and wanting to see it everyday. Or something like that." He tapped the photo. "The different hair color and style caught me off guard. But I definitely recognize that tattoo and can now see *her*."

Ian glanced at Larry whose expression full of understanding mirrored his thoughts.

Real hair concealed under a wig. A unique tattoo in a rather unique spot on the body.

A tattoo they'd never seen due to Denver's early springtime weather that had been favoring winter temperatures the last week or so. The two times they'd seen Nicole she'd been wearing a jacket or sweatshirt.

"Well, *shit*," Larry mumbled. "I can't believe it. We got our ourselves a match."

The tattoo also wasn't noticeable in the original copy they'd printed, but they'd blown the photo up for Perry's sake. It had worked, too, only not in the way they'd expected.

"So that means Nicola is here in Denver." Perry's eyes became round once more. "Am I in danger, too?" He shook his head. "I can't believe this is happening. Of all the women on that damn dating app, I meet the one who belongs in a psych ward."

Larry handed Perry a business card. "I'd be on the look out for Nicole—Nicola—if I were you. Call me if you see or hear from her."

"But I blocked *and* deleted her number."

"Then call me immediately if you see her."

Ian absently followed Larry from the lobby. He then folded the photo copy of Nicole's driver's license and shoved it inside his suit jacket pocket.

Yeah. They had a match. But still too many unanswered questions that began with how in the hell she'd found out about Perry "hooking up" with Felicity in Cancún, Mexico. And he couldn't forget about the elderly Zamoras.

Perry had said he'd escaped Nicola's crazy train, but never thought of her as dangerous.

A chill wound its way up Ian's spine as a new question penetrated his thoughts.

What if Nicola-Nicole was in fact capable of an evil that went far beyond stalking? If so, he would keep Felicity in his home even if he *did* have to handcuff her to a dining room chair.

Chapter Twenty

FELICITY ADJUSTED the box in her arms, lifted her chin, and knocked hard three times.

Seconds later the front door of the condo opened and there stood her very soon-to-be *former* assistant and friend.

Lynn cautiously eyed Felicity while taking in her normal, professional up-do, opened dress coat revealing her business suit, and high heels. The woman, on the other hand, wore nothing but sweats with her long, dark hair piled on her head in a messy knot, this scenario being precisely what Felicity had been envisioning since waking up in Ian's bed.

"Good morning." Lynn gave her a tight grin. "You must be feeling better."

Felicity unleashed her brightest smile. "I had a wonderful night's sleep and woke up with an entirely different perspective." Both statements nothing but the truth, though waking up with Ian still beside her would have made the morning perfect. However, she needed to stay focused on the next several minutes which prompted her to point inside Lynn's condo. "Do you mind if I come in? I think it's time we chatted."

Understanding appeared on Lynn's face, replacing her phony grin.

Felicity's smile deepened.

With wide eyes, Lynn stepped aside.

The woman closed the door behind Felicity. At the sight of taped up moving boxes in tall stacks around Lynn's modest, two-bedroom condo, in addition to the boxes she seemed to be in the middle of packing, Felicity clenched her teeth.

She faced Lynn and managed to politely ask, "Are we moving up in the world?"

Lynn sighed. "You're right. We do need to chat."

"Brilliant. I'll start." Felicity handed Lynn the box she held. "You're fired."

Lynn's eyes became slits before she opened the box and looked inside.

"I took it upon myself to stop at the office and pack up your belongings that were in your now *former* office since I won't have you and your ugliness anywhere near my business again."

Their hard gazes locked.

"I also may have accidentally dropped the framed photo of you and me taken the day we officially opened the office doors of Felicitous Wedding Creations."

In truth, she'd placed it on the floor and shattered it with the narrow heel of her shoe. She'd then swept up the glass pieces and dropped everything into the box…right on top of all the other items the woman had kept in her office.

Lynn released a humorless laugh. "You have been talking to Ian."

And so much more. But she said, "I fiercely defended you before he told me what you said Monday night."

Lynn's eyes hardened.

"And he didn't even tell me until last night." Because he'd wanted to protect her from betrayal for as long as possible. "Then I started to wonder what else I didn't know about my beloved assistant and *friend*."

The woman remained silent.

"So I went into your Felicitous Wedding Creations e-mail because I can."

Felicity sent Lynn a cold smile while her eyes widened.

"I only have one question for you before I walk out of here and never look back." She stepped toward her now former assistant and friend, and leaned forward. "Why?"

Lynn placed the box on the entryway table and crossed her arms. "I want to be in charge and Stacia offered me that by expanding her business into weddings."

Felicity had gathered as much from the slew of e-mails between the two women over the last several weeks, that being the answer she hadn't been seeking. "You could have—*should have*—been honest with me about what you wanted."

Lynn laughed, but there wasn't a bit of humor in the action. "Then what? You would have offered me…a partnership?"

She lifted her chin. "Maybe. But you sure as hell didn't give me that chance."

"You still would have been in charge because it's your business!" Lynn leaned forward. "I'm sick and tired of being nothing more than the *perfect* Felicity Mayhew's assistant and a partnership never would have changed that."

In that moment, the pieces snapped together in Felicity's head.

"You going on vacation in February was the best thing to happen to me because I was able to start putting all of this into motion."

Lynn's cruel betrayal came down to one thing—jealousy.

"Stacia has assured me I will run the wedding side of her event planning business." Lynn smiled. "I'll not only get the title of director and a small staff to manage, but a salary to match. With all of that will come the recognition and respect I've rarely received from *your* clients."

Greed and jealousy. That's all Felicity heard in Lynn's words.

"I can get out of this crappy condo"—Lynn gestured at the space

—"and buy a real home in Cherry Creek. I'm also looking closely at a home in Hilltop."

Two upscale Denver neighborhoods. Felicity's home happened to be in Cherry Creek which led to another realization.

On some level, Lynn wanted Felicity's life.

"The only thing I had to do was feed Stacia everything I knew and had learned from Felicity Mayhew, creator of fairy tale weddings."

Felicity tightened her hands into fists to stop herself from smacking the triumphant smile off of the woman's face.

"It took longer than I thought it would, but I'll finally be sitting down with Stacia and her lawyer to go over the contract Friday morning." Lynn paused before adding, "I'd planned on quitting after working this weekend's wedding with you. But now that I'm fired I think I'll go somewhere and celebrate the fact I am moving up in the world." She shot Felicity an icy smile. "Maybe I'll stay at some fancy resort in Cancún for a week."

Felicity stared at the woman standing in front of her, so full of selfishness and spite.

How had she not ever seen this side of Lynn Delgado? Where had this side of her, the real side, been the last couple years? Then again, Felicity had fallen quite easily for a British bastard whose dark side had eventually emerged.

Seeing the real Lynn for the first time meant Ian had been right last night.

Felicity hadn't done anything wrong; the darkness inside of Lynn had been simmering for God knew how long. She also couldn't help but wonder if Lynn's story about an abusive ex-boyfriend had even been true. Maybe it had been the woman's first of many manipulations on her journey to where she currently stood in her disgusting triumph.

Felicity—and her family—had been played by another narcissistic, worthless human being. Even Scott had been fooled by Lynn, but he'd seen right through Felicity's ex-husband. Though, it could have been due to his protective brother instincts when it came to men in his sisters' lives.

"I have to know one other thing since we're being so honest," Felicity began, already suspecting the answer, "are you or Stacia the ones behind the threatening notes?"

Lynn rolled her eyes. "No." She gestured at Felicity. "I was actually being honest with Ian when I said I thought you were sending them to yourself. But I guess you're not."

It was clear the woman could care less about the notes, too.

Felicity shook her head.

Lynn Delgado and Stacia Marsden absolutely deserved one another.

"If I were you," Felicity replied, "I'd bring my own lawyer to that meeting on Friday. Now that you can afford it?"

A muscle in Lynn's jaw twitched while they continued to glare at one another.

"Stacia Marsden only cares about one person." Felicity grasped the door handle. "Stacia Marsden. You might want to think about that and having someone on your side at that meeting." She opened the door. "I certainly wouldn't want to see you jobless and homeless because you trusted the wrong person." She grinned. "I do love that image, though." She started to step outside when she stopped, turned, and said, "Oh, and if for some reason your deal with Stacia doesn't work out, I do hope you have the good sense to *not* list me as a job reference."

The second Felicity left the condo the door slammed shut behind her.

She headed right, toward the bank of elevators.

The reality of being manipulated for a second time in her life by someone she'd loved and trusted without hesitation would undoubtedly hit hard at some point. She would try her best to not shed another tear over it and the person, too. But right now she needed to make one more stop before heading back to Ian's house since he had no idea she'd gone to the office, then here.

She stepped onto the elevator and pushed the lobby button.

This highly unforeseen problem had been dealt with, but another, much bigger one shadowed her life. And it was possibly much more dangerous. If not for the threatening notes, however, Lynn and Stacia would have held all the power when they finally came clean with their plans and deception.

The doors opened and Felicity emerged.

Despite still being at the mercy of her harasser, she couldn't help but smile at leaving Lynn's condo the true victor and her newest plans for Felicitous Wedding Creations.

LARRY LOWERED his phone from his ear. "So our Miss Zamora isn't a total liar."

Ian dragged his gaze from his partner to check his phone for what felt like the millionth time while they waited for the Zamoras' neighbor to answer her front door.

Why the hell hadn't Felicity replied to his texts? If not for the fact he and his partner stood outside the elderly woman's home, he'd be calling *Ms. Mayhew*.

"The Zamoras' PC doc confirmed everything she said about their health problems, but did add he'd never been concerned about their mental health. Guess we got that going for us."

But the former did slightly help Nicole's case. Something she must have known would support her version of her grandparents' dismal physical life.

The door opened and a small, thin woman with short white hair and thick glasses peered up at them. She gave them a quick once-over. "You look like cops. This about my dear friends?"

Larry showed the woman his badge. "I'm Detective Walsh and this is my partner, Detective Stafford. Are you Doris Milano?"

She sighed. "In all my glory." She stepped back. "Come on in. Starting to get used to having cops in my house."

Ian followed Larry following Doris and closed the door behind him.

He slid his gaze around the compact living room filled with older furniture. A beige recliner angled toward the modest television had a white cat curled up into a ball. The table beside the chair held various pill bottles and a glass of water. At least, it looked like water.

"Have a seat." She gestured toward a beige couch with another cat, only this one was black and watching them with wide-eyed interest. "You can shoo Raven out of your way."

Ian eyed the cat watching him. "I'm good." He grinned at the woman. "Thank you."

It's not that he hated cats. He just didn't like them all that much. And didn't want them anywhere near him.

"This won't take long, Ms. Milano." Larry reached into his coat pocket and withdrew his little notebook. "According to what you told officers on Friday, you and Mrs. Zamora were not only neighbors but good friends?"

"For thirty-plus years." She picked up the white cat and hugged it close.

The action reminded Ian of how Felicity often held the princess.

"We were all friends," Doris continued. "My husband passed away a few years ago."

"I'm sorry for your loss," Larry murmured. "As well as losing your close friends."

"Me, too." The woman leaned forward. "What really ticks me off is that I know it was that bad seed, granddaughter of theirs." She sniffed. "I just can't prove it."

Ian's gaze went to Larry's and back to Doris.

"That girl has been trouble since she hit grade school. My dear friends knew it, too." She frowned. "I said this to the officers on Friday. Were they not listening? I also don't feel they asked me enough questions. Basically popped into my house, then out."

Larry gave her a warm smile. "There was a lot going on that day. We've also learned some new information about Miss Zamora and needed to clarify some things." He opened his notebook, flipped through some pages, then stopped. "I have here in my notes that you said Miss Zamora showed up one day on her grandparents' doorstep after being gone for a while?"

"Yes. Late February. Almost March. Showed up jobless, homeless, and crying over a supposed broken heart." She shook her head. "I tried telling them you gotta have a heart for it to be broken, but they couldn't turn her away and that brat knew they wouldn't."

Okay. The timing matched with Felicity receiving the second note on her *doorstep*. Nicole had also told her grandparents about a broken heart. The tattoo. Perry recognizing her while imagining her with blonde hair. The living in California connection, though her driver's license was from Nevada, another place Nicole had lived.

But she did say something about living all over the place.

This had to be adding up to Nicole-Nicola being one and the same.

"How long had it been since she'd last seen her grandparents?" Ian asked.

"Years. A decade at least."

Which didn't match what Nicole had told him on Friday about she and her grandparents being incredibly close and needing each other.

"When she was fourteen or fifteen, her family in Arizona didn't know what the hell to do with her so they shipped her here." The woman pursed her lips. "It was some young teen age like that because she couldn't get a driver's license, but that didn't stop her from taking the car."

Ian raised his eyebrows and looked at Larry.

Wow. Miss Nicole Zamora was definitely looking more and more *unstable*.

"My dear friends did their best with her. Even when she was little," Doris added. "But you can't fix that kind of badness. The type she was born with?"

Ian nodded.

"But it was Oliver that pushed them over the edge."

Ian froze.

Oliver. Nicola *Oliver*.

Doris squeezed her cat still content in her arms. "That rotten brat treated their cat so badly and then one day he disappeared."

Ian's blood became cold and he somehow stopped himself from shuddering. He caught Larry's wide eyes which meant he, too, had made the connection.

"They knew she'd done something to him, but of course couldn't prove it." She kissed the top of her cat's head. "Didn't stop them from kicking her butt out of their home. My husband and I told them good riddance, too. That was the last time anyone saw her. Until several weeks ago," she hastily added.

Larry pulled out a pen. "Do you—or did the Zamoras—know where she went after they told her to leave?"

"Who knows? Probably some loser friend she had at the time. She didn't have a lot of options since her family couldn't trust or tolerate her."

And there it was. A much stronger motive than an old house in an old neighborhood, on top of the "bad seed" factor.

Ian slid his hands into his pockets as another question hit. "By chance, did Nicole ever go by the name Nicola?"

Doris huffed. "Her grandfather called her that when she was real little and still relatively sweet and innocent."

Holy shit.

Larry angled his head toward the door, took out a business card, and closed his notebook.

"Not sure why he called her that," the woman added. "I guess it was just their thing."

Doris Milano, nosy, concerned neighbor and close friends with the Zamoras, had given them most of the remaining Nicole Zamora puzzle pieces. But none of this solidly connected her to the threatening notes.

"Thank you for your time, Ms. Milano." Larry shot her a quick smile. "We'll be in touch if we need anything more." He handed her his card. "If you think of anything else, please don't hesitate to call me."

"I'd prefer not to go through this a third time, Detectives," she called out to them as they strode toward her front door. "I'll also sleep better at night if that bad seed is put into a jail cell."

Yeah. So would Ian. For many reasons, too.

Once they were outside, Larry pulled out his phone. "I'm calling Gellar. Maybe we can get a couple uniforms to pick up our Miss Zamora and meet us at admin."

As Larry called their captain, Ian called Felicity and not only because he had yet to hear from her. He needed to give her a heads up on Nicole and what she looked like in the now highly strong likelihood Nicole was Nicola and vice versa.

At the call going right to Felicity's voicemail, his jaw tightened.

What the hell was she doing?

He left her a quick "I need you to call me back" message, then ended the call.

"We're all set, " Larry said while they slid into the sedan. "But this time we'll both be in the interrogation room with her. You'll be the charm and I'll be the grump." He started the engine. "We'll get her to crack like Humpty Dumpty."

Ian stared at his phone, not certain someone as cold and manipulative as Nicole Zamora would break that easily. The woman was, for the most part, used to getting away with her manipulations. It had also become clear what had brought her to Denver several weeks earlier.

Righting some things she perceived as wrongs.

But how did Felicity fit into this? Nicole-Nicola had to be the stalker, though he sat on zero, indisputable proof. He also couldn't wrap his brain around how the woman had found out about Felicity or her all-consuming jealousy over a woman Perry had met while on vacation.

Doris Milano had called Nicole a bad seed from the beginning and all but said the woman—and at a young age—had done something terrible to the family pet. And what about the grandparents? In that respect, Nicole being consumed with jealousy over a guy, who she probably considered a catch and who had dumped her in a coffee shop, shouldn't be surprising.

At the end of the day, Nicole Zamora was a sociopath. Her behavior would never make sense to anyone but her. All he and Larry could do was get her to confess and lock her away.

He continued to stare at his phone, willing it to ring or light up with a text.

Hearing from Felicity would certainly ease his mind and help him focus while in the box with Larry and Nicole. Getting that woman off the Denver streets would be even better.

Larry's phone started to ring, forcing Ian back into the now.

He focused on his partner, the man's forehead forming a deep V.

"Well, *shit.*" Larry sighed. "Alight…Okay…Keep me posted." He ended the call and tossed his phone into the center console. "Miss Zamora hasn't been seen at her apartment since Monday evening. This from the pissed off landlord wanting his April rent."

Of course Ian's chat with her on Monday had spooked her.

He sat back and rubbed his eyes. "What about her job?"

"Uniforms are headed there next, but I'm sure she isn't there, either."

Ian stared out the windshield.

All of this meant the unstable woman was MIA…as was Felicity.

Chapter Twenty-One

FELICITY WRAPPED herself in the towel that had become hers while at Ian's house. She then shut the shower door and walked into his bedroom—and halted at the sight of him sitting at the foot of the bed, minus his suit jacket, gun, and holster. He'd also loosened his pale-blue tie.

Stella and Princess Belle sat on either side of him while he glared at her.

She lifted her chin. "Why are you sitting there looking at me like that?"

He pointed at her. "Why are you acting like nothing at all should be wrong?"

She sighed. "Fine. I didn't call you, but I did text you back."

"Hours after the fact. What the hell happened to you?"

Dammit. Getting into this with Ian while wearing a towel happened to be the last thing in the world she wanted right now, but she admitted, "My phone died."

The complete truth since in the turmoil of last night she'd forgotten to charge it. She had a charger in her vehicle, but had been in it only long enough to barely get her phone to turn on.

"So why didn't you charge it? This house contains multiple outlets."

She crossed her arms. "I'm sure you've already figured out that I wasn't here for part of the day. And please stop questioning me like I'm an irresponsible teenager under your care."

Ian stood and closed the gap between them. "And you scared the shit out of me today."

Felicity met his gaze, smoldering with a myriad of emotions, the main one relief.

"I'm sorry," she replied, "but I had to take care of some things. If my phone hadn't died, I would have texted you back right away."

He released a breath without breaking their eye contact. "I asked you to keep your fire in check until we caught your stalker."

"Yes. You did. I never said I would, though." She leaned forward. "I had to go to Lynn's place—with her crap from the office—hand it over, and fire her. It couldn't wait."

His eyes widened. "You went to your office, too? Your office that's right off 16th Street."

She fell silent.

There was no reason to tell Ian she'd also gone home to pick up a few things. That could wait until absolutely necessary. On the bright side, there hadn't been a sixth note waiting for her.

"Felicity, the woman we think is stalking you worked at a restaurant crawling distance from your office. She was probably able to easily watch and follow you because of that."

Her mouth inched open.

"We made that connection today while trying to track her down. She's officially missing, by the way. It's another reason I was trying so damn hard to get a hold of you."

The heat from her hot shower became instantly replaced with a chill worthy of an arctic winter and she shivered.

Ian's frustration vanished and he pulled her into his arms. "I understand you needed and wanted to cut Lynn loose before she could make another move. Believe me."

Felicity slid her arms around his warm waist and hugged him tight.

"But you also have to believe me when I say you can't do that shit again. Especially now when we have no idea where this woman could be."

"Nicole Zamora?"

"Yeah." He rested his chin on her head. "Perry positively ID'd her as the same, unhinged woman he briefly dated in California, only she was going by Nicola Oliver and wore a wig."

Felicity buried her face in his chest that still smelled of his delectable soap. Or cologne.

How the hell could meeting and being with a man in another country while on vacation have caused all of this?

"It was only one week," she murmured into Ian's chest. "How did she even find out?"

Ian tightened his hold. "We're trying to figure that out, on top of looking for her. We're also waiting on a warrant to search her apartment."

A question appeared in her jumbled head and she asked, "Do you think she's dangerous?"

Ian leaned back just enough to catch her gaze. "Yes."

Felicity slowly nodded.

"There's a warrant out for her arrest because we're sure she gave her grandparents a lethal dose of hydrocodone."

Another arctic chill swept over her, followed by a shiver.

"We still need to connect her to the threatening notes, but you have to stay put." He stared at her. "If you can't do that, I'll have no other choice but to handcuff you to a piece of furniture somewhere in this house."

She narrowed her eyes. "You wouldn't dare, Detective."

He smirked. "Try me, Ms. Mayhew."

She started to respond, but he silenced her by pressing his mouth to hers. Her retort became lost as she lost herself in his taste and smell and *him*.

His hands became tangled in her damp hair and he angled her head back, deepening the kiss which caused her to moan. His soft laugh between a kiss made her grin.

The man didn't laugh enough. Neither did she, for that matter.

It was time to change that.

He leisurely brought their kiss to an end and pressed his forehead to hers. "I'm so glad you're okay."

Felicity's eyes drifted shut once more while he lightly brushed his lips against hers.

If he spent the rest of his life doing that, she'd be perfectly content and happy.

"Now that I'm no longer pissed," he added, "what happened with Lynn?"

She opened her mouth to answer, but their extremely close proximity, coupled with their addictive kiss and her lack of clothing, made her say, "No. We're not doing this."

Ian lifted his head. "Not doing what, exactly?"

She cupped his face. "Talking about Lynn right now. Talking in general," she said under her breath. "Not when I'm standing in front of you like this wearing only a towel."

His irresistible mouth curved into that grin of his. "I did notice how fine you looked walking out of my bathroom wearing one of my towels. I wasn't *that* pissed."

She brought his head down. "Then what are we waiting for?" They shared another deep, thorough kiss. "We've already decided we're certifiably insane for doing this and know Scott would never interfere." Another kiss. "Ian, I'm sick and tired of feeling angry and sad and scared. I want to feel good, even if it's only for a moment. Don't you?"

He caressed her lips with his thumb. "Yes. And I swear it would last much longer than a moment."

She laughed softly.

"But I told you yesterday morning that I'm not one to start things I can't finish."

Her humor vanished. "What does that mean, exactly?"

"Felicity, I'm still on the clock and will be until we find Nicole Zamora. I'm also hoping for a call on the warrant to search her apartment."

Meaning his phone could ring at any second and he'd have to leave. The reality of his job, whether in the middle of a case or not. But did she really care about that anymore? Despite her long ago decision following tragedy and being opposites in many ways, she and Ian had developed an unexpected and potent connection.

She also wanted him all to herself for as long as possible.

His eyes, now smoldering with an odd combination of desire and frustration, made her bring his mouth back to hers for several delectable seconds. She then ended the kiss and said, "In that case, we should probably stop wasting time."

His grin came back. "I'm also not one to argue with a beautiful woman standing in my bedroom wearing only a towel and smile." He released her and stepped back. "But our audience definitely has to go." He headed toward the door. "Stella and Princess." He angled his head toward the hallway. "Out! Now."

Stella leisurely climbed off of his bed and walked toward the doorway. Princess Belle hopped up and scurried after her. Once the dogs were in the hallway, Ian closed the door. He next removed his phone from his pocket and set it on the cluttered nightstand. A millisecond later he had his arms around her—tight—and mouth moving with hers.

He turned them around and stepped until Felicity's bare legs reached the bed.

She gripped his dress shirt at the waist and tugged. "You're wearing too much clothing."

"So are you."

They shared a quick laugh around him removing his tie, followed by his shirt. He then guided her backward onto his bed—and something squeaked.

Felicity frowned at him as he gently reached under her and

removed a large stuffed squirrel that he held up and squeezed. The obnoxious squeak filled the silence.

"Stella strikes again."

Felicity laughed at the same time he tossed the toy over his shoulder. Their mouths then fused, hungry and desperate.

She slid her hands up his smooth, defined arms and stopped at his shoulders, savoring his warmth and strength under her fingers.

Ian in turn placed his hand on her bent leg, lightly dragged his fingers up and across her bare thigh, stopping just inside and near *her* now throbbing with need.

"I have to know," he said between a kiss, "if you taste as good as you look somewhere else." He slowly spread the damp towel and placed a soft kiss below her belly button. "I'll try not to take too long."

"You don't have to rush, either," she managed to say around a breath.

He placed a trail of airy kisses down…down…and stopped to nuzzle a spot incredibly close to where she most wanted his mouth. So close she started to lift herself up, but he placed his hand on her abdomen and continued his nuzzling.

"You smell good," he murmured, and she heard the smile in his voice. "I did choose the right soap for you last night." He brushed his lips barely against her as if at her actual mouth.

The action made her even more wet and she deeply inhaled.

While she released the air, Ian kissed her. Then tasted her. Teased her with his tongue. Again…again…and again.

The pressure deep within slowly started to build with each of his tastes and licks.

She gripped the sheets, not wanting him to stop while still desperately wanting and needing the release. "Ian," she practically moaned. "I want you inside of me."

He laughed quietly. "And you will. I promise."

Her mind went blank as his mouth and tongue's teasing intensified. She moved her hips in time with him. Perfectly in tune with each other's wants and needs.

He clearly wanted her to let go—just her—and that's exactly what she needed.

A few thorough, deep tongue licks later her release filled the silence. His entire room.

Felicity took several deep breaths, then started to laugh.

Ian kissed her stomach, laid his head down facing her, and gave her his enticing grin. "In case you were wondering, you do taste as good as you look somewhere else."

She continued to laugh.

He kissed her stomach again and rolled up and off of the bed.

Her smile faded. "Where are you going?"

"Nowhere." He removed his belt. "I'm still wearing way too much clothing and made a promise I fully intend to keep." He unzipped his pants while sliding his gaze across her in a way that reminded her of his gentle touch. "You look so damn good right now I wish I had a camera since my memory will never do this moment justice."

She grinned and rolled onto her left side. "I give you permission to look all you want, Detective."

His smile deepened, followed by his face suddenly lighting up. "I do have a camera."

He reached for his phone. "Don't move a muscle, Ms. Mayhew."

Felicity's eyes widened and she sat upright. "Ian Stafford, it'll be the last thing you do."

"I promise I won't post it anywhere." He held up his phone and pointed it in her direction. "I might print it, though, and hang it in here."

She lunged forward and snatched the device from his hand.

He burst into laughter.

Felicity sat back on her heels, now savoring the sound of his genuine, rich laughter.

No. This beautiful, loyal man with integrity to spare did not laugh nearly enough.

Ian went back to sliding his gaze up and down her body. "I'm definitely ready for more of you." He took back his phone, dropped it on the nightstand, and removed the rest of his clothing.

She lost her breath at Ian standing before her, wearing only that grin of his.

He opened his nightstand drawer and retrieved a very important item. Something she hadn't even thought about until now, though she had protection in her purse.

Ian opened the wrapper and proceeded to sheathe himself, all while barely taking his eyes off of her. Watching her closely. An action so perfect and so *him* her body became hot.

She reached out, grasped his hands, and pulled him forward.

In a blur of greedy kisses and arms wrapping around each other, he slid inside of her.

His moan echoed hers.

"I'm going to be pissed if my phone rings with a work call," he mumbled while burying himself deep within her. "You're so damn *wet*."

"Because of you," she whispered against his mouth. "Let's forget about everything together?" If the universe continued to be on their side, his phone wouldn't ring at all.

"I'm already there."

Their fierce, deep kisses matched their bodies moving in sync. Thrust after mind-numbing thrust. Every inch of Felicity's body started to tingle. But not ready for any of this to end, she abruptly ended their kiss, rolled him onto his back, and straddled him. The action caused him to slip out, but she gradually guided him back into her wet warmth.

His sultry gaze locked with hers and he smiled.

"I like a woman who takes charge."

She responded with her own smile and moving up…and down… back up…and down.

Ian placed his hands on her waist, never breaking their eye contact.

The pressure within started to build once more. Her breathing and his began to match her deliberate movements. Up…and down…up…and down. But then he eased upright, wound his right fingers into her hair, and barely touched his open mouth to hers.

His actions and the different angle pushed Felicity over the edge for the second time. Her release hit hard and fast and obliterated her remaining senses.

Ian's grip on her hair tightened as he went over that same edge.

They remained locked in each other's arms while catching their breath, the world outside his bedroom—his house—no longer existing.

Chapter Twenty-Two

TWO DOGS SLEEPING on the couch. Two glasses each with about a double shot of bourbon. No work calls. No calls at all, for that matter. One *smokin'* hot redhead safe and sound…and naked…in his bed. At this exact moment, everything in Ian's life sat at perfect.

He grinned, unable to recall the last time he'd felt this fulfilled. Easily months, if not much, much longer.

Remembering how Felicity had looked straddling him moments ago, his grin deepened and he picked up the glasses.

He paused on the threshold of his bedroom at the sight of her focused on her phone and propped up against the headboard, her curvy body tangled up in his gray sheets that smelled of them. Her thick hair, now more dry than damp, framed her face while tumbling around her bare shoulders that had a hint of a tan line from her bikini.

Holy shit, if his phone did ring with a work call, leaving her would be physically and mentally painful.

She put her phone beside his on the nightstand and smiled at him. "I feel I should tell you, Detective, how much I like seeing you without your clothing."

He strolled toward the bed. "Ditto, Ms. Mayhew." He handed her a glass, then stretched out right beside her on his bed. "Should I be worried about *your* job interrupting us?" He angled his head in the direction of their phones.

She sipped some bourbon and said, "Absolutely not. I was just e-mailing my new client who I'm supposed to meet with tomorrow morning about changing it to a phone meeting." She lifted her chin. "Happy?"

Between that defiant lift of her chin, her words, and the evening going in a direction he'd never expected, there was only one way to respond. "More than you know."

She curled into his side. "Me, too. And not just because of us forgetting the world tonight." She rested her head on his shoulder. "Miss Emmy Swanson's marriage to Mr. Jason McAvoy is the last *fairy tale* wedding going on my schedule for a while."

He switched the glass to his left hand to wiggle his right arm behind her. "What does that mean for Felicitous Wedding Creations?"

She raised her head and caught his gaze. "You know the name of my business?"

He stared her her. "Yes. I did read your business card. And believe it or not, my captain has even heard of *the* Felicity Mayhew."

Her cheeks became almost the same color as her hair which made him laugh.

"I'm flattered, but I refuse to be that wedding coordinator anymore." She again rested her head on his shoulder. "I've decided on balancing the big, expensive weddings with the small ones that mean just as much to the couples and their families, if not more so."

Ian suddenly remembered a conversation they'd shared last week when talking about Stacia Marsden and Felicity's clientele being "important rich people." There had been something in her voice and words that had implied regret.

"What brought this about?" He hugged Felicity to his side. "Lynn?"

She shook her head. "No. I've been struggling with this for weeks. Before I even left for Cancún, now that I think about it." She sipped more bourbon. "Alyson—the florist Campbell works for?—had this perfectly beautiful, intimate wedding on New Year's Eve. It was all about love, and being with their closest friends and family. That's it." She laughed. "I saw her Monday morning where she was glowing with love and happiness *and* being pregnant."

Ian smiled. "Sassy Felicity Mayhew, the no-nonsense and successful planner of fancy weddings, is a hopeless romantic." His smile faded, though, when his thoughts went to the future and uncertainty of a them beyond moments like this one.

He took a quick drink of his bourbon.

"I lost that side of me for a long time," she murmured. "But it's definitely coming back. A phony, greedy woman like Lynn being gone will make my business plans even more successful."

Lynn Delgado. A woman full of a different kind of darkness than Nicole Zamora, but the scars she left behind would be emotionally deeper and more than likely harder to forget.

Ian frowned. "So now will you tell me how it went with her?"

A long pause fell before, "She was angry, defiant, jealous, and... completely unrecognizable." She looked up at him, her light-brown eyes wide with confusion. "Ian, I don't know how she fooled me and my entire family for so long."

He sighed. "The Lynns and Candaces and Nicoles are damn good at what they do. Trusting people who have real hearts don't stand a chance against them until they've been hurt."

Felicity shifted onto her left side. "Why did you keep that picture of you and Candace with your ex-partner and his wife? Ex-wife," she swiftly added.

He finished his drink and set the glass on a clear spot on his nightstand. "It was taken a couple of years ago at my parents' annual Christmas party as Mr. and Mrs. Mayor. It's also a silent auction to raise money for all of the local animal shelters." He cracked a smile. "Stella and I found each other at one of the shelters that receives money every year."

Felicity's mouth opened. "Stella was a rescue? Isn't she pure bred?"

He nodded. "Yep. But she ended up being way too much dog for the couple who bought and surrendered her. They just wanted her to go to a good home." He laughed. "She's pretty big for a female Bernese Mountain dog. Anyway, that night was fantastic." He rested his head against the headboard. "Candace and I were getting along. Maren and Connor were happy. Great food, open bar, dancing, Christmastime, and lots of money going to a good cause." He hesitated before saying, "Life was perfect that night."

Could that be the last time he'd felt like he did at this moment?

"You said his name."

He blinked twice and focused on Felicity.

"Connor. That's your ex-partner's name?"

Ian stared at her.

"You've never said his name until now."

He racked his brain trying to remember his few conversations about Connor Gregson since December with his family and close friends, including Scott, but couldn't remember ever saying the guy's name.

Until now. Which had to mean something significant.

"It sounds like keeping that picture might be a reminder that life can be quite good." She lifted her shoulders. "I didn't burn *all* the pictures from my time with my ex-husband."

He released a quick laugh and shifted onto his right side.

Yeah. Life could be good. Especially in moments like this after spending months in a black hole and triumphantly emerging.

Ian's gaze caught hers. "Perry paid you a huge compliment this morning and he's right." He reached out and pushed a lock of hair behind her right ear.

Her eyes became round as her cheeks once again turned pink.

"He said you're quite a woman and don't deserve what's been happening." More than the truth, too. He only wished he'd been the one to say it out loud first. He leaned forward and gave her a light kiss. "Stubborn as hell, but still quite the lady."

Her embarrassment eased into a tentative smile. "Ian, Perry really is a lovely man."

And there was that hint of British accent.

It was past time to change the subject.

"Who met the wrong woman on a dating app. Okay. Fine." He hitched his chin toward her unfinished drink. "Need help with that?"

A phone vibrated and dinged behind him.

"That's you." He turned and picked up her phone. "I have a different tone." And thank God it had been her phone that had dinged.

"It's Scott." She looked at Ian and narrowed her eyes. "Yesterday he called wanting to know why he hadn't been hearing from me lately." She held up her phone. "Now he's texting me about spending Easter in Colorado Springs with our mom and older sister."

Ian grinned. "And all of that makes him a great brother." But definitely overdoing it. "Way better than me. I haven't texted my brother in over a week."

"Please stop grinning like that and just admit you told Scott what's happening."

He released a long, heavy breath. "Guilty. But I'm not apologizing."

She replied to Scott's message and handed Ian her phone which he set aside.

"Because you're so damn stubborn," he continued, "and the fact Lynn turned out to be less than trustworthy, I needed someone else looking out for you."

She finished her drink. "Then I forgive you."

He took the glass, also set it aside, and guided her backward onto his bed.

While nuzzling her nose, he quietly asked, "What's happening on Easter in Colorado Springs?"

She gazed up at him. "Dinner with the Mayhews. Scott's also

bringing Peyton and Campbell who has yet to meet our mom, and older sister and her family."

He kissed the tip of her nose. "Scott must have told me about it because that sounds familiar." He hesitated before asking, "What'd you say?"

She slid her arms around his neck. "I'll be there no matter what's happening in my life."

They shared a light kiss.

"Felicity, I'll make sure that happens."

She smiled softly. "I know you will." She lifted her chin which made him grin. "I also know *this* has caught both of us off guard."

Without a doubt.

"And reality can come back at any minute."

More truth.

"But since your family is all the way in Grand Junction, and you might as well be a part of the Mayhew clan, you're more than welcome to come with me. But no pressure," she swiftly added. "I respect the fact you're still working through what happened in Grand Junction."

Yep. He sure as shit was. But it had gotten significantly better… with her help, too.

"Thank you for the invite and the no-pressure clause."

She laughed softly.

"How about we agree to focus on whatever reality brings between now and Easter, then have this conversation again?" Ian couldn't get there. Not now. And for many reasons.

She nodded. "I believe that's more than fair."

He grinned. "You know, it drives me a little crazy when you slip into the British accent."

They shared a longer, deeper kiss.

"It drives me a little crazy when you grin at me like you are right now."

His grin deepened. "So maybe I can grin while you talk to me in the accent?"

She shook her head and deftly rolled him onto his back. "I have a better idea, Detective."

He stared up at her. "And you have my undivided attention, Ms. Mayhew."

She leaned down, pressed her mouth to his, and Ian forgot about everything but her.

A NEARBY RINGING, buzzing phone caused Felicity to stir.

Ian, nestled behind her, reached over and grasped his phone which he brusquely answered.

She rolled onto her right side and squinted at the window with light barely streaming through the closed blinds.

"Yeah," Ian said into his phone while sitting upright. "I'll leave asap." He ended the call and focused on her. "It was my partner. We got the warrant to search Nicole's apartment."

"So early?" she asked around a yawn.

It had to be around five a.m.

He lifted his shoulders. "We just needed the judge's signature and apparently he's an early riser." He sent her an affectionate smile. "I have to get ready for work and go."

She hugged the pillow. "I know. But at least reality didn't come back until now."

At least they'd been given an entire night without a work interruption. An unforgettable night they'd needed and wanted and, most importantly, deserved.

Ian leaned down, and they shared yet another kiss that bordered on desperate need.

A hunger and desire she'd never before felt with a man.

He gradually, almost grudgingly, pulled away, then left his bed, strode into the bathroom, and closed the door. Seconds later she heard the shower start to run.

She continued to hug the pillow tight, imagining it was Ian. She then burrowed under the sheets that smelled of his masculine soap and the more feminine body wash he'd bought her Tuesday night. Unbelievably, it was only Thursday morning. She'd spent a mere three nights here with him, though it felt as if weeks had passed. There did, however, seem to be an end in sight in the form of a faceless woman named Nicole Zamora.

She frowned.

Ian had said Perry met her on a dating app which meant the woman also had to be from California. But she'd ended up in Colorado? And might have done an unfathomable thing to her own— she halted that thought train. Still, the notes had grown increasingly threatening. A stalker graduating to actions much more dangerous was completely in the realm of normal.

She'd left Ian's house yesterday determined to let Lynn Delgado know she hadn't broken Felicity Mayhew in half and she'd achieved it. But based on what he'd told her last night, it may not have been the smartest choice. If the missing Nicole Zamora was her harasser and had done something terrible to her grandparents, she absolutely qualified as dangerous.

Felicity snuggled deeper into Ian's bed.

From this point moving forward, she would do everything Ian asked. She did have a "smaller" wedding this weekend and no assistant, but if absolutely necessary she could ask Alyson—or maybe even Jillian?—to keep Felicity on speaker while they ran things on site. In no way ideal, but what other choice did she have? The fact she had to hire a new assistant would give her something else to do after her phone meeting with Emmy and other business pertaining to this Saturday's wedding.

Hiring a new assistant.

Something she hadn't imagined doing due to her close working relationship and *friendship* with Lynn. No. She hadn't expected Lynn to work for her forever, but she sure as hell hadn't expected the woman's cold disloyalty and teaming with the devil's daughter.

The shower turned off, forcing Felicity back to the present.

At this point, all she could do was take it one minute, one hour, one day at a time while safely in Ian's house with Stella and Princess Belle.

Ian emerged from the bathroom with a towel around his waist and shot her that grin of his. "You look damn good in my bed, Ms. Mayhew. Even this early."

She sat up with the sheet tucked around her as he walked into his closet.

"Ian?"

He walked back into his room holding a blue suit and white dress shirt. "Yeah?"

"I didn't say this last night," she began while he removed the towel and headed for his dresser, ultimately drawing her focus elsewhere.

"My eyes are up here," he replied, pulling on blue boxer briefs.

She dragged her gaze from *him*, ignored the mischief illuminating his eyes, and said, "I promise I won't go anywhere until this is over." She managed a slight smile. "It's been a very rough several weeks and days, but I do love my life. If I have to run Felicitous Wedding Creations from your messy dining room table indefinitely to stay safe, that's what I'll do."

He stepped into his slacks and fastened them. He next swiped his belt from off of the floor. His shirt went on next, followed by a blue tie he draped around his neck.

With a look she couldn't interpret, he stepped toward his bed and sat near her.

He cupped her face. "Okay. We have a deal." He placed a gentle kiss on her lips. "And my dining room table isn't *that* messy."

She breathed his familiar, addictive scent into her mind and soul…and heart. "Only because I partially cleaned it the other day."

He laughed. "Fine. You win. I have to go." He gave her a quick kiss and stood.

In less than five minutes, he stood before her wearing his holster with gun and shrugged into his sharp, dark blue suit jacket. He then fixed his tie.

Detective looked incredibly good on Ian Stafford.

With a deep breath, she scooted out of bed and asked, "Just to be extra cautious, what does Nicole Zamora look like?"

He tilted his head right while checking her out much like she'd done to him.

"My eyes are up here, Detective."

He shook his head and stepped back. "She's thin, average height, short dark hair, blue eyes." He pointed at her. "By the way, you standing naked in my bedroom is a fantastic way to start a day like this." He opened the door and the dogs trotted inside. "I'll check in later."

He disappeared from view. Within seconds the door into the garage opened and closed.

Felicity stared at the dogs staring at her while they wagged their tails. In that moment, she remembered her bag of clothing and some bathroom items she'd picked up at her house yesterday. She'd been in such a hurry to get her phone charging, she'd left everything in her car. Then she'd forgotten all about it, then Ian had surprised her when she'd walked out of his bathroom, then she'd blissfully forgotten everything outside of this room.

With a sigh, she walked into the bathroom to retrieve Ian's sweat-shirt and pants, the only thing she had to wear outside of her business suit. The pajama set he'd been sweet enough to buy hadn't quite fit her curves, another reason she'd needed to pick up clothes at her house.

Once dressed, she padded into the living room with the dogs at her heels.

She removed her car key from her purse and said, "I'll feed you when I get back."

The early, brisk morning air surrounded her while she carefully walked in her stocking feet down the sidewalk. The sun was just starting to hit the horizon. As such, the sky happened to still be favoring night.

She walked around the front of her vehicle and stopped at the driver's side.

"Hi, Felicity."

She yelped and spun in the direction of the voice.

Her eyes locked with a familiar pair narrowed in triumph. And something much darker.

"Oh, my God," Felicity murmured on a breath. "It's *you*."

Chapter Twenty-Three

"THIS PLACE IS CLEANER than a hospital OR." Larry rubbed his goatee. "We're not going to find *shit* in here."

Ian slid the closet door open and peered inside.

Several empty hangers. No shoes. No luggage. But Nicole had left some clothing behind in what had to be haste to get the hell out of the unremarkable apartment not far from the interstate. The outside of the complex, that also boasted "nicely furnished apartment homes," happened to be even more mediocre.

"She kept this place tidier than the entire complex is," Larry continued. "Gotta be more than a neat freak going on here." He sniffed the air twice. "Bleach mixed with pine. Tess uses cleaner that smells the same. Always gives me a damn headache."

A dress buried in the back of the closet caught Ian's attention. He removed the gown, faced Larry, and held it in front of him. "What do you think?"

Larry raised his eyebrows. "Nice. But pink isn't your color."

Ian smirked. "Thanks. But it's kind of a fancy dress for a woman who lives in a place like this and waits tables. Don't you think?"

Larry approached him and inspected the dress. With his latex-gloved hand, he carefully reached inside and displayed the attached sales tag. "Was she going to wear it and return it? But why? Who the hell could she know where she would need a dress that costs more than she probably makes in a month *with* tips?"

"And maybe she already wore it." Ian hung it back in the closet. "Nothing else of real interest in there." But Larry had posed a fair question, for sure.

Ian slid his gaze around the plain and depressing bedroom.

Double bed with a thin, gray comforter and white sheets perfectly made. It reminded him of his time in the military, the bed looked that neat.

Brown, cheap nightstands flanked the bed and held white lamps. The nightstand on the right also had a dated alarm clock.

A dresser that matched the nightstands sat opposite the bed. The shiny, clear top made it obvious she'd cleaned it as well.

The window, with dusty blinds cheaper than those in his house, faced east and barely let in the sunrise light through the semi-open slats.

That happened to be the bedroom; the overall drabness matching the small apartment.

Ian sighed. "It sounds like it's not going any better out there?" He angled his head in the direction of the living area and kitchen.

The place happened to be so small it didn't have a dining area. The bathroom, which contained a narrow shower stall, small vanity with a sink, and toilet, was located to the left of the closet. It contained nothing but a cheap bar of soap.

"Nope." Larry went to the dresser. "I'm telling you, we're going to find diddly squat. She was probably prepared to make a quick escape."

Ian started to sift through what they knew about Miss Nicole Zamora.

Bad seed from Scottsdale, Arizona. Shuffled between family members which would have made her even angrier and defiant. Grandparents—the Zamoras—did their best, but by the time she'd returned to them as a teenager, the damage had been done. No going back.

Doris Milano had nailed it when she'd said you can't fix that kind of badness.

Ian didn't even want to think about what could have happened to Oliver the cat.

Nicole then disappears into the world, never to be heard from again until two months ago.

Clearly the woman had come to Colorado from California with whatever had been in her car, but held a Nevada driver's license. Her car, an older Chevy, was registered in Nevada, too.

An address in Las Vegas had come up in the info they had discovered on her before Ian had sat down with her on Tuesday, but her last known address in California had been in the Los Angeles area. Perry lived in San Jose which was hundreds of miles north of L.A.

Her Facebook page had been even less helpful than her Twitter account. He and Larry had been presented with that info before they'd walked out of the building yesterday evening.

Holy shit, this woman had learned, after her grandparents had kicked her out, how to be visible and invisible at the same time and had spent a decade or so mastering the skill. Turning herself into different people, like Nicola Oliver, had obviously helped, too. But at the end of each day she was still legally Nicole Zamora, the bad seed from Scottsdale, Arizona who no one wanted. In that respect, Ian couldn't help but wonder how many other people she'd become over the years as a way to escape her reality. And at some point she'd snapped.

He would bet his badge it had been when Perry had dumped her in the coffee shop. What Ian couldn't figure out was how she'd found out about Felicity. Their computer guru who'd gotten into her Facebook account had also said she and Perry were *not* friends.

Ian had a hard time believing a computer software engineer

wouldn't have his account secured to keep strangers from all over the place seeing everything he posted.

Larry slammed the bottom dresser drawer shut and stood. "Nothing. Apparently, Miss Zamora didn't come back to Colorado with a whole lot."

Ian headed to the closest nightstand. "Have you by chance heard anything from the unit watching the Zamora's house?"

Nicole would have to be the definition of stupid to show up at her grandparents' house, but he still felt the need to ask. The woman had proven she could hide in plain sight.

"Crickets over there." Larry went to the other nightstand. "Though our Ms. Milano has spotted the unit and seems to be keeping her eye on them."

Ian opened the nightstand drawer.

Nothing. Of course.

He sat on the bed's edge and rubbed his eyes.

The adrenaline from Larry's early call had long since worn off. Fatigue from getting very little sleep during the night seemed to be hitting. He needed an extra-large coffee with a double shot of espresso once they left Nicole's apartment…with diddly squat.

"What's the matter with you?" Larry asked in response to Ian's yawn he'd tried to fight. "My pre-dawn phone call too early for the rookie detective?"

After spending a good portion of his night wrapped around a beautiful redhead with soft, perfect curves, yeah. The call had been way too damn early. But he said, "Late night." Certainly not a lie, either. "Larry, this woman has me stumped. And frustrated." He faced his partner. "She could be in Mexico by now using an entirely different name with a different wig."

Larry opened the nightstand drawer. "It happens. Something else you gotta get used to." He withdrew a bible and held it up. "Really? In this place?" He glanced at their surroundings. "I'm pretty sure God's never been here." He flipped through the pages, but stopped and withdrew a piece of paper folded in half. "Think it's an invitation to hell?"

Ian fought another yawn while Larry opened the paper.

Yep. He desperately needed coffee.

"Well, *shit*." His partner held up the paper. "It is an invitation, but to a wedding."

Ian frowned. "A wedding invite tucked into a bible in a crappy apartment? It's probably been there as long as this place has been standing."

Larry shook his head. "Nope. Wedding date was two weeks." He focused on Ian. "Maybe that's why she needed the fancy dress?"

His frown deepened. "Who got married?"

Larry squinted at the invite. "Emmy Swanson to a Mr. Jason McAvoy at some place in Denver I don't recognize."

Ian froze, the newest yawn being instantly replaced with an adrenaline rush.

"Wait a minute," he murmured. "I know those names." He stood. "Can I see that?"

Larry handed the invite over.

Ian carefully read the formal writing about Mr. and Mrs. Swanson requesting "your presence" to their daughter's wedding to Jason McAvoy.

Miss Emmy Swanson and Mr. Jason McAvoy.

Felicity had said those names last night before talking about her plans for the business. She'd also just finished e-mailing a new client about changing an in-person meeting to a phone meeting for this morning.

"Care to fill me in, Hot Shot?"

Felicity hadn't said who the meeting was with, but her mentioning this particular couple being her last scheduled fancy wedding for a while implied that's who she'd e-mailed.

"Felicity," Ian replied, his mind back to churning. "She has clients by this name. *New* clients," he stressed. "Meaning not married yet."

Larry's eyebrows shot toward the ceiling.

"And we find this tucked away in Nicole Zamora's apartment with the same couple's names, but the wedding already happened?" An invite she'd obviously forgotten to grab in her rush to leave.

His partner pointed at the invite. "We need to bag that and track down this couple."

Nicole had become Nicola with the help of a damn good blonde wig, meaning she'd turned herself into someone completely different with a different name.

Ian had told Felicity what *Nicole* looked like and there had been zero recognition on her part. And Felicity would have definitely said something if Nicole's description had been familiar.

A realization hit and Ian promptly removed his phone from his jacket.

"Calling your lady friend?" Larry asked. "Probably not a bad idea."

Ian chose Felicity's name and said, "I'm almost positive they've met." He held his phone to his ear. "Felicity and Nicole?"

Larry's eyes widened. "You think Nicole posed as *Emmy* marrying *Jason* needing a wedding planner?"

"Yep." Ian followed his partner from the bedroom as he got Felicity's voicemail. "She's not answering." The chill he'd experienced yesterday while they'd spoken with Doris returned.

"Could be in the shower, bathroom, on the other line," Larry said while handing a tech the invite. "Bag this and put a rush on it."

The tech nodded.

Ian took a deep breath. "Yeah. Probably. I'll shoot her a text to call me as soon as possible." She had to be fine because she'd promised to stay put.

But she'd gone out yesterday and what if the missing Nicole had been watching closely?

As he and Larry left the apartment, Ian suppressed the darkness invading his mind.

He couldn't and wouldn't go there. Felicity was fine. She'd call or text him back soon.

In the meantime, he and Larry would locate the real Emmy and Jason. They'd be one step closer to finishing the puzzle and, hopefully, finding the unstable Nicole Zamora.

And he *would* hear back from Felicity.

"NOW THIS IS A CAR." Emmy slid her gaze to Felicity in the passenger seat of her own SUV. "I've never driven a Mercedes, so thanks for letting me drive."

Felicity clenched her teeth and focused on the windshield. "It's not like I had much of a choice."

Before Felicity had been able to fully process the fact Emmy Swanson and Nicole Zamora were the same person, the woman had opened the driver's side door and shoved Felicity inside. She'd then forced her into the passenger seat with something hard and narrow in the small of her back.

Something that had felt like the butt of a powerful weapon.

"It must be nice being someone like you." Emmy-Nicole pulled off the blonde wig, followed by the wig cap, and tossed both into the backseat.

An extremely convincing blonde wig that had fooled not only Felicity but Perry and God knew who else. But Felicity had only seen the woman once and for a brief moment in time.

In The Halcyon Hotel's fireplace room where Emmy-Nicole had been wearing the blonde wig and dressed in a pink gown for the first-class wedding reception Felicity had planned. The woman had also claimed to be a good friend of the bride's.

And Felicity had fallen for every bit of her ruse.

"Fancy SUV," Emmy-Nicole continued. "House in Cherry Creek. Big-time business where you mingle with rich, important people everyday. All that and a pretty redhead."

She lifted her chin. "My life isn't perfect. *No one's* life is perfect."

"Of course you would have two handsome guys wrapped around your perfectly manicured fingertip," the woman added as if Felicity hadn't spoken. "What I want to know is why that hot detective who would clearly kill for you isn't enough?"

Felicity whipped her head in Emmy-Nicole's direction when they reached a red light.

"Why do you also need Perry?" Ice had settled into the woman's stare. "People like you *never* have enough. You take and take until there's nothing left for the rest of us."

Felicity returned her ice-cold glare. "From what I understand, Perry broke up with you before I even met him."

"But he would have been mine again if he hadn't met you in Cancún!" The woman's glare transitioned into disgust. "I saw the pictures. He posted one right after another on Facebook. I didn't deserve that kind of humiliation."

That explained how Emmy-Nicole had found out about Felicity and Perry and why she'd zeroed in on Felicity. But why in the world would Perry have *ever* friended her on social media?

"Perry needed a vacation so I let him go."

The light turned green and she hit the gas pedal. "We were going to get back together once he returned."

Felicity's heart rate gained momentum as the reality of her situation landed in her mind.

She was trapped in her own vehicle, without her phone or a way to defend herself, with a woman capable of causing unthinkable harm to Felicity and anyone else who stepped in her way.

What the hell was she going to do?

"Perry was so over the moon for you I had to do *something*."

Felicity frowned. "I don't even live in California. We never spoke again until he called me about being in Denver this week." None of this made sense.

Then again, this woman clearly lived in a world that wasn't reality.

"He was talking to his friends about you and how much he wanted to see you again." The woman's disgust returned. "He didn't care that you lived here."

Felicity took a quiet breath to settle her racing pulse. "I never knew any of that. I'm also wondering how you would know something like that." The woman had definitely proven she could follow and lurk without detection.

Had that been how she'd learned all this information? If it were even true.

Emmy-Nicole gave her a cold smile. "A mutual friend in San Jose who knows Perry and I belong together. This good friend was also the one who showed me the *disgusting* pictures of the two of you all over each other in Cancún."

They stopped at another red light.

"I had other reasons to come back to Colorado, too." Her nasty smile deepened. "Getting rid of you was simply a fun bonus, but this isn't what I originally planned."

Felicity stayed silent.

If this insane woman wanted to talk, Felicity would let her because she needed to figure out how to get away from Emmy-Nicole without severely hurting herself or anyone else.

The woman also had a weapon hiding inside her coat pocket.

"Before the detective became overly protective of you, we were supposed to meet at your office where *Emmy* would have brought you a coffee out of the kindness of her heart. But it would have been special. Laced with something just for the oh-so wonderful wedding planner."

The arctic chill returned, but this woman would never see Felicity Mayhew shudder.

"Laced with a lethal amount of hydrocodone?" She eyed Emmy-Nicole. "Like what you did to your own grandparents?"

The woman laughed, bitter and hard like the rest of her. "Your hot cop has been busy. Probably talking to that nosy, decrepit bitch who lives across the street." She again hit the gas pedal when the light changed. "And my *grandparents* were a waste of space." She gripped the steering wheel. "I hated them as much they hated me. All of my so-called family, for that matter. My grandparents kicked me out when I was barely eighteen and knew I had nowhere to go." She smiled with cold triumph. "Revenge is best served in a glass of warmed whiskey—their nighttime drink—with *lots* of crushed Vicodin. They were the other reason I came back to Colorado which I'd been planning forever. I wanted to get rid of them sooner, but all of this had to happen when Perry was here for his conference."

Felicity clenched her hands so tight her nails dug into her palms to stop the shiver.

"That he specifically requested to attend because he wanted to see you again."

If that were true, it's not at all what Perry had said to Felicity just last week.

Just last week.

How could her world have flipped on its head like this in one week?

"Someone like Felicity Mayhew has no idea what it's like to have always had *nothing*."

Meeting a good, handsome, successful man like Perry Cantrell must have been akin to winning a lottery worth millions to a woman like Nicole Zamora…who'd been going by a different name *and* look while she and Perry had been together.

Felicity stated, "You were going by a different name and wearing a wig. What were you going to do when Perry discovered you were lying?" She could have cared less, but keeping her talking was her only weapon right now.

The woman lifted her shoulders. "I would have figured it out. And he would have gotten over it because he's perfect and kind and deserves someone like *me* to take care of him."

Whether he wanted her to or not.

Felicity scoured her brain for an idea—any idea at this point—to get away from her abductor who appeared to be driving them into downtown Denver.

Maybe she could somehow unlock her door, then escape at another red light?

Emmy-Nicole handed Felicity a cheap flip phone that she had probably bought in a convenience store.

"We're going to pick up Perry at his hotel and settle this once and for all."

Felicity stared at the phone as her heart again pounded inside of her chest.

"Because he's currently *obsessed* with you," the woman muttered, "you're going to call him and tell him you want to go for a quick coffee before the conference starts for the day. He needs to meet you outside the hotel where you'll be sitting in the driver's side of your car." She dropped the phone in Felicity's lap. "I'll be in the backseat. It's a busy hotel located in a popular spot in down-town Denver so I know you won't be dumb enough to try anything."

Felicity lifted her chin. "I don't have his number memorized. And don't you think he'll be suspicious that I'm calling him from an unknown number?"

Emmy-Nicole grinned. "I do have his number memorized."

Of course she did.

"If he asks about the number, tell him you got a new one. It's that simple."

Felicity glared at her for several seconds before grasping the phone.

Despite what the insane woman had said, maybe Felicity could use this to her advantage.

At Perry's hesitant greeting, she said, "Hi. It's Felicity. I hope it's not too early?"

A pause, followed by, "Hi. Did you change your number because of what's going on? Your detective friend and his partner think it might be this unhinged woman I briefly dated in California. She gave me the name Nicola Oliver, but they said her name is Nicole."

Felicity slid her gaze to Emmy-Nicole shooting her fleeting glances while driving.

"I'm so sorry. I can't believe—"

"It's fine," she interrupted. "I'm starting my work day early and thought you might want to grab a coffee?"

Another pause, then, "The detective told me you're keeping a low profile because of everything when I asked about seeing you. Does this mean they found Nicola?"

Ian must have been the one who told Perry about her "low profile."

She needed to use that.

"No," she sharply answered. "But I couldn't let you leave Denver tomorrow without saying goodbye. What the detective doesn't know won't hurt him." She released a quick laugh that sounded painful to her own ears. "Though I'm sure he'll figure it out with some help."

Emmy-Nicole held out her hand, obviously wanting the phone back.

"I'm already on my way to the hotel. Meet me out front?"

"Okay," he slowly answered. "Felicity—"

"Brilliant. See you soon." She ended the call and somehow stopped herself from throwing the device at Emmy-Nicole. She couldn't risk killing herself or others in a car accident. "Satisfied?"

The woman returned Felicity's ice-cold stare. "He better be alone." She patted her coat pocket. "If I go down, I *will* take you with me."

Felicity faced the window, willing a light to turn red while she set her arm on the door rest which placed her hand near the lock. It was her only option…outside of the hope Perry had figured out what she'd really been saying in that short period of time.

Chapter Twenty-Four

A NEARLY OVERWHELMING sense of déjà vu shrouded Ian while he stared at his phone.

Larry driving them back to work while Ian willed his phone to ring or ding with a text from Felicity. When he'd gone through this yesterday, she'd texted him back hours later. Her phone had not only died, but she'd also—against his wishes—left his house to confront Lynn.

This morning, and after spending an unforgettable night together, she'd made it a point to tell him she wouldn't leave his house. Obviously the reality of what he'd told her about Nicole had hit full force. Her phone must have still been charged this morning. He'd only seen her use it twice. They'd been caught up in each other most of the night, forgetting reality.

So why the hell wasn't she answering today? He couldn't think of any possibilities but two. She'd either gone back to sleep, an absolutely reasonable thought considering their night, and simply didn't hear it ringing or dinging.

Or something was horribly wrong.

He tried calling her again. At once more getting her voicemail, he muttered a choice swear word.

"You know," Larry began, "roosters are barely up at this hour. She could be sleeping."

"I know that." Still, Ian knew where her phone had been all night.

Right beside his on the nightstand. He'd seen it there this morning before leaving her while she stood naked in front of him. He'd called three times and texted twice. The lady would have to be in a coma to not have heard her phone ringing by her head that many times.

Ian tried again.

Nothing.

Dread consumed him.

"Larry, something isn't right. We need to go to my place."

His partner glanced sharply in his direction. "She's been staying with *you*?"

Ian sighed. "Can we talk about it later? I know something's wrong."

The adrenaline rush returned.

Had Nicole been watching closely yesterday? And Felicity, distracted by her anger and disappointment with Lynn, probably hadn't been paying close attention to her surroundings.

Larry's phone started to ring. "Hold that thought, Casanova." He answered his phone.

Ian called Felicity for the fifth time.

His partner suddenly snapped his fingers in Ian's face.

"Hi, Mr. Cantrell," Larry said, his wide eyes on Ian as he braked hard at a light. "You just got off the phone with Felicity…It *wasn't* her number?"

Ian ended the call and faced his partner.

Something *was* horribly wrong.

Larry nodded and listened and finally said, "Head to the lobby and wait there. We're on our way." He hung up. "I'll give you this, Hot Shot, you've got the instincts for this job."

Ian leaned forward. "Is she okay?"

Larry accelerated once the light turned green. "It sounds like she's got unwanted company, but yeah."

Ian released a quick breath.

"Cantrell said she sounded off. And when he mentioned you telling him she was supposed to be keeping a low profile, she laughed weird and said what you don't know won't hurt you. But that you'd figure it out with help."

No doubt the lady's only way of signaling Perry she was in trouble.

Ian put his phone away.

She was okay and they—he—needed to keep her that way. That's all that mattered.

"We gotta beat them to Cantrell's hotel without making a ruckus. That's where they're headed." Larry accelerated even more and went around a slower car. "Your lady friend asked him to go for an early coffee and to meet her outside."

The early-morning hour would help with their haste since rush hour had barely begun.

Ian focused on getting Felicity away from Nicole, then putting the woman in handcuffs. As soon as that happened, his racing heart would return to normal.

Under completely different circumstances, Ian enjoyed the adrenaline rushes from his job, especially as a detective. But this happened to be the first time in years that someone close to him was in danger.

The last time he'd experienced this feeling had been in Afghanistan.

Between Larry's speeding and already being well on their way into downtown Denver, they arrived at Perry's hotel walking distance to the convention center in record time.

Larry pulled up next to the curb and pushed the hazard-lights button. They then emerged from the sedan and jogged toward the hotel's main entrance.

A few cars were parked in the loading-unloading zone.

"What does Zamora drive?" Larry asked.

"An older Chevy." They strode into the hotel lobby. "I don't see a car like that."

Perry, standing near the doors, approached them with round eyes.

Ian couldn't help but feel a pang of sympathy for the guy who'd gone on a dating app because he'd wanted a date for his company's Christmas party.

"I feel like this is all my fault," the guy said, running a hand through his hair. "How does shit like this happen? Felicity has to be scared out of her mind. I never meant—"

"We know, Mr. Cantrell," Larry interjected. "We need you to keep a clear head, okay?"

Larry guided the guy away from the glass doors.

Ian started to follow, but a familiar, bright-white SUV pulled in behind one of the cars parked outside the hotel.

His jaw turned to steel.

The woman had not only abducted Felicity, but had done so in her own car. But how such a thing had happened would have to wait.

Ian stepped behind a tall plant and peered through the branches.

His heart almost stopped at the sight of Felicity in the passenger seat. She then turned toward the driver's side.

"I'm sure you'll want to do the honors?" Larry said from right behind him. "Cantrell's supposed to go out there and meet her."

Ian narrowed his eyes trained on Felicity still facing the driver's seat. "Yeah." He glanced at his partner. "I'll do the honors."

He walked around Larry, toward the glass doors which automatically opened.

The second he stepped outside, his gaze locked with Nicole Zamora's.

Her eyes widened.

He continued his long strides toward the vehicle.

Nicole faced forward—and Felicity grabbed the woman's coat collar and shoved her into the driver's side door. Loud, long honking then exploded from the vehicle.

Ian sprinted to the driver's side, ripped the door open, and Nicole practically tumbled into his arms. Which she immediately fought as if she'd turned into a manic she-devil.

He managed to grip her wrists and force her arms behind her back.

Larry suddenly appeared at Ian's left side, handcuffs out, that he quickly placed on the woman's wrists. And she unleashed a glare so malicious Ian's blood chilled.

The fact her blue eyes had turned black and soulless only added to the malevolence.

Larry smiled. "Good morning, Miss Zamora. It just so happens we've been looking for you. Turns out you've been very busy since arriving in Denver two months ago."

Nicole turned her death stare on Felicity still in her vehicle as she watched them with wide eyes; her mouth slightly open.

"I *knew* that bitch said something to Perry that tipped him off—"

"Stop talking," Ian commanded. He patted her coat pockets. A millisecond later he withdrew a silver pocket pistol from her right side.

He held it up.

Larry's smile deepened. "Well, isn't that cute." He glanced at Nicole. "You? Not so much." He grasped her left upper arm. "I'll put her in the car and call it in." He angled his head in Felicity's direction. "We'll need her to make a formal statement."

Ian stepped toward the open driver's side door.

His gaze connected with Felicity's.

Though all he wanted to do was haul her from the vehicle and hold her tight until someone forced them apart, he went with a warm smile and said, "Hi, Ms. Mayhew. You've had a rough morning."

She slumped against the seat, but stayed silent.

"Officers will be here shortly," he quietly continued. "We'll also need a statement." He leaned forward. "Then we'll be able to get you *home*."

Relief replaced Felicity's dismay before she nodded, their gazes remaining connected, saying so much without one word being spoken.

Approaching sirens caused Ian to step backward.

In a flurry of squad cars and flashing lights and officers, Ian handed over Nicole's weapon. He then grudgingly left Felicity to rejoin his partner and Miss Nicole Zamora, officially in police custody.

Larry looked at Ian across the sedan's roof. "It's going to be a long morning. Think I'll call Tess and have her bring me some breakfast. Want in on that, Hot Shot?"

Ian released a quick laugh. "Yeah. Sounds good." He then took his first deep, head-clearing breath since his initial unanswered call to Felicity that felt like hours earlier.

FELICITY BURROWED DEEPER into the blanket Ian's partner had given her while she'd been giving him her statement, including *everything* Emmy-Nicole had said.

Despite being in Ian's roomy sweatshirt and sweatpants and now shrouded in a thick blanket, she couldn't stop shivering. A powerful fatigue had also taken over as she spoke to Detective Walsh who'd been incredibly kind and patient.

She hadn't seen Ian since being inside her SUV. God knew what had happened to her vehicle, too. Detective Walsh had assured her they'd get her home before leading her out to where she and Lynn had waited for Ian less than two week earlier with the threatening notes. She didn't know the time, either. And as much as she wanted to see Ian and throw herself into his arms, falling into her own bed and curling up with her dog had become a more powerful desire.

Not even two weeks had passed since she'd come here for Ian's help.

How could that be possible?

At that time, she'd hadn't particularly liked him. She'd thought him too handsome and arrogant for his own good, and had encouraged Lynn to ask him out on a date. If he hadn't said yes, he never would have ended up suspecting Lynn of betrayal and warned Felicity. The truly ironic part was the fact she'd warned Ian not to hurt Lynn.

If not for exhaustion and some lingering shock, she probably would have laughed.

And Lynn's betrayal just hadn't been the only thing Ian had suspected.

Emmy Swanson. Nicola Oliver. Nicole Zamora.

Felicity had run head first into another type of devil because of a decision from weeks earlier. She still couldn't comprehend how one seemingly innocent choice had placed her in Denver's Police Admin building on a Thursday morning after being abducted by a mad woman.

She tightened the blanket around her shoulders.

What if Ian hadn't been adamant about her staying in his house until they caught her harasser? Emmy-Nicole had stated she'd planned an altogether different end for Felicity. If not for changing the in-person meeting to over the phone, she would have drank essentially poisoned coffee given to her by an "excited bride-to-be" she'd had no reason not to trust.

Felicity squeezed her weary eyes shut to erase the image.

How could she ever go back to the person she'd been before her trip to Cancún? That Felicity Mayhew had been trusting, and had a trusted assistant and good *friend*. There'd also been no crazy woman leaving her threatening notes while closely watching her.

She also never would have discovered the real Ian Stafford.

They would have never shared last night and forgetting everything but each other.

Now that he had fulfilled his promise to her, she couldn't help but wonder what would happen next with them. She and Princess Belle were safe to return home. She was safe to return to her normal work schedule. However, none of it would be the same.

How long would it take to stop looking over her shoulder? To stop her racing heart as she pulled into her driveway or approached her car? She also had to find a new assistant. She'd trusted Lynn implicitly from the beginning.

After the last several weeks, trusting new people would be an extremely hard feeling to achieve. And she would *never* again blindly give it away.

"Felicity?"

Her eyes flew open and landed on Perry standing in front of her.

His expression appeared to be stuck in shock. Hers couldn't look much different.

"I honestly don't know what to say. Simply saying the words *I'm sorry* would be ludicrous at this point."

She managed a slight smile. "Perry, it's not your fault. And I'm pretty sure you saved me today by calling Detective Walsh." Because he had figured out what she'd really been saying.

"Thanks. But I'm not a hero." He ran a hand through his hair. "Between dealing with this and *Nicola* and my divorce, I think I may need to explore therapy. And take a very long break from women." He paused before muttering, "It'll also be a cold day in hell before I get on another dating app. Anyway, I really did enjoy our time together in Cancún."

She nodded. "Me, too."

"I told you last week over the phone I wanted to call you," he continued. "I almost did call you numerous times, but I couldn't work up the nerve." He huffed. "Then this conference came up and I…lobbied hard to be sent here."

Her eyes widened.

Emmy-Nicole had actually been telling the truth when she'd said the same thing earlier.

"I didn't tell you that because I didn't want to freak you out." He shook his head. "And boy does that sound ridiculous after everything you've been through." He focused on her. "I still have no idea how that crazy bitch found out about you and me."

Felicity sighed. "She told me it was through a mutual friend."

The poor man didn't need to know anymore than that, especially since no one would ever know for certain how much of Emmy-Nicole's statements were the truth.

Perry frowned. "A mutual friend?" His phone started to ring and he withdrew it from the pocket of his windbreaker. "It's work. I have to take this since I have to explain why I'm not at the conference today." He stepped back, disappointment replacing his shock. "I know that all of this has completely ruined whatever connection we had before I left Cancún."

Felicity stayed silent, unable to dispute his honesty for several reasons.

His phone continued to ring while he took another step back. "I'll see you on Facebook?"

She managed another smile. "Of course. Travel safe tomorrow."

With a final, lingering glance her way, Perry answered his phone and headed right.

Felicity rubbed her eyes getting heavier by the second.

What in the world had happened to getting her home? If Detective Walsh didn't come back soon, she'd have no choice but to hunt someone down and demand—

"Hey there."

The quiet, familiar voice caused her to stop the rubbing.

Scott's concerned face slowly came into focus.

"Ian called me." He held out his hand and helped her up. "I'm here to take you back to his place, pick up your stuff and the dogs, then take you home. He'll get your car back to you tomorrow." Her brother smiled. "I'm also supposed to tell you he'll come to your place as soon as he can, but it'll be a while."

Yes. Catching and arresting Emmy-Nicole was just the beginning of his job as detective.

"You should be at work," she half-heartedly scolded.

"Picking up my nosy, stubborn sister from the police station after she was abducted by a whacko is a much more important job for me today." Scott pulled her into his arms. "Ian also told me that you grabbed the woman's collar and shoved her into the door which helped him and his partner. I'm proud of you." He paused, then added, "Dad would be, too."

Between hearing those words from her brother and the warmth of his arms surrounding her, Felicity allowed her dam to crumble. She then released all the fear she'd refused to show while trapped inside her vehicle with a devil no longer in disguise.

Chapter Twenty-Five

IAN PULLED into Felicity's driveway and parked next to Scott's SUV. Another smaller SUV that he vaguely recognized sat outside the lady's home.

He cut the engine, sat back, and slowly released a long breath.

Holy shit, had this day gone in a direction full of still mind-blowing twists and turns.

He'd left Felicity…naked…in his bedroom barely at dawn, met Larry at Nicole's crappy apartment, then the world had turned upside down for what amounted to no more than several moments. But it had felt like a lifetime had passed in the span of time he hadn't been able to get a hold of Felicity because she'd been caught at her car by a crazed woman.

A woman who would never again walk the streets of any city.

He opened the door and hauled himself from his vehicle.

Getting here, to this moment, had been his number-one motivation all day. This and putting Nicole Zamora into a jail cell.

Ian knocked on the door and two distinct series of barks reached him outside before the door flew open.

Scott gave him a shrewd once-over. "You look like shit."

Ian smirked. "Thanks, Professor. Are you going to let me in?"

He stepped aside.

Ian became surrounded by Stella and the princess, both vying for his attention.

"Hi," came a warm voice from Felicity's living room.

He gave the dogs final, vigorous pats and looked up to find Campbell smiling at him.

"I don't think you look like shit," she said, shooting Scott a pretend glare.

Ian walked into the living room and they shared a tight hug.

"The fact you're here, too, must mean Scott's been running his big mouth."

They released one another.

Scott walked up and stood beside his girlfriend. "It turns out this lady right here can be more persistent and scarier than my sister."

Campbell lifted her shoulders. "And it turns out this guy right here is a terrible liar."

Ian grinned. "Truth."

"I also thought Felicity may want some positive female energy after such a horrible day."

He shrugged out of his trench coat and draped it over the back of a plush chair. "How's she's doing?" His grin faded as he next removed his suit jacket.

That happened to be the most important question right now.

The dogs surrounded them.

As Campbell picked up the princess, Ian rubbed his dog's head.

"When Felicity and I got here," Scott murmured, "she took a shower, changed her clothes, and fell into bed. She's been sleeping on and off most of the day."

A good sign, for sure.

"I just saw her Monday morning." Campbell rubbed the princess's head. "I can't believe she was going through all of that and keeping it to herself. I mean, she seemed a little less...*Felicity*... when she was in the shop, but nothing dramatic." She paused. "But then Alyson did burst into tears after Felicity gave us the bonus and told her she's pregnant."

Ian removed his gun from the holster. "Bonus?" He looked around for a safe place to keep it and spotted a drawer in the table by the front door.

"She gave us a one-year-anniversary-you're-so-amazing bonus."

He placed his service weapon in the drawer and closed it. "Wow. Sounds generous." Also not surprising now that he knew the lady much better.

Loyalty apparently ran strong in the Mayhew bloodline and happened to be something Ian fully appreciated. Something he couldn't ignore as he and Felicity eased into...what?

Campbell set the princess on the couch. "It was generous because she's amazing. And after everything she's been through with this stalker and that despicable traitor, Lynn, you better not hurt her, Ian Stafford." She leaned forward. "Because if you do, you'll not only have to answer to Scott, but you'll also have to deal with *me*."

Ian angled his head back, then looked at his buddy.

Scott shrugged. "Truth." He grabbed his jacket off of the couch as the princess trotted toward it. "I told you she's scary." To Campbell he asked, "You ready? I was thinking I'd pick up something to eat and we can meet at my place so I can give the babysitter the rest of the night off." He smiled at Ian. "And if it makes you feel any better, I like you a whole hell of a lot more than the last guy my sister dated...then married."

"Gee, thanks." Still, having Scott's support when it came to Ian dating his sister did make him grin, though it wasn't at all surprising.

Dating *the* Felicity Mayhew. Yeah. Ian couldn't help but like the sound of that and getting to know her even more. Especially after the last twenty-four or so hours.

Scott and Campbell shrugged into their jackets.

"Tell her I'll check in with her tomorrow." Scott clasped his girl-friend's hand.

When they reached the small foyer, Scott paused and focused on

Ian. "If you keep saving the important women in my life, I'll have no choice but to do something nice for you."

"Great idea. How about you start by getting the hell out of here?"

Scott laughed and opened the door.

Once they left, Ian locked the bolt and handle, and released another deep breath.

Now he could start focusing on the lady.

After removing his holster, he headed in the direction of her bedroom which he remembered from his only other time in her house —the night she'd received note four while at dinner with Shannon and Peyton. Also the night he'd realized Lynn couldn't be trusted.

Though it had only been a speed bump in time, Ian couldn't believe he'd actually been interested in Lynn Delgado who happened to be a different type of Nicole Zamora.

People like that were damn good at lying and manipulation to get what they wanted, not caring about the mental and emotional destruction they left behind.

Ian stopped on the threshold of Felicity's extremely feminine bedroom with light-wood furniture, pastel bedding, and quotes inside gold frames that said "Own the Day" and "You've Got This," among others.

He smiled at her curled on her side under a pale-pink blanket, body moving up and down in deep sleep. He didn't like the thought of waking her, but could no longer not be next to her.

Especially after the last twelve or so hours.

Keeping his gaze trained on her, Ian made his approach and eased onto the bed.

She curled deeper under the blanket.

His grin deepening, he stretched out beside her, then rested his head on a pillow.

Her deep red hair framed her serene face.

Another round of relief surged through Ian at seeing her so peaceful, looking nothing like she had in her SUV before and after Nicole had almost fallen out of the vehicle and into his arms. Unmistakable fear mingled with dismay.

It would be a long time before Ian would get that image out of his head.

He reached out and gently brushed aside a loose hair—her eyes fluttered open.

"You're here," she murmured, blinking several times.

"Yeah. Finally." He tucked the hair behind her right ear. "Sorry for waking you."

"I'm not," she said around a huge yawn. "Scott and Campbell?"

"Just left."

"And the dogs?"

"In the living room. I should probably take them for a walk."

"No. Not yet." She grasped his hand and scooted closer. "And Emmy-Nicole?"

His grin faded. "Is in a jail cell where she'll be for a very long time."

"What happened?"

He kissed the top of her hand. "She made our job ridiculously easy by confessing to everything." He frowned. "But it's not like she had much of a choice, considering your statement to Larry and Perry identifying her in person as Nicola Oliver. On top of everything else we had."

"So it's over for now?"

He slowly nodded. "For now." He leaned forward and placed a soft kiss on her lips.

She gave him a sleepy smile and damn him if that wasn't something he could get used to seeing on a regular basis.

"Nicole, Nicola…" Felicity peered at him. "Where did she get the name Emmy?"

Right. Yet another section of the one-thousand piece puzzle now complete.

"Emmy Swanson is a real person who did marry a guy named

Jason McAvoy a couple of weeks ago. We found that out after finding their invite stashed in Nicole's apartment."

Felicity's eyes widened.

"The real Emmy worked with and befriended Nicole at that restaurant. The one crawling distance from your office that she chose because it was close to *you*."

She shuddered.

"Real Emmy did give Nicole the invite, but added she never saw Nicole at the wedding."

"Emmy was just another pawn in Nicole's game," Felicity murmured.

"Yep." Ian placed his arm across her waist and shifted toward her. Once her head was tucked under his chin, he added, "That's not even the last part of the Nicole puzzle."

"I don't think anything would surprise me at this point when it comes to her."

The final chunk had sure shocked the shit out of him and Larry.

"It turns out Nicole had an unlikely ally in California."

Silence before Felicity said, "She told me about a friend she and Perry shared being the one who showed her the pictures he'd posted on Facebook while we were in Cancún."

"And that very good friend happened to be the one and only Clara Cantrell."

Felicity leaned back and their gazes locked.

"Perry's ex-*wife*?" she nearly shrieked.

Truth really could be stranger than fiction. Yet another thing Ian happened to be learning the hard way as a rookie detective.

"How did they even meet?"

He propped himself up on his right elbow. "Nicole utilized her blood-hound tracking skills to *cross paths* with the ex-Mrs. Perry who, as it turns out, is not on his side like she told me Wednesday night when she called me back."

"So she lied." Felicity sat up and crossed her legs. "I don't understand."

"Because of what Nicole told us about Clara, we had to get a hold of the San Jose PD to haul Clara in so we could get her side of the story." Ian lifted his shoulders. "After she tried denying everything Nicole confessed to us, two San Jose detectives eventually got her to crack. She admitted not-so-perfect *Perry* cheated on her, the real reason for their divorce."

Felicity's mouth fell open.

"According to her statement, she saw *Nicola's* instability as a way to get back at him for cheating, then had zero hesitation throwing the woman under the bus after spending weeks feeding her crazy. Now, the ex-Mrs. Perry has her own legal problems because of *her* crazy."

Silence descended.

On some level, Ian's head was still spinning from the way this puzzle had come together.

"Ian, I swear Perry didn't tell me any of that."

"Why would he volunteer he'd cheated on his wife and she left him?"

She sighed. "Fine. He's not perfect. But he still didn't deserve all of this."

Ian also sat up. "Neither did you. And you're all I care about."

Her eyes became round. "Does Perry know that his ex-wife isn't really his friend?"

"Don't know. Don't care." Ian cupped her face. "The guy obviously needs to start making better choices when it comes to women."

She lifted her chin which made him grin.

"He chose me. I'm nothing like either of those women."

He pressed his forehead to hers. "You don't count because you're way too good for him."

Felicity tilted her head up, and their mouths fused.

Greedy and desperate and picking up where they'd left off early this morning as if the harshness of life had never happened.

Ian grudgingly ended their kiss due to nothing more than needing air.

"And what about you, Detective?" she breathlessly asked. "Am I too good for you?"

He lightly rubbed her bottom lip, plump and red from not only their kiss but his thicker than usual scruff. "No." He grinned. "But I'm starting to realize you might be good for me."

Unfortunately, it had taken Felicity being abducted by a highly unstable and unpredictable woman for the realization to hit him upside the head.

"I like the sound of that." She returned his grin. "I feel that way about you, too."

"Then we agree to take this one day at a time?" He tugged her forward and into his lap. "Felicity, I wish I could offer you more than that, but—"

She placed her fingers over his lips. "One day at a time since we're both in odd places after being betrayed and discarded by people we loved and trusted."

He kissed her fingers. "Okay. We have a deal."

The same peace he'd experienced last night replaced the day's insanity and he tightened his hold on her.

She shook her head. "Not quite." She raised her chin. "Where's your phone?"

He squinted at her. "In my suit jacket. Why?"

Felicity untangled herself from his arms, stood, and headed into the living room. Within seconds she returned holding his phone.

"You never said you deleted Candace's voicemail message."

He froze.

She held out his phone. "I think it's time you listened to it, then start to really let her go."

He held up his hands. "Felicity, I appreciate what you're trying to do—"

"You know you need to do this." She sat beside him. "We'll listen together."

You know you need to do this.

Scott had said something similar to him last week while talking Ian into a Friday night out in Denver.

"Persistence seems to also run in the Mayhew bloodline."

She stared at him. "You're just now realizing this?"

Ian hesitated for several seconds before grasping his phone.

Maybe Felicity was right. Maybe this could be the final step away from what Candace and Connor had done to him and Maren that no longer felt as painful. But that would depend on the message she'd left him that must have been important to her since she'd called twice.

With his gaze locked with Felicity's, he went into his phone and tapped the voicemail icon. He then put his phone on speaker and held the device between them.

"*Ian, it's me,*" Candace began, her voice no longer familiar and a part of him or his life. "*I had a feeling you wouldn't answer, but I wanted to call and tell you the news, hopefully before Maren does.*" She sighed. "*I'm pregnant, and Connor and I are getting married.*"

Maren had of course gotten to Ian first, but he remained silent and focused on Felicity.

"*For what it's worth, I did want this with you and there's a part of me that still thinks this should be us.*"

Felicity grasped his free hand and squeezed.

"*But we let it die, and I found someone else. I never thought it would be Connor.*"

Ian shook his head.

"*I really do hope Denver treats you well.*"

The line went dead.

Ian stared at his phone. "She's right." He deleted the message and put his phone aside. "We did let it die and should have ended things a long-ass time ago." But it's not like he hadn't already admitted that to Felicity.

She grasped his face and forced him to look into her eyes. "You made a mistake. She and your ex-partner made a much bigger mistake. But you have to start letting it go, Ian. And not just because of us."

He nodded, fully understanding what she *wasn't* saying. She, too, happened to be right.

"I also think you need to finish unpacking." She smiled. "Put out the rest of your pictures? It might really help."

He guided her backward onto the bed. "You going to help me with that?"

She started unbuttoning his shirt. "I can be terribly bossy, Detective."

And of course there was that hint of British accent.

He helped her out of her pink hoodie sweatshirt. "I've figured that out, Ms. Mayhew."

She, with his help, removed his shirt. "We'd probably end up strangling each other."

Her matching pink sweatpants joined her sweatshirt on the floor. "Yeah. But I'm willing to take that chance if you are. Especially if you boss me around in that British accent."

His pants came off, followed by his boxer briefs.

"I guess I'm helping you finish the unpacking."

Their mouths came together for a long, thorough kiss that lasted until he said, "Please tell me you have protection nearby."

She laughed. "Top nightstand drawer."

In under a minute, their moans surrounded them while he slid inside of her, going as far as he possibly could.

He barely brushed his open mouth against hers. "And I guess I'll be your date for Easter."

"Okay," she breathed. "We have a deal."

Ian grinned, then lost himself in Felicity.

A beautiful woman with fire in her hair and heart and soul.

FELICITY SMILED at Jillian and Jackson swaying on the dance floor to their wedding song.

The Fireside Room of the Boettcher Mansion glowed with candlelight, overhead light dimmed to warmth, and spots of deep purple and sunflower yellow provided by the flowers that of course had come from Daisy's Bouquets. Most importantly, the room glowed with romance and genuine love coming from the small number of guests the bride and groom had invited, as well as the couple.

A full champagne flute appeared in front of her face, followed by a deep, irresistible voice murmuring in her ear, "I think you've earned this, Ms. Mayhew."

Her smile deepened as she grasped the glass. "My first intimate wedding in too many years to count does seem to be a success, Detective."

When Jillian and Jackson had become engaged not too long after Easter, Felicity had surprised the couple by offering to plan their intimate, fall wedding as a gift and a way to get back into what she wanted most for Felicitous Wedding Creations—to create weddings of all sizes that expressed the true love between a bride and groom, no longer accepting clients who were only interested in showing off their money.

Though she hadn't reneged on the *fairy tale* weddings she'd taken before officially making the change, she now, and with help from her partner extraordinaire, chose the couples more carefully.

Ian slid his right arm around her waist and hugged her to him. "Next up, Scott and Campbell."

"But he just proposed and they're in no hurry."

Felicity's smile slipped when her gaze landed on Jackson's frail mother talking with Alyson and her husband, David. The older woman then smiled while placing her hand on Alyson's very pregnant belly, the couple being only a month away from their due date.

Mrs. Lovett's battle with cancer had taken a sad turn the last couple of months. As such, the day and night had taken on a bittersweetness most of the guests were successfully putting aside not only for her, but for the glowing couple.

Ian angled his head in Felicity's direction. "Then there's my brother and his fiancée who want you to help them with their wedding in Grand Junction." He drank some champagne. "Is it just me or has this been a big year for engagements?"

She laughed. "It's not just you." She faced him. "Are we forgetting anyone else planning on marrying in the next year?"

"I don't think so." He faced her and unleashed that enticing grin of his. "But I'm wondering where that leaves you and me?"

She lifted her chin. "I thought we were taking it one day at a time."

Ian pressed her close. "That was six months ago."

She fought a smile. "And?"

"And I'm in love with you, you're in love with me…" His grin grew.

"*And?*"

His grin transitioned into a smirk. "You drive me crazy."

"Ian Stafford, if that's how you propose to a woman—"

He silenced her with a kiss, then said, "I want to marry you, but I don't think I can wait until after Scott and Campbell, and my brother and his fiancée."

She sighed as he pressed his forehead to hers. "I accept your proposal."

"Fantastic. But I have to ask again, where does that leave us?"

Felicity placed a light kiss on his lips. "Detective, surely you've heard the words *elopement* and *destination wedding*?"

He brought back his grin. "And I accept *your* proposal, Ms. Mayhew."

They shared a quick laugh before sealing their commitment with a kiss while surrounded by true love and romance and promises intended to last forever.

~The End~

Author's Note

I hope you enjoyed the final book in the Timing is Everything Series. Each book can stand alone, but it's recommended they're read in series order for maximum enjoyment.

And if you have a moment, please leave a rating and brief review at wherever you purchased the book. Authors always appreciate and need honest reader reviews.

Acknowledgments

Felicity and Ian's story ended up not only being the final book in my first Adult Contemporary Romance series, but my **tenth** published book. As such, there are people I must thank.

Kim with the Kim Killion Group has produced every cover and brilliantly captured each series and story within the series. I feel blessed to have lucked into finding such a talented designer and group, overall. I hope to continue our working relationship for another ten books (and more).

Over the course of writing ten books the last handful of years, it's been a journey in itself to find the right editor for my stories and writer's voice. But I believe I have finally found her. A huge thank you to Megan Records who respects my writer's voice and offers invaluable, thorough, and professional advice. I hope to continue our working relationship for the next ten books (and more.)

A huge thank you and hug for my mom who encourages and listens and pushes during my highs and lows of being a full-time author. She's also a proofreader extraordinaire!

Finally, for those who have been with me from my very first book, an immense thank you for your continued support. It means more than you could ever know.

About the Author

Christine Miles is a full-time writer living in Albuquerque, New Mexico.

An avid reader and writer since elementary school, her passion for literature inspired her to pursue a BA in English and an MA in Creative Writing. She writes YA and Adult Contemporary Romances with sassy, independent heroines and swoony heroes who love them for their strength.

When not writing romances, she loves traveling, binge-watching shows on streaming apps, reading mysteries and thrillers, listening to music, and spending quality time with her family, friends, and dog.

You can find her on Facebook and Instagram. Sign up for her newsletter to get ARC's and updates at www.christinemilesauthor.com.

facebook.com/ChristineMilesAuthor

instagram.com/christinemilesauthor

amazon.com/author/christinemilesya

bookbub.com/authors/christine-miles

goodreads.com/christinemilesauthor